"WE DON'T HAVE ANYTHING THAT PUTS HIM IN THE BAD GUYS PILE."

"Except for what Givens calls the Project," Kurtzman countered. "I don't see why the file is so heavily encoded. I had a hell of a hard time breaking into the outer layer of their computer security systems. Hunt's working on the code, which just happens to look like a DOD system used to guard nuclear weapons sites."

"Okay," Price stated. "I'll try to get Hal on board."

"It's not Hal I'm worried about. As far as I'm concerned, the President's a little too close to this thing. I know he was good friends with Bowers, but putting us to work on something like this is outside the envelope. It makes me wonder why we were given the assignment."

Price had also asked herself that question.

DON PENDLETON'S
MACK BOLAN.
STONY MAN.
JUDGMENT IN BLOOD

THE
ARMAGEDDON
PROJECT

BOOK I

A GOLD EAGLE BOOK FROM
WORLDWIDE.

TORONTO • NEW YORK • LONDON
AMSTERDAM • PARIS • SYDNEY • HAMBURG
STOCKHOLM • ATHENS • TOKYO • MILAN
MADRID • WARSAW • BUDAPEST • AUCKLAND

First edition December 2000

ISBN 0-373-61934-0

Special thanks and acknowledgment to
Michael Kasner for his contribution to this work.

JUDGMENT IN BLOOD

Printed in U.S.A.

JUDGMENT IN BLOOD

CHAPTER ONE

Saudi Arabia

The sun was setting over the Red Sea when the three Bell UH-1N helicopters roared over the coast south of the port city of Jidda. The choppers had flown only feet above the wavetops on the way in, and now they had to gain altitude to clear the sand dunes and foothills of the mountains on Saudi Arabia's western border with the Red Sea.

The Hueys were boldly marked with the green-and-white rondels of the Royal Saudi Air Force on their desert camouflage paint. They were also squawking RSAF IFF codes so the ever vigilant AWACS aircraft spotting for the MiG Cap guarding Saudi skies wouldn't mark them as enemy. But the choppers weren't Saudi and neither were the pilots or the dozen and a half troops on board. They were all mercenaries being paid very well to do a very dangerous job.

Once clear of the foothills, the three choppers flew into the mountain passes heading directly for the holy city of Mecca forty miles inland.

A member of the Royal Saudi Air Force stationed at the ground radar installation on the mountain of At Taif picked up the flight of the three choppers as they made a beeline for the holy city it guarded. As per procedures, he flashed them a IFF query on the guard channel.

When the pilots didn't immediately reply, the radar operator instantly punched the bandit button. The attack alarm flashed to both the F-15 flying cover over Mecca and the Triple A sites scattered throughout the town.

"I think we just got painted," the man in the right seat of the lead chopper said in English as he studied his electronic countermeasures board.

"ETA?" the pilot asked tersely.

"Six point five."

The pilot tried to twist the throttle grip up against the stop, but it didn't budge. The turbine was already screaming.

WHEN THE LEAD Huey reached the outskirts of the town, it dropped to rooftop level, and the other two ships followed it in a trail formation. They were two minutes from the holy sanctuary of the Kaaba when the RSAF F-15 on MiG Cap over the city acquired the blips on his look down–shoot down radar and locked up the trail ship.

"I am Fox Two," he called to the radar installation as he pressed the launch trigger on his control stick twice.

Both the F-15 and one of the town's rooftop Stinger

gunners locked on the target Huey at the same time. The Eagle pilot foxed off two AIM-7 Sparrow missiles just as the shoulder-fired Stinger left its launch tube.

Since it had the shortest distance to fly, the heat-seeking Stinger reached the chopper first. This was one of the Block 31 upgraded missiles, so its warhead detonated a yard from the chopper's turbine exhaust. The explosion sent several dozen pyramid-shaped, hardened steel projectiles slashing into the transmission and the turbine at supersonic speeds.

The resulting destruction of the compressor blades sent them knifing through the chopper's fuel tanks, and the red-hot burner cans ignited the spray. When the projectiles punched through the transmission housing, the whirling gears and clutches disintegrated, tearing through the cowling panels. With the JP-4 fuel burning and the Huey coming apart in the air, the Eagle's radar-guided Sparrows couldn't miss.

The first one flew through the open side door and detonated as it passed through the chest of one of the men sitting on the deck plates. This warhead contained almost one hundred hardened steel rods, each one a quarter of an inch in diameter and half an inch long. It had the effect of turning a 7.62 mm minigun loose in the cargo area with the trigger held down.

Everyone in the chopper was shredded an instant before the second Sparrow flew straight through the cockpit canopy and detonated against the rear bulkhead. Burning wreckage and bloody chunks of what had once been men fell from the sky.

By now, the two lead ships were so close to the holy enclosure that the Eagle pilot had to refrain from lighting them up. Dumping his flaps and throttling way back, he cursed all infidels as he went onto a low, mile-wide screaming orbit over the most sacred site in all of Islam.

EVEN THOUGH the Stinger gunners on the rooftops around the Kaaba couldn't fire on the two aerial intruders for fear of damaging the shrine, the Saudi guards in the enclosure itself were under no such restraint. They started firing long before the choppers got within effective range of their small arms.

The troops in the open doors of the two remaining Hueys had their assault rifles blazing on full-auto as soon as they cleared the walls of the enclosure around the Kaaba. Tracer fire flashed back and forth like fireflies gone berserk.

Both choppers had door gunners in the rear compartments, Vietnam Air Cav style. Their Sagami-mount M-60s hammered out a steady stream of 7.62 mm suppressive fire as the choppers flared out in front of their intended landing sites on top of the sacred Kaaba itself.

A Saudi guard with an RPG-7 on his shoulder sighted on the lead chopper and fired his antitank rocket. It wasn't the best anti-aircraft weapon in the world, but had been used in this role both in Vietnam and Afghanistan with great success. This time, though, the 85 mm rocket missed the intended target. But, as it flashed past the lead chopper, it hit the mast head of the following ship. The armor-piercing shaped-charge warhead blew the entire rotor assembly off the mast, sending the crippled Huey crashing to the ground.

Emboldened Saudis poured fire into the burning wreckage. More than a dozen FN assault rifles riddled every square inch of it and the crew inside.

While most of the defensive fire was concentrated on the downed chopper, the pilot of the third aircraft huddled behind his seat armor and brought his helicopter to a landing. As the skids touched down, he yelled into his throat mike, "Go! Go!"

Five men leaped from the chopper, pulling a 250-pound cylindrical object with them, a shaped-charge cratering device designed to penetrate the Kaaba and blow it into a hundred pieces. Retractable legs were snapped down and the charge placed squarely in the middle of the roofed structure over the sacred rock.

The guards had been momentarily stunned by this outrage, but they recovered quickly and directed their fire toward the intruders. It was as if the mercenaries had walked into a lead hailstorm. The demo man trying to set the timer for the detonator didn't get within a yard of it before he was blown apart.

Looking over his shoulder through the open side door, the pilot saw the last demo man go down. He had kept his turbine screaming and his rotor at max RPM so, when he hauled up on the collective, the lightened Huey leaped into the air. The beating rotors were clawing for airspeed and altitude when another RPG rocket took off the tail boom.

With the tail rotor gone, the ship went into a crazed dance in the sky. More fire streamed into it as it barely cleared the enclosure walls and crashed.

BY DAWN, the wreckage of the Hueys had been removed from the sacred compound. Work crews were busy repairing the damage where bullets had chipped the tiles and intricate stonework. Other crews were scraping up the burned and bloodied sand and taking it outside to be buried.

The remains of the attackers and their weapons had been collected as well as could be and were being examined. Of the unburned bodies, most of them were dark-skinned and dark-eyed. One of the pilots' bodies had also escaped the inferno of burning jet fuel, and he was light-skinned with blue eyes and blond hair. None of them carried any kind of identity papers nor anything of a personal nature. They were faceless men with guns.

The raiders' uniforms were Russian-pattern camouflage, but the pilots' helmets were American. The weapons were standard Soviet-issue AKM assault rifles and U.S. M-60C machine guns for the door gunners. The cratering charge that had been delivered was custom-made, but contained Czech RDX filler, a favorite tool of "freedom fighters" all over the world. The Huey choppers, of course, were American. But they had been refitted with French instruments, which indicated that they had seen previous service outside the United States.

All of that material could have been purchased from

any of a hundred black market arms dealers throughout the world. So could the Bell helicopters. In the shadowy world of illegal arms deals, serial numbers weren't usually recorded. But, if money could buy arms, it could also buy information and the Royal House wasn't short of cash.

Even so, it would be a long time before these men and their weapons could be tracked down, if they could be. It would be even longer before those responsible for this outrage could be brought to justice.

CHAPTER TWO

Los Angeles, California

The United States senator from Indiana, Robert Bowers, was a man on a mission, the most important mission he had ever undertaken. The only person in the world he loved more than himself was his eighteen-year-old daughter, Jennifer. The fact that for the past five years she had been living with her mother in California and used her maiden name didn't matter.

As a politician from a Bible Belt state, he'd had a hard time hanging on to his Senate seat after the very public breakup of his marriage. Only his high-profile involvement in his church had turned aside the wrath of his traditionally minded constituents. It had also helped that his ex-wife and daughter had gone to live in California. The old out-of-sight trick had worked to buy him enough time to let the scandal fade from the voters' radar.

When Jennifer graduated from high school, even though she'd been an indifferent student, he'd had no trouble getting UCLA's board of directors to ignore her less-than-stellar SAT scores so she could be admitted. No one who was as dependent on federal funds as the president of a public university wanted to anger a powerful senator. It just wasn't smart.

Bowers sincerely doubted that his daughter was ever going to become a career woman, and knew that the education would be wasted on her. But UCLA was a good place for a girl like her to hunt for a suitable husband. Her mother had taught her to enjoy the good life, and she was going to need to find herself a promising young man who could afford her.

While UCLA was a university of academic superstars, it had more than its share of diversity quotas and less-than-bright celebrity offspring. To keep the standard of the UCLA degree up where the university's chancellors thought it should be, they didn't use a sliding scale of grades based on race or family connections. If the unqualified had the proper family or ethnic connections, they could get into UCLA easily enough. But, if they wanted to graduate with the school's coveted degree, they had to perform.

Unfortunately, Senator Bowers's very good looking but intellectually mediocre daughter hadn't been able to swim with the academic sharks. After months of being ridiculed by professors who expected her to be smarter than she was, she disappeared into the smog of Southern California.

When Senator Bowers received a notice that Jennifer had been put on academic probation for failure to take the term's final exams, he went ballistic. When he was unable to contact her in California, he went from an angry father to a frightened one. With Congress in recess, he booked a seat on the first plane to California.

Bowers had barely stepped off the United 747 in LAX when he started to call in his political markers to start the search for his missing daughter. By the time his limo delivered him to the administrative offices of UCLA, he had learned that Jennifer hadn't been seen on campus for more than a month.

FOR A MAN KNOWN for his political acumen, Bowers let it all hang out when he walked in to the conference room full of university officials. They had just started to express their lukewarm concerns when he exploded.

"I don't know what kind of organization you people think you are running here," he said bluntly, "but I am holding you responsible for Jennifer's disappearance."

"Senator," the university provost broke in when Bowers paused for breath, "may I remind you that—" he glanced down at the paper in front of him "—Miss Wayne, I believe it is, is not our only student from a distinguished family. We don't provide special oversight for these students because our job is to educate, not to baby-sit wayward adult children."

That was exactly the wrong thing to say to Bob Bowers. He was silent for a moment and when he spoke, it was in a low, level voice. "Gentlemen, it's apparent to me that you aren't in the least bit concerned with the whereabouts of my daughter, and I will discuss that with you later. Right now, I have to make a phone call.''

The officials sat in silence as the senator walked to the phone on a side table, punched on the speaker and quickly dialed a number.

"Federal Bureau of Investigation, how may I help you?" a young woman's voice said over the speaker.

"This is Senator Bob Bowers," he said. "Is the director in?"

"Just a moment, sir."

The senator didn't have to wait long.

"Bob, how are you?"

"Not too good, Richard. I have a problem."

"What's wrong, Bob?" the head of the nation's premier crime fighting organization asked his good friend.

"Well, I'm calling from UCLA, and it looks like the stupid bastards who run this place have allowed my daughter to be kidnapped."

The director didn't miss a beat. "Hang on for a second, Bob, I want to get Rick Johnson on the line for this."

"But, Senator," UCLA's president sputtered, "there's no proof..."

"Mister," the normally mild-mannered Bowers snapped, "if you don't want to find yourself the primary target of a National Security investigation, I suggest you keep your fucking mouth shut."

Bowers swept his eyes around the table of academics. "And that goes for the rest of you morons as well."

"Bob," the director finally said, "I'm back and I

have Johnson on the line with us. I don't think you've met him, but he's in charge of National Security investigations for the Bureau. Tell him the situation."

Bowers was concise with his briefing. Jennifer had been missing for more than a month and the university hadn't even noticed that she was gone. "I don't have to tell you what the risks are if she's been kidnapped," he concluded.

"I'll have a task force at UCLA within the hour, Senator," Johnson assured him, "and they'll have the necessary warrants in hand to start the investigation immediately."

"Thank you." Bowers felt a lot better. "And if you have to tear this place apart brick by brick to find her, do it."

"We will be thorough," Johnson promised.

The officials were in shock when Bowers put the phone back down. "But, Senator…" the president tried to say.

"You had your chance asshole," Bowers said, his voice cutting like a razor. "Now it's my turn."

AN HOUR LATER, squads of FBI agents armed with federal warrants were swarming over the UCLA campus, canvassing both the faculty and the student body. By late afternoon, they had their preliminary findings and a prime suspect in custody.

The suspect was one Jason Donahue, twenty years old and a sophomore in the school of engineering. He was being held on suspicion of being an accessory to kidnapping and was singing like a manic canary, trying to stay out of jail. The fact that he was no longer enamored with one Miss Jennifer Wayne also had a lot to do with it.

"Apparently," the agent read from his notebook as he briefed the senator in the FBI command post trailer, "Mr. Donahue was intimate with your daughter on several occasions. According to him, she was the one who initiated the—"

"I don't care about that," Bowers cut in, and he didn't. His daughter had lost her virginity years before, and her mother's lack of concern about it had been one of the final battles they'd had before the divorce. His ex had blamed it on his being an absent father while he insisted it had happened because she had failed to instill morals and a sense of decency in the girl. "Anyway," the agent continued, "Donahue claims that after he introduced her to a new age cult group in town called Rainbow Dawn, she dumped him flat and took up with a man, name unknown at this time, from said group. We're following up that lead right now and should interview him soon."

"Have you learned where she's living?"

"With the assistance of the LAPD, we came up with an address, but haven't yet attempted contact. We thought you might like to do that yourself."

"Get me a warrant in case she isn't home."

The agent reached into his briefcase. The director had given him explicit instructions not to hump the pooch on this one, and he was ready for any possible request the senator might make. "I already have it."

"Get those local cops and let's go."

"JESUS CHRIST," Senator Bowers said when he saw the rundown apartment in a seedy part of town. "Are you sure this is the place?" he asked the FBI agent.

"Yes, sir," the agent replied. "We've got her name on both the rental agreement and the phone hookup."

"Let's go."

Three cars full of LAPD officers were waiting when Bowers and the FBI agents stepped out of their cars. The precinct sergeant in charge reported to Bowers as they walked up to the door of number 14.

"There's no sign that anyone's home, sir," the cop said. "We knocked on the door and checked the windows. The manager says he hasn't seen her in several days."

"Take the door down," Bowers ordered.

Since the senator had a valid federal warrant, the cops had no choice but to put their shoulders to the flimsy wood. The cheap lock disintegrated, snapping the door open.

One whiff of the smell in the airless room told the cops the story, and they tried to keep Bowers outside. But he wasn't a man who was accustomed to taking orders from anyone.

"Out of the way," he snarled as he rushed in.

An instant later, he sincerely wished that he hadn't. When he got a good whiff of the stench, his gag reflex kicked in. But before he could turn away, he saw his daughter slumped over in a chair with a syringe in her arm. Dull shrunken eyes in a bloated face told him that she had been dead for a couple of days. On the coffee table in front of her was a heroin junky's kit, with a half-used bag of white powder. From the expression on the dead girl's face, the cops knew the drug would turn out to be high-grade China White.

WITH THE HIGH PROFILE of this case, the investigation took off at lightning speed. To all appearances, Jennifer Wayne had died of a drug overdose, but Bowers was confident that she had never used drugs. When he was honest with himself, he knew that she had been frivolous, willful and not very smart, but she'd been deathly afraid of drugs. The older sister of her best friend in high school had ODed, and Jennifer had been with her friend when the body had been discovered.

Because of that, when the medical examiner declared her death to be an OD, Bowers asked his good friend the director to have the FBI look into the case.

A DAY AFTER the FBI started investigating Jennifer's death, Senator Bob Bowers was driving his full-sized rental sedan in the right lane of the I-5 freeway north through L.A. Since he was talking on his cellular phone as he drove, he didn't notice the white Chevy van coming up behind him in the middle lane at a high rate of speed. He only caught a flash out of the corner of his eye before he was hit.

The blow knocked the phone from his hand and snapped his attention back to his driving. "Idiot," he muttered as he glanced into his rearview mirror.

When the senator saw a dented chrome grille coming at him again, he stomped on the gas to try to get out of the way. But the four-door American-made lead sled he had rented needed a few minutes to change speed, and the van's driver didn't give him that time.

The van slammed into the left side of Bowers's rear bumper, causing the car to skid to the right. Bowers fought the wheel, but land barges weren't sports cars and the overweight sedan didn't respond well. After another shove, he lost control completely and the heavy car left the road, slamming into an overpass abutment. At the speed it was traveling, it turned into a steel casket around the senator before it burst into flames from a ruptured fuel tank.

The freeway confrontation and resulting crash were taped by a California highway-department traffic monitor camera. The next day, a burned-out van was found that matched the one seen in the video. When the VIN number was traced, the CHP realized that it had been stolen the day before the crash.

The death of a powerful senator stayed in the news for more than one day. Flags were flown at half-staff, his funeral was a televised event and three proposed laws punishing road-rage crimes were offered on the floors of both the House and the Senate within days of the crash. Jennifer Wayne's funeral, however, went almost unnoticed.

CHAPTER THREE

Los Angeles, California

The day after Jennifer Wayne's funeral, a press conference was held at the corporate headquarters of Rainbow Dawn. Any communication to the media, much
less a press conference, was a rare event with this organization. Roy Givens, the group's leader, didn't appear in public. But the high-profile death of Jennifer
Wayne had brought his group under intense scrutiny.

With the media sharks circling, Givens knew that he
had to do something to get them off his back. The last
thing he needed right now was to have these nosy bastards looking at his organization too closely. So, in the
glare of the TV camera lights, Rainbow Dawn held a
press conference, but Givens did not appear himself.

Instead he sent his press officer, a polished, relaxed
middle-aged man, to read his prepared statement ex-
pressing regret for the dual tragedy.

"...The loss of two such people is always a tragedy," the PR flack concluded, "and it should reawaken

all of us to the fact that life is a fleeting gift and should be celebrated every moment of the day and night.''

The spokesman took his glasses off and looked up from his prepared statement. ''I'll take a few questions now.''

''Are you praying for Senator Bowers and his daughter?'' an older female reporter asked.

''I cannot speak for individual members,'' the PR man said. ''But Rainbow Dawn isn't a religious organization. Prayer is something that is left to the individual.''

''Do you guys take in a lot of drug addicts like Miss Wayne and try to straighten them out?'' a man in the back row called out.

''We weren't aware that Miss Wayne had substance-abuse issues when she decided to join us,'' the press secretary said smoothly.

''What would you have done if you had known that she was using?'' the reporter pressed.

''Rainbow Dawn isn't a twelve-step program,'' the PR man replied sternly. ''When we discover that one of our members has a substance-abuse problem, we recommend that they deal with it outside before returning to us.''

''So you're saying that you threw Miss Wayne out then, right?''

''We do not 'throw' anyone out,'' the PR man stated, his tone hardening. ''In this case, when Miss Wayne learned that Rainbow Dawn wasn't a place to hide her drug use, she left us of her own accord.''

A female reporter held up her hand and was recognized. "What about the statement from her mother that Jennifer had never used before she joined the Dawners?"

The PR man smiled thinly as he reached for his papers. "Ladies and gentlemen, thank you very much."

IN HIS PENTHOUSE OFFICE, Roy Givens watched the press conference downstairs on the in-house video system. While he wasn't a hundred percent satisfied with how it had gone, it hadn't been the disaster it easily could have been. Rainbow Dawn had powerful friends in the State House as well as inside the Beltway, but they couldn't protect them from something of this magnitude. The only way that this could have been worse would have been if the silly little bitch had been the daughter of an ex-President.

He was not at all amused with the blunder over Jennifer Wayne. He knew the reasons why she had slipped through their screening—the girl had used her mother's last name and had never been involved with her divorced father's political life—but they didn't matter. The failure to investigate her parentage before giving her access to high-level material was inexcusable. He was aware that Miss Wayne's physical attributes and the way she had freely shared them had had a lot to do with the haste with which she had been brought inside.

That mistake had also earned the staff member who had recruited her a fatal accident as well, a swimming tragedy in his case. Mistakes weren't tolerated in the upper levels of Rainbow Dawn, particularly not then. The Project, as it was called in-house, was about to be launched, and nothing could be allowed to interfere with it. Particularly anything that drew attention to his group.

For a cult leader, Givens was a surprisingly true pragmatist. While there was no way that he could put Humpty Dumpty back together again, he could distract the sharks. A couple of high-profile publicity stunts should put them off the scent. There were more than a few low to midlevel celebrities among the ranks of the Dawners: sports figures, actors and wanna-be actresses, so-called recording artists and other medium-high profile types.

He'd tap a handful of them and put on some kind of dog-and-pony show for underprivileged kids, heavy on the diversity, of course, with lots of media coverage. Then, he'd have the organization publicly donate a truckload of money to some drug rehab center in the girl's name. He could donate a million dollars and not even miss it, but that would buy a lot of condoms, needles and methadone for the local junky population.

The media would eat it up with a spoon and, in a month, no one would remember Jennifer Wayne. Or, if they did, they would confuse her with the next would-be-starlet found with her veins full of poison. It might be a new millennium out there, but L.A. was still L.A. and the attrition rate for the young and talentless was still pretty high, particularly for the women.

IF ANYONE BOTHERED to take the time to check him out, Hal Brognola was listed as a high-ranking official in the Justice Department assigned as a special liaison officer to the White House. This made him just another one of the thousands of well-tailored, bland, faceless Beltway hacks who made Washington what it was.

In the shadow world of covert operations, however, he was the director of an organization hardly anyone had ever heard of. To the mere handful who did know of it, it was called the Sensitive Operations Group. The sensitive operations part of the title meant exactly that, when the problem was too sensitive to be handled through normal channels, SOG was given the job. In this case sensitive meant something that could never be allowed to see the light of day.

The Sensitive Operations Group had been designed to be completely free of petty politics. It was to be the extralegal clandestine arm of the sitting President, whoever and whatever that particular President happened to be. In theory, the only way SOG could do its job successfully was if it was tasked without political consideration. Nonetheless, over the years, SOG had gotten pulled in on a fair number of politically fueled missions. It went with the territory.

Since Brognola had been a high-level Justice Department official, he'd been a practiced D.C. player before being tapped to take on SOG and he knew the game. On more than one occasion, he'd gone head-to-head with the man in the Oval Office to try to keep SOG clear of politics. Sometimes he'd won, sometimes he'd lost, but most often he'd been able to fight to a draw that allowed his organization to sidestep much of the political in-fighting. This time, though, he had readily offered SOG's assistance with something that had absolutely nothing to do with their primary mission. Senator Bob Bowers had been an honorable man, and his death, while being publicly mourned as a road-rage accident, needed looking into.

When the Man asked him to take this task on as a personal favor, he'd had no problem accepting the job and was now making the ninety-mile flight to the Shenandoah Valley of Virginia to see that it was carried out.

AT A SMALL FARM in the Blue Ridge Mountains of Virginia, a man named Buck Greene made yet another tour of his area of responsibility. To all outward appearances, the patch of land that went by the name of Stony Man Farm was a prosperous agricultural enterprise, and in fact, it was. It was more than that, though, much more. Stony Man Farm was one of America's most closely held secrets. This little farm was home to Hal Brognola's Sensitive Operations Group, and Buck Greene was Stony Man's security chief.

This day Greene was touring the farm's new Annex. This was a forty-eight-acre parcel of land adjoining the eastern boundary of the original farm, which had recently been acquired so SOG could expand its operation. Stony Man Farm had had humble beginnings. Hiding a clandestine, high-tech operation in a small farm had been a good idea. But the operation had long ago outgrown its modest layout.

In the beginning, the farm house had been adequate for the purpose. But the never-ending march of technology had created equipment and techniques not even dreamed of when Stony Man first went active, and the original space was crammed full. To keep pace with the expected further technical developments of the twenty-first century, the time had come for the farm to expand beyond its original boundaries.

The Annex, like everything else at Stony Man Farm, wasn't really as it seemed. The land had been planted with fast-growing poplar trees to produce wood pulp. When they were grown, the trees would shield anything that went on from casual view as well as providing a convenient place to hide a network of sensors, video cameras and warning devices to protect the new perimeter.

The centerpiece of the Annex was, of course, the wood-chipping mill, situated on a small knoll close to the old perimeter fence. It was the obvious excuse for having planted all the poplar trees. As a one-stop wood processing operation, the trees would be grown, cut down and ground into wood chips, all on-site. The mill building and storage bins, however, were really nothing more than camouflage for the new Stony Man facilities located in the basement of the building.

Above ground, the wood-chip mill was a single-story flat-roofed concrete-block building with the mill taking up half of it and an office the other half. The mill side was open on the north end for trucks to bring the wood in and had an adjoining two-story wood-chip storage silo. Like everything else at the farm, though, what you saw was not what you got.

Behind the concrete-block facade of the building was a six-inch layer of the same armored concrete that was found at missile launch complexes. The chip storage silo's outer skin was plastic sheeting over EM invisible composite. An inner chamber in the silo could actually be used to store chips, but most of the space inside contained the antennae needed for Stony Man's worldwide communications net. New data-link transmitters allowed the farm to shoot signals carrying voice, video and electronic data to a remote mountaintop re-transmit site. An additional small, but powerful antenna, looking for all the world like a commercial satellite TV dish, was mounted outside the office half of the building to handle satcom radio traffic.

The floor of the surface building was three feet of reinforced concrete, which also served as the roof of the two level subterranean structure. The top floor of the underground structure held Aaron Kurtzman's new cyberkingdom. This modern facility was big enough to hold more powerful mainframes that would allow the computer room crew to have data on hand that they used to have to go out-of-house to acquire.

Sharing the top floor was a new communications center replacing the crowded, isolated rooms the comm people had been stuffed into before. The old radio room in the farm house had been in a room barely twelve feet long on each side with another even smaller auxiliary comm room below it in the basement. Now that the farm was able to reach out anywhere on earth through the satellite network, the equipment had to go somewhere and it made sense to have it all in one place.

The lower floor held the new security operations center, capable of monitoring everything that went on in, around and above the farm.

Adjoining the center was a soundproofed room full of generators. For safety, the fuel tanks had been buried outside the walls. On the other side of the generators, huge vent fans drew air in through the false wall of the silo. Since electronic equipment generated a great deal of heat, this was important. The hot exhaust air was vented well away from the building so as not to show an IR signature.

The original farm house retained the primary offices and living quarters for the crew, so the Annex was connected to it through a thousand-foot-long reinforced concrete tunnel sunk twelve feet into the ground. The tunnel was tall enough for the Stony Man crew to walk the distance, but a small electric railcar made the transit quicker.

The biggest drawback to the new facilities was that Barbara Price's and Hal Brognola's offices were still in the farm house and, in a crisis, they would have to make the trip through the tunnel to be personally on the scene. Their offices, however, were hard-wired to the computer room, so information could be sent directly to their workstations.

After a long, sometimes heated discussion, it had been decided that the War Room would also remain in the farm house. It was more of a briefing room than an operations center and, since it was already in the basement, it was safe in event of attack. Under a serious threat, the farm house crew could withdraw to the underground Annex.

Buck Greene finished his second inspection tour of the day with only two comments on his gig list. Even though the Annex had been operational for some time, he wasn't a man who took his duties lightly. He still wasn't satisfied with each and every last detail of the new security arrangements and probably never would be. But his paranoia was professional rather than personal, and went with the job. There would come a time, though, when he wouldn't walk the area three times a day, but that time hadn't come quite yet.

As USUAL, when Barbara Price received the call that Hal Brognola's chopper was inbound, she walked out to the farm's landing pad to meet it. In a place where nothing looked like it really was, Barbara Price was no exception. Since fashion models usually weren't found on farms unless they were visiting for a fashion shoot, she couldn't be a model. And, certainly not in washed-out jeans, scuffed cowboy boots and a man's shirt, with her honey-blond hair tied back in a ponytail. She more fit the mold of a rich man's trophy wife who had taken up hobby farming. The last thing in the world she looked like was Hal Brognola's second-in-command

and the mission controller for the Stony Man action teams.

Also as per procedure, three blacksuit guards from the boots and jeans detail were waiting in their dusty Jeep for the incoming chopper. For all the world, they looked like run-of-the-mill farmhands in well-worn work clothing, although they ranged in age from their late twenties to midforties and looked even more fit than hard-working laborers. At closer inspection one would have seen an alertness in their eyes, and looking inside the Jeep would have revealed a small armory. Anyone who tried to hijack Brognola's chopper for a ride to the farm wouldn't make it more than two steps from the pad.

Price briefly turned her back to the rotor blast as the unmarked Bell JetRanger helicopter touched down on the pad. When she turned back, she saw that, for a change, Brognola didn't look harassed as he stepped down from the aircraft. She hadn't received advanced notice that he was coming until the chopper had radioed its request to land and, since there was nothing on the threat board, she had no idea what this visit was about.

But, as she well knew, that usually meant that he was bearing bad news with a smoldering short fuse attached. "What's the story this time?" she asked.

Price knew that Brognola's ritual was never to mention the mission until he was safely inside the farm house, but she always tried to see if she could sneak past his guard.

"Actually, it isn't an emergency at all. We're just

going to do the President a favor and conduct a little background investigation on something.''

Price was so shocked that she almost stopped and asked him if he was feeling well.

CHAPTER FOUR

Stony Man Farm, Virginia

Brognola looked across the War Room's conference table at Price and Kurtzman. "You know, of course, about Senator Robert Bowers and his daughter?"

"Of course," Price answered. They were both familiar with the broad outline of what had happened to the senator and his daughter. One would have had to have been in a coma to have missed the media frenzy.

Even so, Brognola quickly hit the high points to refresh their memories before going on to the President's request. "Basically, he wants us to take an in-depth look at both the girl's OD and the senator's car crash."

"Is there any reason to think that it didn't go down the way it was shown on the news?" Kurtzman asked.

"Not really." Brognola slid a couple of photos across the table. "But, considering the senator's chairmanship, he just wants to make sure that there are no loose ends that might affect national security."

"Pretty girl." Kurtzman stared down at the photograph of Jennifer. "And a nasty way to die."

"They're all nasty ways when you're that age," Price said as she slid the photo aside.

"I can get Able Team working on this tomorrow," she told Brognola. "They're already in California and they just wrapped up their current operation."

"Needless to say," Brognola cautioned, "the FBI is already working this, as well as every other state, local and federal agency. I don't think HUD has a team on board yet, but I'm sure they have alerted their top building inspectors in the area to be ready to move in should someone find a structure that isn't in compliance."

"Isn't this a classic example of publicity-driven federal overkill?" Price asked. "I mean, I realize that Bowers was a big man on the Hill, but errant children of politicians are almost a cliché, and they have been for years."

"That's true enough," Brognola acknowledged. "But Bowers was a personal friend of both the President and the director of the FBI, as well as being the chairman of the Armed Forces Committee. That's a lot of juice up there. And, on the off chance that this was something nefarious, we'll get to the bottom of it months before the FBI does."

"If they ever do," Kurtzman said.

Brognola grinned. Even though he had a long association with J. Edgar's boys, he knew their faults in detail.

"Speaking of which—" he took some files out of his briefcase "—I have their preliminary reports for you to go over. They're thin, but they do have a few names that bear looking into. The CHP report pretty much covers the same ground, but focuses more on the freeway crash.''

"What happens if we don't turn up anything?'' Price asked as she reached for the files.

Brognola shrugged. "If we don't, we don't. And don't let this get in the way of anything else. If a shot comes across our bow, we drop this and go to work instantly.''

"I'll get on it,'' Kurtzman said.

KURTZMAN HAD BARELY gotten back to his workstation in the Annex when he started experiencing an odd sensation. The brightly lit, open areas of the new computer room were driving him crazy. He couldn't shake the feeling that he had somehow mistakenly wheeled his chair onto the set of some kind of techno-thriller movie. He was used to working in an eighteen-and-a-half-by-seventeen-foot room with three other people and enough electronic equipment to fill a couple of moving vans. His new quarters, freshly painted, were more than twice that size with a high ceiling. It was going to take a while for him to get used to it.

Kurtzman had promised Brognola that he would look into the deaths of the senator and his daughter, but he wasn't going to make a project out of it. He already knew about Rainbow Dawn. As part of his post-Y2K activities, he was still keeping an eye on the die-hard leftover millennium wackos. The fact that Y2K hadn't

ushered in the end of the world didn't stop a certain
class of people from working hard to bring about the
Apocalypse. A total cataclysm that would bring the
peace of the grave to the entire world was still appealing to some.

Despite the overall decline of doomsayers, he had
noted a dramatic membership increase in one quasi-
religious cult, the so-called Rainbow Dawn. While hundreds of thousands of men, women and their children
had engaged in serious millennium madness, the Dawners, as they liked to call themselves, had remained calm
and rational. They didn't isolate themselves from the
world; they lived and worked completely unnoticed in
society.

Rainbow Dawn's founder, Roy Givens, wasn't the
usual wacko cult leader who made the headlines of the
supermarket tabloids. To all appearances, he was a
fairly rational man who believed that he could lead his
followers to greater inner peace and happiness. That
made him no different than any number of well-
regarded preachers, gurus, politicians or self-help talk-
show hosts on the national scene. He just had a slightly
different rap.

Kurtzman figured that it wouldn't take long to go
through anything Rainbow Dawn might have on the
short time that Jennifer Wayne had been with them. A
quick cybersurf through their files should suffice to sat-
isfy the requirement before going on to issues that were
more pressing to him. But when he tried to get in, he
ran into a wall right away.

A quick recon showed that Rainbow Dawn's computers were guarded by one of the highest-level security systems he had ever seen in a nongovernment application, and that was like waving a red flag at an angry bull. But rather than charging his way through, he worked cautiously.

For a man who went by the nickname of North America's largest predator, "Bear" Kurtzman could be very delicate when he wanted to be. And he was never more delicate than when he was working in cyberspace, and supreme delicacy was what was called for this time. Anyone who had gone to such lengths to protect what should be routine business files would have installed hacker alarms as well.

As he expected, once he went below the skin, he started hitting the firewalls and trip wires, but they only made him even more determined to find out what this secretive group was doing that required so much security. Fortunately, the cutting-edge mainframe computers that had been installed in the newly operational Annex would make this relatively easy.

It took awhile to hack his way in, but after all that work, he found only one possible reference to Jennifer Wayne. In the minutes of a weekly meeting that had taken place three weeks before her death, he found a note that a "Jennifer" had been added to the Project Team. Now, the fact that a large percentage of the women in Miss Wayne's age group had been named "Jennifer" meant that he might not have found her.

And, even if this did refer to her, rather than answering any questions, the note brought up two more instead. What was the Project Team? And what, if anything, did it have to do with her death?

As much trouble as it had taken him to get that far into Rainbow Dawn, when he tried to track down the Project, he really hit a wall. Normally, he'd enjoy working at the edges until he got a corner loose enough to let him in, but he just wasn't up to it this time.

"Hunt," he called out across the room, "can you come over here for a minute?"

Huntington Wethers had once been a renowned professor of cybernetics before Brognola and Kurtzman had lured him away to join the Stony Man team. But although the professor had been taken out of academia, he hadn't completely shed academia. He didn't have Kurtzman's flashes of intuitive genius, but he was doggedly persistent in the old-fashioned mode.

"Take a look at this." Kurtzman nodded at the display on his screen.

"That looks like one of those multipulse-phased security links that DOD developed for classified weapons plants," Wethers said. "When the government finally decided that they really should try to do something to keep foreign spies from stealing the nation's secrets, this is what they came up with."

"How do I hack into it?"

The distinguished black man looked thoughtful for a moment, as if he were pondering the secrets of the universe. "I'll tell you what. Shoot that over to me and I'll start working on a cracker program. I think I have access to the matrix that was used to design that system.''

''How long do you think it'll take?''

''Hard to tell,'' Wethers said cautiously. ''It might take a couple of weeks.''

''How about doing it in three or four days so we can get Hal off our asses on that Bowers thing.''

The request didn't faze Wethers. It only made the challenge more interesting. ''I'll see what I can do.''

WHEN BARBARA PRICE walked into the computer room that afternoon, she saw that one of the TV sets over Kurtzman's workstation was tuned into a popular daytime program—*The New Frontier with Mellanie Mitchell.*

''I can't believe you're watching that garbage,'' she said, sounding disgusted.

''Mellanie Moonbeam's one of my best sources of information.'' Kurtzman grinned. ''I have to know when I need to get my stuff together so I can get it all to the landing zone in time to meet the spaceships. If I'm going to make the great leap into the New Beginning, I have to be ready for it. I don't want to miss the boat, or the flying saucer in this case.''

Price shook her head. ''Aaron, Aaron, Aaron. Of all the people I have ever known, you're absolutely the last person on this planet the galactic overlords will chose to go anywhere. They'll take one look at you and hit the reject button.''

''Why do you say that?'' Kurtzman feigned injury.

"My heart is pure, and I see a glorious future for humankind as soon as we leave the darkness of ancient hatreds behind. I haven't been inside a church except for a funeral or a wedding since I was a kid, so I'm not contaminated by the virus of religious violence. I don't believe that supernatural powers can affect my life if I give my money to men who prey on ignorance."

"That's what I mean, you're too damned rational to get sucked into that crap. This woman's worse than the fruitcake who ran that Heaven's Gate scam. At least he was easily recognized as a nutcase and offing yourself to catch a ride on a comet doesn't have very wide appeal. But she sounds almost rational. Except for the alien landing bit, her predictions make a great deal of sense."

"And that's why I'm taping every last word she says," Kurtzman said, dropping the idiotic grin. "Her predictions of the collapse of the 'Ancient Evils' sound a hell of a lot like an operations plan to me. Her program is a concerted effort to prepare the people of the Western World to live under a new order that doesn't include the three monotheisms. According to her, rationality and pragmatism are to be the new gods of this bright future, not Bronze Age deities."

"But why would anyone want to attack religions?"

"Well," Kurtzman replied, leaning back in his wheelchair, "I can think of several million reasons, each one of them being someone who was killed in sectarian violence, and that's just the body count since the end of World War II. And, to be honest with you, I agree with much of what she says. I just don't know why she's saying it.''

Price picked up on the tone of his voice. "What do we know about her?"

"That's the problem," he replied. "Damned near nothing. Before her 'conversion,' her name was Tammy Wright and she was a high-priced stripper. Then, according to her press releases, during the millennium madness, she had a conversion and realized that the evils of the world were almost all the result of religious hatreds. She says that she got a message from the future, and it gave her the ability to look into the things to come."

"Right."

"She also says that once she could see all of the paths that were open to humankind, she felt an obligation to guide us lesser beings into the light."

"Every time I hear that crap," Price said, "I hold onto my purse."

"But she doesn't ask for money," Kurtzman pointed out.

"That makes me even more suspicious."

"Which is why I'm taping her," he said. "This is a telescam, no doubt, but it's the best one I've ever seen and I'll be damned if I know what she's up to."

Price shifted gears and got to her original reason for her visit to the Annex. "How's the code-breaking going?"

"Slowly," Hunt Weathers spoke up from across the

room. "Multipulse-phasing isn't some simpleminded code that any good sixteen-year-old with fifty bucks' worth of off-the-shelf software can hack into. But I have to admit that finding this used in a nondefense-industry is intriguing."

"Hal's waiting, so let me know when you get in."

MELLANIE, AS SHE WAS known to her production crew, held the smile until the red light on the cameras winked out. Another edition of the *New Frontier,* the surprise hit of the first season of the new millennium, was over. Then the star's smile vanished and she snapped at her aide waiting off camera, "Get me the stupid bitch who designed this goddamned dress."

As the aide vanished, Mellanie turned her back to one of the stagehands who had come to change the set and roared, "Unzip this goddamned thing."

"Yes, ma'am." The stagehand hid a smile as he unzipped the skintight costume.

Mellanie let out a sigh as soon as the pressure was released and turned back to the young man, measuring him with a practiced eye. When she liked what she saw, she dropped the top of her dress, freeing her bare breasts. With a practiced wiggle, she slithered out of the dress and let it fall to her feet, revealing that minimalist thong panties were all she wore underneath.

Nudging the crumpled cloth with the toe of her high-heeled shoe, she smiled. "Could you bring that to my dressing room for me?"

Grinning like an idiot, the stagehand blushed as he

reached down and collected the dress still warm from her body. "Sure thing, ma'am."

"That's a good boy," she purred.

Mellanie's impromptu striptease was no big thing for her. She'd made her living as an exotic dancer and part-time companion to rich men before finding her new profession as a TV prophet. It had the effect, however, of dropping a grenade on the set. It went completely silent. Every man, and most of the women, froze, following her with their eyes as she marched across the stage to the exit. The grinning stagehand followed behind her like a willing lamb being led to the slaughter.

She wasn't unaware of the effect she was having. She had always prided herself on her body, and there was something about wearing thong panties with high heels that was more erotic than if she had been completely naked. Givens had cautioned her about doing things like this, but she'd had just about all she could take of the Goody Two-Shoes persona she had been forced into. If a girl couldn't shake her tits every now and then, why the hell have them?

She'd been living off her tits and ass since she was sixteen, and she wasn't about to stop now. In fact, if she didn't look like a blond reincarnation of the goddess of love, she wouldn't have this job. She'd been doing an act billed as the Living Venus when she got a call from Givens offering a job that paid too much to refuse. The money was great, but having to maintain a low profile was starting to wear on her. A girl needed to relax every now and then.

WHEN THE AIDE finally found the dressmaker who had made Mellanie's costume and escorted her to the star's dressing room, the sounds from behind the locked door weren't those of anger. When the aide knocked on the door, the sounds of pleasure got only louder.

The aide sniffed, a look of sour distaste on her face. "I guess we'll just have to talk to her later."

The dressmaker had no argument with that. Maybe the afternoon delight would mellow the woman a little. Working on this crew paid well enough, but trying to keep Mellanie happy was a second full-time job, and she wasn't getting paid enough to do both of them.

CHAPTER FIVE

Los Angeles, California

Carl Lyons was a happy man because he was doing something he did very well. He usually used his skills to track down the bad guys for Stony Man Farm, but this case was different. He wasn't after a terrorist or a threat to America's security. He and his team had been asked to dig into Senator Bowers's death, but so far, it was going slowly.

"This is lame, Ironman." Hermann "Gadgets" Schwarz sat in the back seat of their rental while Rosario Blancanales canvassed the run-down Hispanic neighborhood where the hit-and-run van had been found. They had been parked for more than an hour, and Schwarz had long since lost interest in the proceedings. "A fairly decent first year LAPD detective should be doing this scut work, not us."

"But he wouldn't be able to bust heads the way we can," Lyons replied cheerfully. "As soon as we can prove that this was a hit and not an accident, we'll be able to swing into action and start kicking ass and taking names.''

Schwarz shook his head. ''Morons who talk on their cell phones while they're driving get drop-kicked off the freeway down here every day. Just because the senator was a big-time guy on the Hill doesn't mean that he didn't have his head up and locked when he got hit. He was just unlucky enough to find a bridge abutment in front of him when it happened to him. It's no big deal.''

''Then why was that van wiped clean as a baby's butt before it was burned?'' Lyons asked. ''Usually the drivers of hit-and-run vehicles don't go to that much trouble to cover their tracks. And they usually don't have the presence of mind to burn their rigs. They just lose them.''

''Maybe the driver has other problems. He could have had wants and warrants out on—''

Lyons interrupted with a laugh. ''Really, a wanted man in L.A.? I've never heard of such a thing.''

''Cut the crap, Ironman,'' Schwarz said. ''You know what I mean.''

''Sure, he could have been carrying a load of dope in the van or he could even have been talking on his own cell phone when he ran the good senator off the road. But the fact remains that we have a dead senator and Hal wants us to find out how and why he died.''

''And you're getting off on playing Dick Tracy.''

Lyons grinned broadly in the rearview mirror. ''You

got that right, but why are you bitching? We're on vacation here. No one's shooting at us.''

"Not yet."

"You've got to make up your mind, Gadgets. If this was just another road-rage tragedy like the media called it, why would anyone want to kill us?"

"You know what I mean. If Hal sent us down here to gather seashells from the beach, you know we'd have to watch out for land mines and snipers. He's a sneaky bastard.''

"Coming from you, that's a compliment.''

WHEN ROSARIO Blancanales walked back to the car, he wasn't smiling. "I'm starting to get the impression that someone really doesn't want us to find out who was driving that van. I'm batting zero again.''

"Get in,'' Lyons told him.

"I don't know what the deal is here,'' Blancanales said, settling himself into the front passenger's seat of their rented Pontiac Grand Prix. "That van had to have burned for at least half an hour, and that's to say nothing of the gas tank exploding. Everyone within a two-block radius had to have known what was going down. But no one, and I mean absolutely no one I talked to, heard or saw anything. Zip, zilch, nada.''

"What do you think's going on?'' Lyons asked.

Nicknamed the Politician for his winning ways with people, Blancanales was known for being able to coax information out of anyone. Only the most hard core failed to succumb to his persuasive ways, or people who were afraid for their lives. To strike out like this in a primarily Hispanic neighborhood was unheard-of for him.

"I'll be damned if I know. The obvious is that they do know who was involved, but they're afraid to say anything."

"Could they have been paid off?"

Blancanales shrugged. "I didn't see any new big-screen TVs or air conditioners in any of the houses, so I doubt it. A more likely scenario is that the local gang-bangers were involved, and they put the word out that they'd bust heads if anyone opened their mouths."

Intimidation by the local criminal element was always a factor when investigating a crime. Particularly in an ethnic neighborhood such as this. It was a factor that could be impossible to overcome.

"Now that Dick Tracy and Sergeant Friday have struck out," Schwarz said, "what's next?"

"What in the hell's he talking about?" Blancanales frowned.

"Never mind him," Lyons replied. "He's mixing metaphors again."

"What I am is bored shitless," Schwarz replied.

"Okay," Lyons said. "Let's switch tactics here and go back to working on the girl's case. I think that's got a lot more to it and adds up even less than the car crash."

"And talk to the nut-jobs at Rainbow Dawn again?" Schwarz asked.

"Why not?"

Since this was such a high profile case, the farm had provided him and his Able Team partners with a number of covers, all of them well supported. One of the covers was that of insurance investigators. Both the senator and his daughter had been covered for major amounts of money, and no insurance company liked to put out that kind of cash if there was any way they could wriggle out of it.

IN HIS PENTHOUSE suite at the Rainbow Dawn headquarters, Roy Givens reached out and hit his intercom. "I need the latest market share figures for Mellanie's show."

"Yes, sir."

Mellanie Mitchell's program was an important adjunct to the Project. It was doing a lot of the preparatory work needed to help people make the transition after the Project was initiated. The show was fluff, but it was firmly planted in the mainstream of American popular culture. People like her had been shaping public opinion since the invention of the boob tube. In fact, there was no aspect of American culture than hadn't been influenced, if not outright created, by what the public watched night after night on TV.

What people wore, what they said, what they ate, what they drank, what they drove, what they believed, who they voted for, the list was endless. A lot of it came directly from television.

So pervasive was TV in shaping American culture that few, if any, even bothered to rage against its influence anymore. Sure, every time some psycho slipped his chain and went on a rampage, the criticism flew again. But it was all PR spin-doctoring, full of sound and fury and signifying exactly nothing. The public soon turned it off and went back to watching the one-eyed monster to find out what they were supposed to be thinking and doing.

The best part of it was that, like a horror-movie virus, the influence of a successful show infected everything around it. And that was already happening with Mellanie. A ton of money was being poured into her program, and the writing was carefully crafted to pass a particular message to people who couldn't even spell the word *message*.

But the main thing that had made her show so successful was the oldest grabber in the world, T and A. As had been proved over and over, tits and ass were the biggest draw on television, and not just for men. The statistics for Mellanie's program showed that a vast majority of her viewers were women in the targeted demographics, twenty-one to fifty-one.

On top of that, her show was being copied and referred to so often on the talk shows and magazine shows that her message was reaching out well beyond her own viewers. She also had her detractors, but their rebuttals were so lame as to be laughable, which only reinforced her message.

By the time the Project was activated, the vast majority of the American public would be ready for it and those who weren't simply wouldn't matter anymore.

They would join the Flat Earthers and public ridicule would drive them into impotency and obscurity.

Mellanie Mitchell would find her name in the history books before this was over.

WHEN ABLE TEAM went back to the Rainbow Dawn headquarters later that afternoon, Rosario Blancanales again took the pointman position. He had made a previous visit to the Dawners in his insurance investigator persona looking into Jennifer Wayne's death before his company paid off on a large policy. On that trip, he'd been able to verify that she had indeed signed on with the organization and had been given an entry-level job. But that had been about it. Roy Givens hadn't been available to him that day.

This time, the receptionist in the lobby gave him the same song and dance. "I'm sorry, Mr. Reyes but Mr. Givens isn't available without an appointment."

"Can I get an appointment with him this afternoon?"

"I'm sorry," the woman replied as she pretended to look down at a dayplanner, "but his schedule is full today."

"No problem," Blancanales said, smiling before glancing over at the couch in the waiting room. "I'll just wait here in case he has a cancellation."

He had barely started on the most recent copy of the company rag, *A New Dawn,* when a young woman walked up to him. "Mr. Givens can see you now, sir."

Blancanales smiled widely. "Thank you."

GIVENS ROSE from his chair, all charm, and held out his hand when Blancanales walked in. "How can I help you, Mr. Reyes?"

"As I'm sure your receptionist told you, I'm representing United Annuities in an investigation of Jennifer Wayne's death."

"Yes," Givens said with the proper intonation, "a tragedy. I understand that you've been here once before. What brings you back today?"

"This time, I'd like to take a look at the personnel file on Miss Wayne's supervisor. Mr. Dale Williams, I believe."

"I'm afraid that's not possible." Givens tented his hands in front of him. "I'm sure you can understand that our employee records have to be kept confidential. The privacy act and all of that."

"I can get a court order to examine the records if I have to," Blancanales said smoothly, "but my company doesn't want to open old wounds. It would be so much easier on the senator's widow if we didn't have to go that route. Going into open court with our request would create a media circus that wouldn't benefit anyone but the tabloids. I'm sure you understand."

Givens knew exactly what the slick bastard meant. In the case of a policy payoff this high, the insurance company wasn't going to put out the money without a fight. If they could show that Jennifer had been introduced to drug use while she had been employed by Rainbow Dawn, they would have a good case to try to recover the amount of the policy payoff from him.

"Were Mr. Williams still alive, of course," Blancanales said, "I could interview him and we wouldn't have to go to these lengths, but as it is..."

"What do you need to see?" Givens asked in capitulation.

"Does he have a discipline file?"

"We don't keep records of that kind here at Rainbow Dawn," Givens replied. "Our employees are also members of our group, and we don't believe that recording a person's missteps on their journey to enlightenment serves any purpose. When a mistake is made here, that person isn't punished, instead they are shown a better way to do whatever it was they faltered on."

Blancanales looked at Givens like the man had just spoken gibberish, which of course he had. "So you're saying that no one is ever fired here?"

"Not in the sense that you mean, no," Givens answered. "People do make mistakes, certainly. But, when they do, they are helped, not punished."

"Like Miss Wayne was helped by being shown the door?"

For an instant, the professional smile vanished from Givens's face.

Gotcha! Blancanales thought.

"Mr. Reyes," the cult leader said, his smile back in place, "I think you're smart enough to know that we didn't throw Jennifer to the wolves. When we discovered that she was using drugs, we—"

"By the way, how was that discovered?"

Givens didn't miss a beat. "One morning when she

came to work, Dale Williams noticed that she didn't seem to be acting normally. And when he asked what was wrong, she confessed that she was using.''

''I see,'' Blancanales said and he did. It was more than a little convenient that Williams was also no longer among the living.

''And,'' Blancanales said, rummaging through his papers, ''you have stated that she left here of her own volition?''

''Yes. She said that she intended to seek treatment, but…'' Givens shrugged. ''You know how difficult that can be even with the best of intentions.''

''Do you know which treatment center she was visiting?''

''I'm sorry, but that was a private decision on her part and we weren't privileged to that information. Is there anything else I can help you with today?''

Blancanales locked eyes with him. ''I'd still like to see Williams's personnel file.''

Givens lost the staring contest and reached out for his intercom button.

BACK IN Able Team's motel suite, Rosario Blancanales briefed Lyons and Schwarz on his visit. ''Williams's file didn't have anything of value,'' he said. ''In fact, it looked a bit too new for someone who had worked there for almost two years, if you know what I mean. My gut tells me that something's wrong there,'' he concluded. ''I just don't know what it is.''

''Has anyone stopped to ask why anyone would want

to off this girl?'' Schwarz asked. ''I mean, from the FBI profile we have on her, she wasn't too bright, but she wasn't a basket case either. She was damned good looking and apparently didn't mind sharing her goodies. People don't off party chicks who look like her. It's counterproductive.''

Blancanales laughed.

''I'm serious, man,'' Schwarz said. ''While you were in there, I've been surveilling the foot traffic, and none of the women I saw going in or out of that place looked anything like her. Now, it's true that there weren't too many out-and-out trolls or whales, but I can tell you that most of them spend their nights in a kennel, not a disco.''

''When did you get so picky, Gadgets?'' Lyons asked, grinning. ''I've seen you take the flea collars off some of your dates before taking them out in public.''

Blancanales started to howl.

''Dammit, guys, all I'm saying is that they should have been overjoyed to have a girl like her even walk through the door, much less one who liked to get down, or what-the-hell-ever they call it nowadays.''

''He has a point, Pol,'' Lyons said, suddenly getting serious. ''Whatever kind of scam Givens is running, it's something that appeals to the age group that's still focussed on getting it on. They aren't the one-foot-in-the-grave crowd of most pseudoreligious cults. From what we know, celibacy doesn't seem to be one of Givens's hang-ups, so they're probably humping each other all night long around there. And, since everybody likes to sample the new chick, particularly one who looked like she did, I don't think they got tired of her that fast.''

Blancanales nodded. ''Damn, Ironman. I'm the guy who's supposed to pick up on stuff like that, not you.''

Lyons grinned. ''You'd better get to work on it then, hadn't you?''

''Doing what?''

''Work her supervisor's background.''

''I was afraid you were going to say that.''

CHAPTER SIX

Los Angeles, California

The more Roy Givens thought about it, the more uneasy he became about the insurance investigator who wasn't willing to stop looking into the Jennifer Wayne incident. Before he had become a spiritual leader to thousands, he had sold insurance himself and he knew the greasy bastards who populated that business. This guy who was calling himself Rudy Reyes wasn't a typical insurance guy, not even a company investigator. In fact, for all his polish, he had a cop's mind, and Givens also knew cops, but from the other side of the badge.

Givens didn't need this, and he sincerely wished that he had never heard of Miss Jennifer Wayne, but he had to play the hand he'd been given. That didn't mean, though, that he wouldn't keep trying to improve the odds in his favor. The senator's crash had been accepted as a road-rage incident and had gone down in the records that way. Dale Williams's drowning in a place known for its nasty riptides was also a matter of record. The only thing that kept coming back to bite him was Miss Wayne's OD story. It had made it into the official record, too, and he needed it to stay that way. In retrospect, he should have arranged her demise differently, but how could he have known that she'd never done drugs?

Pick a hundred So Cal hot-pants sweeties at random and a hundred and one of them were at least recreational users of something. When he had given the orders on her, he hadn't had a clue that she was a drug virgin. Reyes was sniffing around to find out who'd gotten her cherry, and that meant he needed his action man again.

Givens's action man was a street thug named Hoop Stringer. Stringer had a small record, but nothing that would alert an investigator. He was also a sociopath, which made him perfect for this kind of work. Being completely unemotional, he never did anything more than was absolutely necessary to get the job done. He hadn't laid a hand on the delectable Miss Wayne beyond giving her the "hot shot." Jennifer had been a real looker, and many guys might have wanted to sample that before offing her, but not Stringer.

Reyes had written a local contact number on the back of his business card, and it was the number of a small motel. It wasn't a Ramada Inn or an Embassy Suites, but was what was most often referred to as an "economy" motel, a flea trap. That was a strange place for a company man on an expense account to stay. Who and whatever he was, though, Reyes had to be taken out of the picture.

It would have to be done carefully and might even have to involve a subcontractor or two, but he'd leave that decision to Stringer. Givens hated using subcontractors, but sometimes they were necessary to insure success and to add local color. Reyes was staying in a bad neighborhood, and it wouldn't raise an eyebrow if he was fatally mugged in the parking lot of his own motel.

As ROY GIVENS had said, Leroy "Hoop" Stringer was a sociopath. The fact that he had never heard the word and wouldn't have known what it meant if he did made no difference to him. As far as Stringer was concerned, he was a player who was smart enough not to have gotten caught too many times. His early busts had all been juvie, and he hadn't done any serious time. He had, however, been locked up long enough to know that he didn't want to go back for a serious stint.

That kept him out of L.A.'s primary industry, the drug business, but there was no way that he was going to spend his life making minimum wage in some loser job. Instead, he put himself in business as a one-stop fix-it shop for those who couldn't deal with their problems on their own. He and his small organization could handle almost anything a paying client wanted done.

If a person wanted his girlfriend's boss beaten up for hitting on her, Stringer could see to it, for a price. If a person wanted a new Range Rover delivered to Mexico, he could handle that, too. If a business competitor needed to be burned out, he had the means to see it done. More serious problems, things like seeing that someone had a serious accident or disappeared altogether, could also be done, but the price was higher.

That was why he liked getting phone calls from Roy Givens: the man had money. This time, he wanted Stringer to take care of another serious problem, and so he would. As before, Givens didn't insult him by suggesting how it should be done. All he ever said was where he wanted it to happen and asked what it would cost. Stringer was smart enough not to get too greedy, and the man always paid up-front.

This job didn't look any more difficult than the last two he had done for Givens. An insurance investigator was asking too many questions about things that were dead and gone. Stringer believed that the dead should stay dead and that speaking of them wasn't wise.

WHEN ABLE TEAM checked into a motel, one of the first things Gadget Schwarz always did was to hook it up for video surveillance. They had no known opposition this time and nothing to watch out for, but old habits died hard. He put in his usual hardwired sensors and pickups covering the door and back window before they had even unpacked. Then he placed a couple of miniature remotes to keep an eye on the parking lot and one on the breezeway that led past their second-story door.

HOOP STRINGER LOVED action adventure and spy movies. He fancied himself kind of a combination of Action

Jackson and Mr. T, but more subtle. He knew the value of patience and good surveillance before making a move, and he was being patient this time. Givens wanted this guy taken out as soon as possible, but kicking down his motel-room door and beating him to death wouldn't be cool.

Instead, he had two of his men—teenagers actually, but he always called them men—keeping an eye on the target for him. He had another group of three teenagers close by the motel, waiting for word that the target was coming out. Since the guy's room was on the second floor, by the time he reached the parking lot, he could have his people in place.

The plan was for his men to take the target down, bust his head, grab his wallet and keys and hijack his car. That would fit in with the neighborhood, and the car could be driven out into the Valley and burned like the van had been. That would meet the client's requirement quite nicely.

ROSARIO BLANCANALES rummaged through his briefcase for a moment before getting up and putting on his coat. "Where are you going?" Carl Lyons asked.

"I left something in the car."

Schwarz glanced over at his video monitors as Blancanales opened the door and walked out onto the breezeway. Everything was clear.

WHEN STRINGER'S lookouts told him that the target was on the way to the parking lot, he sent in the rest of his troops. Five teenagers should be able to take down an insurance guy.

He tagged along behind the first wave to make sure that they did their work properly.

A smile crossed his face when he saw that the target was halfway down the stairs and his men were in place in the shadows. In the next few seconds, he would earn another fat paycheck.

SOMETHING ON the monitor caught Schwarz's eye, but when he looked, he didn't see much. When he switched over to night vision, he thought he caught a flash of something hiding behind a car.

"Is Pol wearing his com link?" he asked Lyons.

"I don't think so," Lyons answered. "Why?"

"I thought I had something down there."

"I'll check it out."

When Lyons stepped outside, Blancanales was approaching the car. Lyons scanned the poorly lit parking lot, but didn't see anything. Suddenly, two punks jumped out from behind a car with what looked like pipes in their hands.

"Pol!" he shouted. "Behind you!"

"I'm on them," Blancanales yelled back as he spun on his left foot and sent the right crashing into his first attacker's chest. A metallic clatter sounded as the length of pipe the punk had been carrying hit the pavement.

That warned Blancanales about what he was facing, so he went defensive with a strong offense. The second punk hesitated in midswing, and that's all it took for Blancanales to kick him in the crotch. His scream startled a couple more punks out of hiding. One look at their buddy writhing on the ground clutching what was left of his family jewels told them they wanted no part of this.

"Hey! Assholes!" Lyons called out from the top of the breezeway when he saw four figures rapidly fleeing the scene. "Stop right there."

When they didn't, a tall black man stepped out of the shadows, a glint of chrome-plated steel in his hand. Hoop Stringer's paycheck was fading quickly, and he couldn't allow that to happen. Holding his pistol sideways like they did in the movies, he snapped off two quick shots at the second figure on the breezeway before turning to his primary target.

Lyons didn't flinch as the 9 mm rounds sang past his head. His hand dived into his left armpit and came out holding his .357 Colt Python. As the pistol cleared leather, he thumbed the hammer back for a smoother first-round trigger pull. A micro-second later he was on target and dropped the hammer.

The roar of the .357 echoed from the building on the other side of the parking lot as the heavy slug took the gunman high in the left chest. His aim had been spot on, so Lyons didn't need a second shot.

Stringer staggered backward from the blow to his chest, a look of confusion on his face. This wasn't supposed to have happened. He was dead before he hit the ground.

The shot hadn't yet echoed away when the thug Blancanales had put down with the crotch shot rolled over and came up with a shiny .25-caliber hideaway in his hand.

"Pol!" Lyons yelled as he instantly retargeted. The roar of the Python sounded again, and the .357 punched the thug back down to the ground.

The curtains in a few of the motel rooms had been pulled back an inch, but no one was opening their doors on an urban firefight.

"I owe you one, Ironman," Blancanales said as he got to his feet, having dived to the ground at Lyons's warning.

The big ex-cop holstered his weapon. "Put it on my tab."

SINCE THEY HAD created a pair of corpses in a rather public place, the Able Team trio produced their FBI IDs and went through the drill when the LAPD showed up.

"Do you have any idea who the gunmen were?" Lyons asked one of the cops.

The cop pulled back the sheet as the paramedics were about to load the body into the meat wagon. "This one's name is Hoop Stringer, a local wanna-be hood who ran a loose-knit gang of street punks. They never got into the big-time stuff, so they didn't get much attention from us. They just terrorized the hell out of the locals, but you know how that goes."

The cop hooked a thumb at the second body being

zipped into a rubber bag. "That's one of his homies, but I'll have to print him to find out who he is."

Lyons wasn't surprised at the cop's admission that while these thugs were known, they had done little about them. From his days on the force, he knew that a cop had to prioritize. Petty thuggery and neighborhood terrorism didn't stack up against the major urban criminal pastimes—drugs, murder and gunrunning.

"With the ringleader down, the locals should be able to breathe a little easier for a while."

The cop snorted. "Until some other asshole moves in here and picks up where he left off."

While Lyons was talking to the cop, Blancanales was talking to the LAPD sergeant on the scene. "We're just finishing up the last of the Bowers investigation," he said, "and I'm sure the director would appreciate it if we didn't get mentioned to the media. He wants us back doing something useful instead of wasting more time around here."

The sergeant had put in more than his share of overtime hours on the Bowers incident, and he understood the Fed's concern. And, since he seemed like a nice guy, he wouldn't make life any more difficult for him that it already was.

"I don't think that'll be a problem," the sergeant said. "With your witness statements and the forensics from the perps' guns, this will go down as a good shooting. The DA might want an affidavit later, but you should be able to do that from Washington."

"I appreciate that."

The cop grinned. "We owe it to you for giving us a hand here. That Stringer asshole has been a neighborhood problem for years, but we could never get anything worth booking him on that the DA wouldn't throw out."

"Glad we could help."

AS SOON AS the cops left, the trio went to their room and started to pack.

"I think we've hit a nerve," Blancanales said. "Getting shot at is always a good sign of that."

"We've sure as hell hit something," Schwarz stated, sounding indignant. "This was supposed to be a mail-it-in investigation, man. No one said anything to me about people shooting at us."

"We're supposed to be investigating a string of mysterious deaths, remember?"

"But none of them were shot."

"I think we need to get the Bear digging into this for us," Blancanales suggested. "It's about time that we know who and what the hell we're really up against here."

"Don't worry," Lyons said. "As soon as we get packed up and check out of this flea trap, I'll have a talk with Barbara and tell her that we're going into full-contact mode and that I want full mission support."

"You got that right," Schwarz said.

WHEN ABLE TEAM'S incident report came in from L.A., Hal Brognola and Barbara Price had a secure minitelecon. Since they weren't dealing with a national crisis this time, Brognola stayed in his Justice Department office instead of moving his briefcase to the farm for the duration.

"Do you want me to send Lyons some reinforcements?" Price asked him. "Striker and Phoenix are on stand-down."

"Leave McCarter and his boys in place," Brognola replied, "but you might want to ask Striker if he would mind checking in with Carl. Since we still can't prove that this is more than what it looks like on the surface, I'd like to leave it at that for now."

Mack Bolan, a.k.a. the Executioner, and Hal Brognola went back a long way, to a time when they had been on opposite sides of the law. That was ancient history now, and the two men had long since joined forces. In fact, the concept of Stony Man Farm had been born out of that partnership, and while Bolan wasn't an official part of SOG any longer, he still used the farm as his base camp. Even the lone warrior had to have someplace he could go to rest up, work on his hardware and find congenial company. The farm fit all of those requirements quite nicely.

This relaxed relationship actually worked well for both parties. Bolan used the farm as his resupply point and operations center. Also, having the resources of the farm to call on had become a vital part of the Executioner's operational mode. Kurtzman could run an address and print out a map in minutes instead of his having to recon the area himself. Additionally, Brognola often invited him to participate in SOG missions. Even though he was under no obligation to do so, more often than not he joined up with Phoenix Force or Able Team.

When Bolan wasn't taking care of business, he kept in touch with the farm as a matter of routine, both to keep informed and to talk to Barbara Price.

"He checked in the day before yesterday," she replied, "so I know where he's going to be for the next few days. I'll give him a call and see if he wants to lend a hand."

"Good," Brognola concluded. "Give me a call when he's on-site."

"Will do."

CHAPTER SEVEN

Seattle, Washington

It took Barbara Price a couple of tries before she caught up with Mack Bolan at his motel in Seattle's Pioneer Square district.

"How'd you like to get in out of the rain?" she asked after they passed pleasantries.

He glanced out the window at the typical Seattle weather. "What'd you have in mind, someplace where the sun shines maybe?"

"How'd you know?" She laughed. "Carl is in L.A. working on that Senator Bowers case, and I think they could use some backup. Someone set them up to be ambushed."

Like the rest of the nation, Bolan hadn't been able to avoid exposure to the media storm over Senator Bowers' death and the OD of his daughter. He had been in a coffee shop in Seattle when he had first seen Jennifer's photo in a copy of *USA Today*. When he scanned the story, it had appeared to be just one more in an endless line of pretty, young people he had seen over the years who had died with poison in their veins. But if Able Team was working the case, there had to be more to it.

"What's the deal?" he asked.

Los Angeles, California

CARL LYONS WAS ON HAND in the Alaska waiting area at LAX to meet Bolan and saw him come out of the jetway with a large carryon in one hand and his usual small bag in the other. He was surprised to see him turn back to a good-looking blonde and help her put the bag she had been carrying into a luggage cart along with the one in his hand. They shook hands before Bolan turned away.

"I'm glad to see that chivalry isn't dead." Lyons looked in the woman's direction when Bolan walked up. "Who's the item?"

"A seatmate."

"Did you get her phone number? If you forgot, I'm sure I can catch up with her and get it for you."

Bolan's eyes smiled.

Seeing that he wasn't going to get any more out of the Executioner on that topic, Lyons led the way out. "Gadgets has the car waiting in a no-parking zone."

"The old Justice Department 'official business' drill?" Bolan asked.

"It works like a champ."

Even in a madhouse like LAX, both the passengers and hustlers in the terminal made way for the two men.

But this time, they made twice as much room to let them pass. It seemed to be the right thing to do.

AFTER THE MOTEL incident, Able Team had relocated to new quarters, this time in an upscale hotel. A suite of corner rooms on the second floor had been set up as a mini–command post and comm center for the duration.

As soon as Bolan walked in and dropped his bag, the four Stony Man warriors went into a skull session. After filling him in on their activities so far, Schwarz briefed him on the main target, Rainbow Dawn. He had snapped a series of photos of their headquarters and had blown them up to eight by eleven's in a photo shop's instant enlargement machine.

"As you can see," he said, "that place is an urban blockhouse. There are no windows at all on the bottom floor and no doors except for the main entrance and a fire door in back. They have an antenna farm on the roof—" he moved a long-range shot to the top of the pile "—and a lot of it's stuff I haven't seen before, but I think they're talking to someone on noncommercial channels."

"Have you tried to listen in yet?"

"I've got a shipment of farm goodies coming in by overnight courier," Schwarz said. "When they arrive, I'll do what I can to tap into whatever they've got going on over there. From the shape of the wave forms on the dishes, my guess is that most of it's data link."

"What do you have on Givens's home turf, Carl?" Bolan asked Lyons.

"We've got the address, but we haven't scoped it out yet."

"I'll take that tomorrow," Bolan said.

"Do you want me to go with you to tackle the security?" Schwarz asked. "If he's set up at home like he is at his office complex, it'll be dense."

Bolan shook his head. "This will just be a drive through. I don't want to try a penetration until I have a better grip on the situation here."

"While you're doing that," Lyons said, "I'm going to take Pol with me and work the manager at the girl's apartment. We know the guy's been grilled by both the FBI and LAPD just for starters, as well as having been hounded to death by the media, but I want to talk to him again."

Bolan smiled. Lyons had a way of getting people to talk. "Good cop—bad cop?"

Lyons grinned. "I was thinking more in the line of bad Fed—badder Fed. He owns that flea trap she died in, and we might be able to lean on him big-time. You know, health and safety violations, that sort of thing."

"That works for me."

Bolan went on to the next topic. "How're we fixed for hardware?"

"We came down here pretty light," Lyons replied, "because we weren't expecting to have to fight our way through town. But I can't let people shoot at us and get away with it, so I put in a call to Cowboy Kissinger to send us a full mission pack, and it's on its way.''

"I'm also going to need a car," Bolan said. "A Beemer, a top-of-the-line Accura, something like that, with a little speed, good handling, electric windows and a sunroof."

"Sounds like you're planning on going to war, Striker."

"I guess we'll see, won't we?"

ROY GIVENS WASN'T happy to hear about Hoop Stringer's failure. He never liked to hear of failure, and certainly not about something as important as that. As near as he could find out, some off-duty cops had been in the vicinity and Stringer had made the mistake of shooting at one of them. Stringer's demise wasn't half as important to him as the fact that the insurance man had survived. With Stringer dead, though, he had no fears that he might be tied to the attempt on Reyes's life. He knew that he was bulletproof on that as well as everything else that Stringer had handled for him. With the cutouts he had used, there was no way to tie Rainbow Dawn into any of it.

Rainbow Dawn was exactly what it appeared to be, a group of people who had freely banded together to try to improve their lives by expanding their narrow view of the world. Unlike so many other cults, the Dawners didn't dabble in either guns or drugs, they didn't embezzle, nor did they have the members empty their bank accounts into the organization's coffers.

Those were all things that could backfire and bring ruin, and Givens was smarter than that.

His personal life as Roy Givens was equally bullet-proof. The fact that he hadn't been born with that name was of no consequence. In his official Rainbow Dawn bio, he admitted to knowing nothing of his heritage because he had been adopted. The fact that he had adopted the name he currently used long after the fact would never come to light because the original Roy Givens had also been adopted, and his parents had died in a tragic fire. Roy himself had died not too long after that and his badly decomposed body had been found carrying the ID of an up-and-coming teenaged petty crook named Frank Medan. Changing identities with a corpse cleared his file, and taking a Greyhound to California changed his life.

Once in L.A., the newly renamed Roy Givens found himself in a brave new world of unlimited opportunity. Many of these opportunities were on the other side of the law, but there had been more than enough semilegal scams that didn't lead to hard time for him to keep busy. One of the biggest moneymakers of that time was anything connected with the New Age movement that was just picking up steam.

He quickly made a name for himself, along with a bundle of cash, by running New Age scams ranging from self-help seminars to crystal healing sessions. Every time the New Age racket took a different turn, he was right on top of it, milking the new angle for all it was worth. His running into Grant Betancourt, though, had been the thing that had finally catapulted him into the big time.

The billionaire had attended one of his seminars and, after the session, had approached him. Betancourt wanted certain things done and Givens was a man who had proved that he could do things, so an agreement was quickly struck. Out of their deal came two things: one of them was Givens' personal wealth and the second was the foundation of the organization that was now known as Rainbow Dawn.

In the beginning, Givens hadn't known where Betancourt intended to take the organization he was putting together. All he knew was that his benefactor wanted him to recruit certain kinds of people and create a place where they could be trained in technical fields and put to work in private industry. It was only when the members were out in society that things had become clearer to him.

Grant Betancourt had no connection to Rainbow Dawn now whatsoever. The money he fronted for things like Mellanie's TV program was funneled through offshore trusts as donations from anonymous donors. In fact, since their first few private meetings, the only way Givens had to communicate with his boss was through a scrambled phone. And it was that phone that he picked up now to make his report.

"I WANT YOU to get out of this immediately," Betancourt told Givens at the end of his report. "If Reyes returns to your headquarters, deny him access beyond your lobby and refer him to your attorneys.''

"He's pretty persistent," Givens warned.

"I'm sending you an executive security team, and they'll take over your internal security, effective immediately. I want you completely out of it. Once more, it's obvious that you can't handle it.''

"I'm not sure that I really need outsiders here," Givens said cautiously. "We run a pretty loose organization, and they might upset my people.''

"I don't give a damn what you or your people think," Betancourt snapped. "You wouldn't be in this mess if you hadn't wanted to screw a senator's daughter.''

"I didn't know who she was," Givens said weakly.

"If you'd vetted her properly, you'd have screwed her on your own time and she wouldn't have been brought in on something she never should have been given access to. You were warned about that sort of thing before.''

Givens hadn't bothered even to try to tell Betancourt that he hadn't gotten close to Jennifer. He had watched a video of her in action, though, and had decided to add her to his personal shortlist. But he had been waiting until she had been properly broken in and trained before he bedded her. That he hadn't been able to get his shot at her was the real tragedy of this whole affair. Nonetheless, Rainbow Dawn was never short of young women who were willing to give till it hurt. None of them were quite in the same league as the late Miss

Wayne, but what they lacked in the looks department, they made up for in enthusiasm.

"I warned you once about turning your building into your own private whorehouse," Betancourt said, "and I won't do it again. The next time something like this happens, you won't live to regret it. Do you understand completely?"

"Yes, sir."

"Nothing," Betancourt grated, "not you, and certainly not anyone in your organization, is going to get in the way of the completion of the Project. Do you understand that?"

"Yes, sir."

BETANCOURT PUT down the phone and looked out the one-way glass of his suite's windows. It was more than apparent that he had made a serious mistake when he had recruited Givens. It had seemed a good idea at the time, but the past month had proved it a serious mistake, one of the very few he had ever made in his life. But he hadn't gotten where he was by not knowing how to correct mistakes. He reached for his phone again.

CHAPTER EIGHT

Los Angeles, California

By the time Bolan returned from his recon the next morning, the members of Able Team were back from their missions as well.

"Did you get anything from the apartment manager, Pol?" Bolan asked.

"Not a hell of a lot," Blancanales replied. "According to him, Wayne didn't have a lot of visitors. The ones she did have were all male, though, and he picked out the photo of Williams as being the guy he saw there most often."

"That follows the established story," Bolan noted. "What about any signs of drug use?"

"That one caught him completely by surprise. He said that he hadn't figured her for even a casual user as he hadn't seen or heard any of the signs. Running an apartment building, he claimed to be somewhat of an expert on the subject."

"Again, that agrees with what we have from the FBI report."

"What *is* new," Carl Lyons said, "is that we got the tox screen on Williams back from the medical examiner and he had no traces of drugs in his system when he died. Not even ethanol. He was either a piss-poor swimmer or he had a little help drowning."

Bolan smiled grimly. "Considering how this is shaping up, do you want to place your bets on that one?"

"Not a chance."

"We do have something new at the Rainbow Dawn building," Gadgets Schwarz reported. "I spotted uniformed security guards, and they didn't look like rent-a-cops, more on the order of professional hard guys. They have the haircuts and polished boots of some kind of disciplined unit, not just a collection of individuals."

"Why doesn't that surprise me?"

Bolan looked at Lyons. "Do the Dawners have any kind of internal paramilitary security unit like the Nation of Islam has?"

"Not that anyone has reported," Lyons said. "But that doesn't mean anything. We really don't have good information on what's going on inside there."

"At least I didn't see anyone like them on my two visits," Blancanales confirmed.

"The good news," Schwarz said, "is that I got the interception gear in place in an apartment with a good line of sight to the roof of Givens's building. The bad news is that so far, I'm getting diddly that I can break. I got two hours' worth this morning, but it's all encrypted. I'm going to have to send it to Kurtzman and let him have a crack at it."

"What do you think, Carl?" Bolan asked.

The ex-LAPD cop shrugged. "Part of me just wants to call in a confirmation of the official findings, kiss the ass of the FBI and go find something more useful to do. I mean, this is L.A., right? An OD, a car crash and a drowning. What's new?"

"But?"

"My gut says that this thing stinks."

"Then go with your gut."

AFTER GOING OVER the latest Able Team update, Aaron Kurtzman put in a video call to Barbara Price. It was almost as good as being in the room with her.

"The question," he said, "that we're not looking at hard enough isn't how was Jennifer Wayne killed, but why. We've been focusing on the senator, but it's obvious to me that he was killed to keep him from looking deeper into her death."

"What do you think happened to her?"

He leaned forward in his wheelchair. "Okay, let me lay it out the way I see it. A not-too-smart, but rather sporty girl goes to college, quickly gets bored and finds a boyfriend to brighten her nights. He invites her to join his cult and, because of her personal form of therapy, she's instantly accepted. And playing New Age devotee is a hell of a lot more fun than UCLA. Somehow, though, she comes across something she's not supposed to see. She gets excited about it, talks to the wrong somebody and it gets back to Givens. He pushes the panic button and has her set up to go down as another Southern California drug OD.

"Then—" Kurtzman raised his right index finger "—just when he thinks he's home free, the excrement is dumped in the ventilation by the truckload. He suddenly discovers that this bouncy little Miss Fun and Games isn't just another Southern California party girl. She's the daughter of a very powerful United States senator. So, when the angry, grief-stricken father shows up with half of the FBI in tow, he has a freeway accident. Are you with me so far?"

Price smiled. "Yes, Aaron, I'm somewhat familiar with the outline you've proposed."

"Okay. Now one thing that hasn't been factored in is Dale Williams, the boyfriend who introduced her to the Dawners and was also her supervisor. He also has a very Southern California accident. He's screwing around in the surf and gets swept away. That's rather inconvenient for anyone who wants to find out about Wayne's sojourn with the Dawners."

"But the police report has no indications of foul play in his death, either."

"You know, it would take me a while to run the numbers on how many people die in L.A. in any given period of time and break it down by type of death. But let me assure you that if I tried to run the stats on this many people who are connected dying accidental deaths within a two-week time frame, I don't have a big enough computer.

"Then," Kurtzman continued, "if that isn't enough,

we get an attempted hit on Rosario after he starts grilling Givens about the girl. Everything keeps going back to the girl. The only question we need to answer is why she was killed. If we learn that, this thing will open up like a sardine can.''

''Aaron, I know you get your hackles up about groups like this, and I understand it. But we really don't have anything yet that puts them in the bad-guys pile.''

''Except for what they call the Project,'' he countered. ''And, if it's just another peace, love and tie-dye plan to build playgrounds in the bad parts of town, I don't see why it's so heavily encoded. What's that old saw about the guilty fleeth when no man pursueth?''

He shook his head. ''As you know, I had a hell of a time breaking into the outer layer of their computer security systems. I'd have had an easier time reading the President's personal mail. Hunt is still working on the Project security code, which just happens to look a hell of a lot like a DOD system used to guard nuclear weapons sites.''

''Okay, I believe you,'' she said. ''And I'll try to get Hal on board.''

''It's not Hal I'm worried about,'' Kurtzman replied. ''As far as I'm concerned, the President's a little too close to this thing. I know that he was good friends with Bowers, but putting us to work on something like this is outside the envelope. It makes me wonder why we were given this assignment.''

Price had also asked herself that question, but had

just chalked it up to the President wanting a third opinion from people he knew he could trust completely.

It HADN'T EVEN TAKEN a day for Roy Givens to get real tired of Grant Betancourt's storm troopers. Within hours of their phone call, an entire security unit had been flown in and had taken over the Rainbow Dawn headquarters. And, from the moment they arrived, things had started rapidly going downhill.

Rainbow Dawn was a spiritual haven for talented free spirits, not an R and R camp for black-combat-suited Nazis. Their mere presence was disrupting enough, but their condescending behavior toward the members was a more serious problem. It was impossible to reach a mediative state with men like them talking loudly about airheads and crystal freaks.

But he knew that he was stuck with them for the duration. Betancourt had made that abundantly clear when he had ordered them in to take over his security. And that included their leader, who went by the single name Miller and who had set up shop in Givens's office.

"You've been suckered big-time, Givens," Miller said as he looked up from the report his survey team had just completed. The first part of any job was to survey the situation.

"What do you mean?"

"What I mean is that your insurance guy is either a cop or a Fed, and I'm betting on him being some kind of Fed."

Givens went cold. "What are you talking about?"

"Well, for starters," Miller replied, "he's got a couple of sidekicks he's working with, and one of them has been keeping us under electronic surveillance."

Givens was stunned. "You're kidding."

"I wouldn't shit you about something like that, mister," Miller snapped. "They've got a number of receivers and long-range scanners listening in on us from a building over on the next block. They're catching everything you send out on land line or sat-link."

"What are you going to do about them?" Givens felt himself going into a panic.

The security man smiled. "Flat-ass nothing."

"But why?"

Miller took a deep breath. Why was it that every time he was assigned to work with a civilian, the guy turned out to be a complete idiot?

"Well, if we bust their surveillance site, they'll just put their receivers somewhere else where we might not be able to find them. If we leave them alone, we know where they are, but they don't know that we know. Got that?"

"But what are you going to do to keep them from spying on us?"

"Like I said," Miller replied. "Nothing, because they can't hurt us."

"But I don't understand. You said that they were listening in on us."

The security man took a deep breath and continued the explanation. "I'm not going to do anything because they're not getting shit for their efforts. Like I told you before, everything that goes out of this building is scrambled and there's no way they can break the encryption."

Miller laughed. "In fact, not even the government can break it because while Mr. Betancourt supplies the coding programs to the Feds, he always keeps the latest version for himself. It would take a couple of mainframes and the best code crackers in the world to make sense out of it."

Like most people who used modern cybertechnology, Givens knew how to use it, but had no idea what made it work. If it worked when he turned it on, he didn't need to know how it worked, because he had someone on his staff to fix it when it didn't.

"Are you going to do anything at all about those men?"

"That has to be cleared through the Phoenix headquarters," Miller shrugged. "Then, if I get a go, we'll take them out."

BLANCANALES HAD PUT his voice mail number on the card he had left with Givens and when he checked in, he had a message from the cult leader. "Mr. Givens, Rudy Reyes here," he said when he called back. "I got a phone message that you wanted me to call you."

"Glad you called back. I have some information that might help clear up your questions about Miss Wayne's stay here. Some of my people were cleaning out Dale

Williams's room and they found some material pertaining to her that you might find interesting.''

"What kind of material?"

"Well," Givens said hesitantly, "to be honest, it's a series of photographs. Not exactly the sort of thing I can release to the media, but I think they may explain many things for you."

"When can I see this stuff?"

"This evening if you'd like," Givens replied. "Say eight?"

"I'll be there," Blancanales said.

"How'd I do?" Givens asked the man in the black jumpsuit with the headphones seated behind a monitor screen.

"The guy's cautious." Miller looked up from his voice-analysis readout. "He doesn't believe you for a second. The needle was almost jumping off the scale here."

"Will he make the meeting?"

"I think so."

"What do you want me to do when he gets here?" Givens asked.

"Just exactly what you were told," Miller said. "Nothing more and nothing less. My people will do what is necessary, and you don't need to know anything about it."

Givens was no stranger to necessity, but he had hoped that the need for it was finally over. He had tried to do the necessary to Reyes once before, but fell woefully short.

"CAN YOU SPELL *setup*, children?" Schwarz quipped. "I've never heard such crap in my life."

"What kind of photos, I wonder?" Lyons mused. "A couple of bare-ass shots of Wayne and maybe an action shot or two to prove that she was a party girl. And, of course, her partner in those will be the guy who went swimming without a lifeguard. That way, no one will be able to question the circumstances of the shots."

"That's true," Schwarz agreed. "And they don't even have to be legit. They can easily have been doctored. All it takes is a computer with a photo-enhancement program. They take one of their girls who is roughly her size and shape, get her to drop her pants for a couple of candid shots. Then they do a cut-and-paste job from snapshots of Wayne taken at, say the Christmas party, and you have her face on that body. No one questions what they see and they have established her as a slut."

"Except I don't think these guys do Christmas," Lyons said. "It's not New Age enough."

"Dammit, you know what I mean," Schwarz growled. "Any photo that shows her full face can be used. The programs do a bit map that can be manipulated to show either side and can change expression. That will give them powerful material in case—" he smiled at Blancanales "—some insurance company tries to play hardball."

"No matter where they came from," Blancanales said, "I'm going to take the meeting."

"You're out of your rabbit-assed mind, Pol." Schwarz sounded disgusted. "How much plainer does it have to get? Are you waiting for a fish wrapped in yesterday's paper to be delivered to our room? You're being set up, man."

"You're right. I'm being set up. But is it an ambush if I know that I'm being ambushed?"

"Are you going to be any less dead for knowing it?"

"Look, here's how I see it. The photos might be a come-on, but I don't think so. I think that they actually have something, Whether they're doctored or not, it doesn't make any difference. They have something and they want to give it to me. So, I go in there, get the material and leave. If they're going to try to take me out, it'll be after I'm back on the street. They'll need to be able to say that I made the meeting. They'll have videotapes showing me leaving the building and driving away. They're not about to do anything on the premises."

"He's right, Gadgets," Bolan said. "This is a good way to find out how far they want to take this."

"You're both nuts."

With Blancanales committed to making the meeting, it was time for the team to go to work. The maps came out and they planed a route from the hotel to the Rainbow Dawn building that would allow them to keep him covered without being too obvious. As soon as the route was laid out, they checked their hardware.

"I'm going to put a skin tag on you." Schwarz dug into his little bag of goodies for a personal radio tracer transmitter that looked like a nicotine patch. "They're not as good as the subdermal tracers the military uses, but they're better than trying to wear a wire. They'd have to strip you to find it."

"I don't need that," Blancanales said. "Like I said, I don't read Givens as having enough balls to try something like that on his home turf."

"That was before he got those new security people," Lyons pointed out. "Until we know who they are and what their mission is, we can't take chances on them. Just because this is some nickel-and-dime investigation we shouldn't even be doing doesn't mean that we can't get whacked doing it."

"Okay, okay, I'll wear the bug."

"I also want voice-activated commo in your car," Bolan said. "If this does go down the way you think it will, you're going to be too busy driving to dial us up."

"Good point."

CHAPTER NINE

Los Angeles, California

Lyons and Schwarz were already in their car and positioned on the street when Blancanales pulled out of the parking lot of the hotel. They held their position until he was two blocks away, but no one pulled in behind him to follow. When they left the curb, they still maintained the two-block distance, keeping tabs on Blancanales all the way to the Rainbow Dawn headquarters, but no one made a move to follow him.

"You're still clear, Pol," Schwarz radioed.

"Okay," Blancanales radioed back. "You guys can pull back now. I'm right around the corner from the building."

Bolan had driven ahead and was on station close to the Dawners' headquarters and saw Blancanales making the turn. "Roger, Pol," he radioed. "I've got you in sight. You're covered all the way into the building."

"Thanks."

When Blancanales pulled into the public parking

spaces in front of the building, Lyons and Schwarz drove past before taking up their surveillance position.

ROY GIVENS MET Blancanales in the lobby and escorted him to a small meeting room on the first floor. "As I'm sure you'll understand when you see these photos," he said, "this is an awkward situation. I, of course, was completely unaware of the existence of them until we cleaned out Dale Williams's room. Because of Miss Wayne's unfortunate death and, of course, the subject matter, normally this would be handled with utmost sensitivity and privacy. But I think you need to see them so you'll have a better understanding of what Miss Wayne was like when she was here."

The dozen photos Givens handed over turned out to be exactly as Schwarz had predicted they would be. Half a dozen of them showed a young woman playfully doing a striptease in what looked to be a small apartment. The face was plainly Jennifer Wayne's, but he couldn't ID the body. By the fourth photo, the woman was naked and posing provocatively, leaving nothing to the imagination. Four photos later, she had been joined by a young man and the shots were what could only be called hard-core porn.

"You say these were taken on the premises?" Blancanales asked.

"In Williams's apartment here, yes," Givens replied. "Some of our senior staff work long hours, and we have a few small apartments on the upper floors reserved for their occasional use. He had been assigned

one of them at the time. I can show it to you if you
wish.''

"That won't be necessary," Blancanales answered.
It would be a waste of his time. No matter how the
room had looked when Williams had lived there, it
would be exactly as it appeared in the photos now.

"These copies are for me?" Blancanales asked.

Givens hesitated. "Surely you can understand that I
wouldn't want to see these photos fall into the wrong
hands.''

He sounded very concerned. "If a tabloid got hold
of them, it would cause Miss Wayne's family unnec-
essary embarrassment and renewed grief. But, since
they are germane to your investigation, it might be useful for your employers to know of them.''

"Thank you," Blancanales said as he slid the photos
back into the envelope and put them in his briefcase.
"I think they will be useful.''

LYONS AND SCHWARZ were keeping a close watch on
Blancanales' parked car when a pedestrian rounded the
corner in front of the Dawners' building and walked up
to it. When he was half hidden behind the rear fenders,
he paused and leaned down as if to pick something up
from the sidewalk. A second later, he straightened and
continued on.

"Bingo!" Schwarz called out. "Rosario's ride has
been tagged.''

"I've got him," Bolan radioed back. "He's rounding
the block headed for the rear of the building.''

"There's a fire door back there," Lyons told him.

"Pol's coming out," Schwarz announced.

"I've got him," Bolan replied.

As the Stony Man warriors watched, Blancanales got into his sedan, started up and pulled away from the curb. "I've got the goodies and they're what Gadgets said they'd be," he radioed. "But it went too easy, much too easy."

"We know," Lyons called back. "They put a tag on your car while you were inside."

"Bastards."

"We know," Lyons sent. "Now we go to plan B."

THIS TIME, plan B was for Blancanales to cruise through the streets, keeping within the speed limit. They planned to give it at least an hour before breaking off. Again, Lyons and Schwarz kept two blocks back while Bolan leapfrogged ahead and reconned the side streets before pulling over to let the other cars pass him again.

Blancanales spotted Bolan parked at the curb and drove past him without a glance. He was halfway down the block when an SUV with four men in it raced out of an alley and squealed to a stop crosswise in the street right in front of him. As he slammed on his brakes to avoid a collision, a full-sized sedan pulled away from the curb behind him.

"This is it," Blancanales said calmly as he took his MP-5 submachine gun from the passenger's seat.

If the Stony Man warriors hadn't been prepared, the

carjacking might have worked. As it was, they went into counterambush mode almost before it got started.

From his position on the curb, Bolan had a clear line of sight to the men in the SUV and snatched his MP-5 subgun from the floor beside him. Sticking his head out of the open sunroof of his BMW, he drilled a 3-round burst into the driver of the blocking sedan. The thug never made it out of his car.

"I'm going in for him," Lyons radioed over his comlink.

"Got you covered," the Executioner replied as he switched his fire to the SUV.

The ambushers obviously hadn't expected to have to deal with more than one man and were thrown off their timing. When Bolan opened on them, all they could think to do was duck for cover. And that was the wrong move.

They were only armed with handguns, but they put out a good volume of fire, most of it aimed at Blancanales, trapping him in his car. Even when Bolan put another one of them down with a short burst to the chest, they didn't back off.

As Lyons roared up the street, Schwarz added to Bolan's covering fire with bursts from his H&K. When Lyons came up beside Blancanales' car, he jammed on his brakes and threw the Pontiac halfway across the street in front of it.

With the side of his car shielding Blancanales, Lyons opened the rear door. "Get in!"

Blancanales scrambled in and slammed the door behind him "Go! Go!"

Lyons spun the wheel to the left, hit the gas hard and popped the clutch. Schwarz lay on the trigger and dumped an entire magazine as the back end of the Pontiac swung around in a bootlegger turn. In a few seconds, it was headed back the other way at sixty miles an hour.

Bolan ripped off another long burst from his MP-5 to cover Lyons's withdrawal, but at least three of the opposition were down and they didn't seem too anxious to keep playing a losing hand.

As soon as Lyons's car disappeared around the corner, he slammed his BMW in reverse and dropped the clutch.

"I GUESS THAT'S the end of the insurance investigator scam," Schwarz remarked when they returned to their hotel suite.

"It's also the end of screwing around with those guys."

Carl Lyons turned to Bolan. "What's that you like to say about three times being enemy action?"

"But this is only twice."

"I'm not going for three, man."

"Which means we go proactive."

"If I can break into this conversation," Blancanales said, "we've gotten way off track here."

"What do you mean?" Lyons asked.

"We came down here to rubber-stamp the official

investigation into a string of mysterious deaths to make the Man happy. In the process, we, or at least me, has become a target. I think we need to clear the board and start all over with a new focus."

"Such as?"

Blancanales turned serious. "I want to talk to Hal or Barbara about what we're doing here. Mack's right. We need to get serious about those Rainbow people, at least with the storm troopers they imported. But I want to clear it with them and set up our covers first. We left bodies and a shot-up car on the street this time and—" he grinned at Lyons "—even the LAPD is bound to notice something like that."

"Goof!" ex-LAPD cop Carl Lyons growled.

"He's right," Bolan said. "We need to get our butts covered before we take this any further."

MILLER'S AMBUSH TEAM had also been radio-equipped and he learned of the aborted hit on Rudy Reyes almost as soon as the last shot died away. Of the five-man team he had dispatched, two were dead and a third wounded. Reyes's cover team had been pros, and he knew damned well and good that they weren't dealing with the usual black-shoe Feds.

Miller knew his men were good, some of the best operatives in the States. But they'd been sucked in and chopped up like dumb-ass street cops. Whomever the opposition was, they were too good for his taste. Then there was the fact that they'd used full-auto weapons and had fled the scene rather than calling for backup.

Those weren't the actions of an official unit, federal or local.

He needed hard intel on these people before he found himself on the wrong end of the stick again, and that meant getting help from the Phoenix office. But he would wait until the survivors of the ambush got back before calling in. He had to have his facts straight before he reported this.

Stony Man Farm, Virginia

NOW THAT Barbara Price's office was more than a short trip away from his workstation, Aaron Kurtzman made sure to check in at least twice a day to keep her updated. The fact that he had always checked in with her periodically when she didn't stop by didn't matter. The physical distance between them now loomed in his mind as a barrier that had to be overcome.

"Price," she answered her phone.

"Kurtzman here," he said. "I'm going to borrow an NSA satellite to try to find out where Givens's electronic traffic is going. Even his cell-phone transmissions are encrypted, and we're having a hard time getting through the code. It might help me figure out what kind of encryption he's using if I know who he's talking to."

"I thought your new toys were going to make this sort of thing easier."

"They are. If I was trying to do this with our old

machines, I'd be completely blocked. But even with the extra power, this is tough going."

"Go ahead," she said. "And keep me updated."

"Will do."

When Kurtzman hung up, Price went back to the stack of work on her desk. Since they didn't have a real ongoing mission, she was spending most of her time trying to catch up with the day-to-day work that was required to keep the farm running. When, and if, this California situation turned into a full-bore mission, she'd be more than glad to abandon her bookkeeping chores and put on her mission controller hat. In fact, she'd relish it.

"AARON," Hunt Wethers called jubilantly from his workstation. "I've got it."

"That was fast," Kurtzman replied.

"A little over forty hours total elapsed time." Wethers glanced at the clock icon on his screen. "As I thought, the code turned out to be a copy of one of the recent DOD multipulse phase ciphers. The hard part was finding the access codes for that particular one, but we're ready to roll the tapes."

"Great, send it over."

While Wethers transferred the program, Kurtzman unlocked his chair and rolled himself over to the coffeepot for a steaming refill. By the time he was behind the keyboard again, he was charged and ready to go to work. Accessing the copies he had made of Rainbow Dawn's files, he started opening them.

WITH WETHERS'S cracker program, it took no time at all to break into the Rainbow Dawn's Project files. It took some time, though, for Kurtzman to put it all together and understand what they were about. He wheeled over to the coffeepot for another neuronal jolt before reading through the material a second time.

In its bare form, the Project was simple. The Dawners had formed three groups of technicians who were on contract with three American firms working in Vatican City, Jerusalem and Saudi Arabia. The Vatican archives team was to set up a decontamination and conservation system for the manuscripts and books in the archives. The Jerusalem group was to conduct an archaeological survey using a new type of ground-penetrating scanner. The third group, a construction team, was to revamp the pilgrim facilities at Mecca. The jobs all looked like legitimate contracts tendered to well-known American companies. And, while scientific firms often had tight computer security, he didn't understand the level of secrecy on this by the Dawners.

Also, the three areas the Project focused on bothered him. Vatican City, Jerusalem and Mecca were the centers of the three most prominent religions in the world. Judaism didn't have the numbers behind it that Christianity or Islam did, but it was the grandfather of both of them. And, of the three sites, Jerusalem was the most important because it was a holy city to all three faiths.

With his brain freshly bathed in high-test caffeine, Kurtzman started to look into the bills of lading for the Vatican team and found something that didn't look kosher to him. Included in their supplies was a large quantity of chemicals for use in an on-site decontamination chamber to treat the mold, fungus and insect infestations in the ancient books and manuscripts. The problem was that those chemicals could also be combined in a certain way to create a persistent nerve agent.

When he checked the supplies for the Jerusalem group, he found that they were importing a large amount of nuclear materials for their neutrino geological mapping equipment. The amount was so substantial that a special export licence had been required by the Energy Department for its transport. But the administration had readily signed off on the shipment as had the Israeli government.

Nothing seemed to be too out of line with the gear the Mecca construction team had imported to do its work. Except for the fact that the group was using eco-friendly, but dangerously explosive propane-powered excavation equipment in the world's largest oil-producing nation. Eco-awareness was all very fine and good, but propane had other uses besides inefficiently powering internal combustion engines. It was half of the equation for an FAE—fuel air explosive.

Of all the nonnuclear explosives available, FAEs were the most powerful. A few hundred pounds of propane could do the damage of several thousand pounds of high explosives. It was only the fact that FAEs were rather difficult to control that limited their use to specialized military applications. It would, however, be a great way to eradicate Mecca from the face of the earth.

Kurtzman's job required that he be a professional paranoid and he took that part of his job description very seriously. And this time his gut was telling him that something nasty was going on.

"Barbara," he said as he hit the intercom line to Price's office in the farm house, "you need to get Hal down here."

"What did you find?"

"I'm going to pull a Brognola and keep it for the briefing, but he needs to hear this ASAP."

CHAPTER TEN

Phoenix, Arizona

Billionaire industrialist Grant Betancourt's private office resembled a NASA launch control room more than it did a place to conduct business. But it was the control room for his worldwide business empire and his business was cutting edge, high technology usually expressed in aerospace and defense applications. His BII logo could be found on a wide range of items from deep-space satellites to laser-guided ammunition and a thousand things in between.

Not only was Betancourt a billionaire, he was a poster child for the boomer generation. He was a tall, athletically fit man in his early fifties who looked a decade younger. He had a full head of hair worn long and full, clear, piercing blue eyes, and a ready smile for a good-looking woman. The winning smile and piercing blue eyes, though, served him as more than just a way to attract women. They were weapons that had served him well along the path to where he was now.

The smile hid his thoughts, and the eyes had unblinkingly watched the aftermath of Senator Bowers's death closely. Bowers had been the chairman of the powerful Armed Forces Committee, and Betancourt had known him well. The two men had spent a great deal of time together both on and off the Hill. Socializing with the nation's power brokers was part of doing business, but he had actually enjoyed Bowers's company. That hadn't, however, stopped him from ordering the senator's death after his daughter had inadvertently learned of his plan to create a new world.

Betancourt wasn't the kind of man anyone would ever think harbored dreams of the Apocalypse. The owners and CEOs of high-tech industries and prominent inside-the-Beltway figures who were as welcome in the halls of Congress as they were in the D.C. black-tie and cocktail set usually didn't dream of the end of the world.

As was common among the nation's wealthy and powerful, Betancourt felt that he had an obligation to do what he could to make the world a better place. His political contributions were matched only by his generous charitable giving. But, unlike most Fortune 500 philanthropists, he was acutely aware that he couldn't reach his goals by giving money to causes, however worthy. Men who poured tons of money into endless rat holes disguised as worthy causes might as well have burned the cash for all the good it actually did.

Betancourt's support of politicians and charities was simply the price he had to pay to maintain his position as one of the nation's richest and most powerful men. And maintaining that position put him outside the petty laws that governed lesser men.

Betancourt fully intended to change the world, but he was going to do it the old-fashioned way, the only way that had ever proved to be effective. He was going to destroy the part of the world that he felt had no value. And, as a man who personified the world of high-tech science, his enemy was anything that didn't promote the triumph of technology for the benefit of humankind. In his mind, the main thing that stood in the way of the twenty-first century becoming a utopia was the Bronze Age mentality that still clouded men's minds in the name of religion.

After untold centuries of mindless violence in the name of one particular god or the other, humankind had learned nothing from it. From India and East Timor, through the Middle East past Eastern Europe and all the way to Northern Ireland, religious warfare was still the greatest killer of modern times. While there was no place on Earth that hadn't suffered from this mindless slaughter, Betancourt was only concerned with the future of the West and the Middle East. With the exception of Japan, Taiwan and maybe South Korea, the rest of the world would have no significant part to play in the future that was coming.

While the future belonged solely to the science and technology of the West, the Middle East couldn't be left out. Even though that region was also hopelessly mired in ancient hatreds, it was as critical to the future as was the industrial West.

As he saw it, there was only one way to free men's minds from the shackles of religious violence. If the twenty-first century wasn't to be a repeat of the blood-bath that had been the twentieth century, Mecca, Jerusalem and Vatican City had to be eradicated. Once these age-old sources of festering hate were gone, humankind could finally concentrate on the future. If peace was to ever come to the world, humankind had to be forced into a different thought pattern.

Even though this dream had been borne in his mind, Betancourt wouldn't be involved in this himself. He had created Roy Givens and his Rainbow Dawn to handle the Project for him. And when the job was done, Givens and his minions would follow their victims to the grave. In the world of science and reason he envisioned creating, people like Givens had no place. A truly rational human being didn't join a cult, any cult, even the Dawners. Until then, though, they would play their part to bring the Project to fruition.

The slow pace, though, was wearing on him. In his haste to see results, he had deviated from his carefully thought-out plans and had hired a crew of mercenaries to test the defenses at Mecca. They had been completely annihilated to the last man, proving that his main program was his best bet to see results, and it was finally in operation.

The Vatican archives team was already in Rome to kick it off. Though the members of that team were all

Dawners, the VAT wasn't linked to Givens's Rainbow Dawn in any way. It was operating under the banner of a famous scientific lab and that cutout was what made this job possible. The second phase of the Project, the Jerusalem mapping group, had finished its training and was being deployed now. Again, half of the staff of that group were Dawners, also unassociated with Givens.

It was only the Mecca team that was behind schedule and that was the sticking point. Early on, Givens had warned that he was having trouble recruiting team members. That's what had prompted Betancourt to make the raid. When that had failed, he had been forced to switch gears, and the plan now was to use an all-American contracting company and infiltrate enough Dawners into the workforce to do what had to be done.

The purpose of the Project was to drive home one point—that God had no existence except in the minds of men who used fear to control the lives of their followers. The destruction of Vatican City, Jerusalem and Mecca would once and for all break the spell of fear that had been spun for so many thousands of years.

Doing that had its risks, though. The predictions of what would happen when millions of believers no longer had a place to focus their fears ran the entire gambit from stunned immobility to mindless worldwide destruction. It would take a few years for the realization that humankind was finally free to fully sink in and for peace to return.

But when it did, a true new age would dawn over

most of the world: the reign of peace that so many millennialists had hoped and prayed for.

ALONG WITH putting the Project into action, Betancourt had taken a page from the Vatican and had created an office of propaganda to prepare the religions of the world, and their followers, for what was coming.

Like any successful man, Betancourt was well aware that perception was nine-tenths of the battle. To win this war for the future of humankind, he had to fight perceptions that had been hundreds of generations in the making. The fact that these perceptions were groundless and were cruel manipulations for the power of a few made no difference. To the people who held them, they were real. But perceptions could be changed, and were changed everyday.

Modern America was a nation that had been built on unsubstantiated perceptions. The entire economy of the United States had been created by an advertising industry that worked to change perceptions. Everyday, countless consumers spent millions of dollars on things they didn't really need simply because they perceived that they did.

Through his clandestine media connections, Betancourt was feeding two kinds of stories. One was simple, scientific and straightforward, that the new millennium hadn't started and wouldn't arrive until the year 2001. The fact that there had been no year zero in the Christian dating system was fully explained, and the years counted from one to two thousand. It was a simple concept and even the simplest of minds, no matter how clogged with dogmatic garbage, could grasp it. For all its hype and horror, Y2K had been only a rehearsal for the real thing that was coming.

His other story line was much more subtle, but was also tied in with the announcement of the "real" millennium. Throughout the world, psychics and mystics were predicting that major changes were coming. These changes, though, were nothing like the thousands of failed predictions that had been made during the Y2K hysteria.

Y2K had been a complete bust for those who had quaked in religious fear as they fervently waited for whatever they had been promised. And they had been promised much. About the only thing the faithful hadn't been promised in the new millennium was a chicken in every pot and a Ford in every garage. But when the sun rose on the world of the first of January of the year two thousand, all those promises had turned to dust.

Angels hadn't appeared to snatch the righteous and fly them up to heaven. The world hadn't erupted in blood and flame, nor had the Four Horsemen of the Apocalypse ridden through the nations. The sun hadn't even stood still in the sky for one short second. In short, Y2K had been the greatest example of FDR's old axiom that "The only thing we have to fear is fear itself."

In these new predictions, the "saved" still weren't going up to heaven, sinners still weren't going to punish sinners and the final battle for men's souls still wasn't going to take place on an ancient battlefield in Israel that had originally been named Har Medigo.

Instead, the new predictions were simple and foretold that when the real millennium arrived, humankind was going to suddenly awaken from a two-thousand-year-old nightmare. A new world would be born that would be free of the hate that had clouded men's minds for so long.

Since it wasn't enough to simply say these things, Betancourt's crowning coup was that apparitions were appearing all over the world predicting the same thing. Since he had access to some of the world's most sophisticated technology, it was child's play for him to stage these apparitions. That they had no more reality than any other collection of coherent light particles made no difference to those who saw them. They were designed to appear to the gullible, and the eyes of the gullible never looked far beyond their own fears.

THE ONLY PART of Betancourt's plan that wasn't progressing as expected wasn't even really a part of the Project. Roy Givens's clumsy handling of the Jennifer Wayne situation had turned into a real mess. Were it not for the fact that he still needed the Dawners, he would simply have wiped out Givens and his followers. A fire in their headquarters would work perfectly for what he had in mind. But that would have to wait.

Instead, he had turned the operation of Rainbow Dawn over to Miller and a security team from Security Plus. Miller was one of his best specialists, but even he wasn't getting a handle on it. While a failure, the car-jacking episode had shown that someone was a little too interested in the inner workings of Rainbow Dawn. This would have been discovered much earlier if Givens had bothered to take the time to investigate the credentials of the so-called insurance investigator. Miller had checked them, and the company Reyes claimed to work for didn't exist. But Givens hadn't done that, and now the situation couldn't be ignored.

His agents hadn't been able to find any indication that the Dawners were being investigated by any official agency, state or federal, which left either private parties hired by the family or one of the nameless contract groups that fringed in the shadows of government. From the information he had about Susan Wayne, the widow of the late senator and Jennifer's mother, she wasn't likely to have hired anyone to look into her daughter's demise. That left the contractors.

He had his best people at Security Plus looking into who might be interested enough in Rainbow Dawn to hire an expensive team to investigate it, and who obviously had a tie to the late senator or his daughter.

The one ace in the hole he had was a standing invitation to drop in on his old college roommate, the President of the United States. If these contractors were somehow connected with the government, he would know about them. He would have to approach the subject carefully, as the President knew nothing of Betancourt's connection to the Dawners, but it could be done.

He would also send a specialist team to Miller with

orders to track down the contractors and eliminate them. As a rule he didn't like employing that kind of direct action in the United States because it created problems, but this was one of those exceptions. Nothing could be allowed to impede the progress of the Project.

AFTER AARON KURTZMAN'S briefing, Hal Brognola had to agree that Roy Givens and Rainbow Dawn's "Project" needed investigating immediately. If they were working up some kind of post-Y2K doomsday plot, the three greatest religious centers of Europe and the Middle East were at risk, and the danger to international stability if even one of them was attacked was beyond measure.

"I'll present this to the Man," he said. "But I have to warn you that he usually doesn't put much credence in this kind of thing. I'll try, though, to get the point across."

Kurtzman snorted. "He'd sure as hell pay attention if a group of Arabs was behind something that looked as suspicious as this."

"That he would," Brognola readily agreed. "But that's because we have a long track record of those people trying to do that kind of thing. These are American companies setting this up, and I'm sure that the bottom line with them is just the bottom line, not some kind of religious terrorism."

"That's an assumption," Kurtzman countered. "And if you'll remember, Hal, to assume is to make an ass out of you and me. Don't forget Jonestown, David Koresh and the Heavens Gate wackos, and that's just in recent years. Americans have a long history of leading the pack when it comes to religious lunacy. Anytime I find Americans overly mixed-up in religiously oriented plans like this, I smell a scam.''

"Point taken."

"Also," Kurtzman continued, pressing his point, "you might want to have the Man ask someone how a private nonprofit organization, a wacko cult if you will, got access to a Department of Defense cybersecurity system. That alone should be enough to get him off his apex."

"I'll mention that, as well."

"And the attempts on Able Team," Price added. "If we need any proof that something's wrong, that's it."

"I'll bring that up, too."

CHAPTER ELEVEN

Stony Man Farm, Virginia

On the chopper flight from Washington, D.C., to Stony Man Farm, Hal Brognola had a tough decision to make. When he had mentioned Aaron Kurtzman's concerns to the President in his morning briefing, he had been surprised to find that the Man already knew all about these projects. He had been told that all three of the projects had been cleared at the highest level of the UN and were being overseen by the UN Commission on Cultural Heritage. Even when he had presented the information Kurtzman had gleaned from digging into Givens's Rainbow Dawn files, the President hadn't been concerned.

In recent years, bitter Congressional partisan battles had been waged over the UN. Even though the U.S. was by far the major financial supporter of the organization, the liberals wanted to give them even more tax money. The conservatives, however, either wanted to get America the hell out of the UN entirely or cut the U.S. contribution to something a little less ruinous to the national debt. Recently, though, the war had gone to the UN supporters.

Part of the current administration's attempts to get back into the good graces of the international body had been to pay off a large chunk of the back dues owed, with interest. Another ploy had been to underwrite a number of UN pet projects and this was only one of them. Of all the money being spent in this very public arena, the President was particularly proud of this project because the costs were being underwritten by his old college buddy and good friend Grant Betancourt instead of the taxpayers.

Just hearing that man's name made Brognola shudder.

Brognola knew Grant Betancourt and had never liked him. He had a visceral dislike for the man without being able to state a clear, rational reason for it. Regardless of the impressive commercial empire the man had built from nothing, his social generosity and his heavyweight friends on the Hill, Brognola always wanted to wash his hands after just being in the same room with the man. Shaking hands with him was completely out of the question.

The big Fed served as the director of SOG at the President's pleasure, which meant that he had no job security. It also meant that he could leave anytime he wanted. That was the only way he would have taken the job. He had come close to calling it quits several times and had equally come close to getting canned on a number of occasions, as well. This was going to be another one of those times.

The President hadn't specifically ordered him to leave Givens and Betancourt alone. If he had been told that, he would have been honor-bound to either do exactly as he had been told or resign his position. But he had been given some wriggle room, and this wasn't the first time that Stony Man had operated on wriggle room. He would take the opening this time as well, but would keep it out of his weekly White House briefings as long as he could.

His instincts told him that he had no choice but to do it this way, and he would follow his gut on this one.

AS WAS HIS CUSTOM, Hal Brognola waited until everyone was at their place in the War Room of the old farm house before he laid out the situation for them. "Aaron," he started, "I went over your concerns with the Man and he said no. Now—" he held up one hand "—before you start berating me, let me add that I am not in agreement with him this time."

"Thank God."

"I did, however, learn a bit more about the background on these three projects. They're being administered under the auspices of the United Nations. In fact, they originated with the Cultural Heritage Commission, and the administration got involved on the funding at the request of the Secretary General himself. With the President's strongest approval, an American industrialist named Grant Betancourt stepped in to pick up the tab.''

"Where does that leave us?" Price asked. "Do we fold our tents and slink off or what?''

"What I want," Brognola said, his voice tight, "is a full-court press kicked off immediately. And if you find what you think you're going to, I want Phoenix Force standing by locked and loaded to deal with it.''

Barbara Price found herself in the odd position of having to question a decision to go against the President's orders. Usually it was her calling for an all-out assault no matter what and Brognola trying to keep her reined in.

"Are you sure about this, Hal?" she asked. "If these projects were vetted through and are being sponsored by the UN, aren't we leaving ourselves wide-open if we get involved and the Man finds out?''

Brognola blinked as if he had just swallowed a fish bone. "Did I just hear you trying to cut the UN some slack, Barbara? I thought you had strong views about the U.S.'s involvement?''

"I have to put personal opinion aside. The Cultural Heritage Commission is composed of very competent people who have been drawn from a wide range of professions and academic disciplines. I can't see them as being involved in any apocalyptic cabal.''

"If I may interject," Kurtzman said, raising one hand.

Price and Brognola disengaged and looked at him. "The thought just occurred to me that we may be dealing with a very real millennium apocalyptic plot here. As anyone with any scientific knowledge knows, the third millennium doesn't really start until New Year's 2001. And that is the date when all three of these projects are due to be completed.''

That brought a thoughtful silence.

''And,'' he continued, ''as Barbara knows, I've been keeping track of post-Y2K phenomena as they have shown up. One of the biggest trends that's developed is that a lot of different people ranging from talk-show hosts to psychics are talking up the scientific fact that the new millennium doesn't start until January 1, 2001.''

''But we heard all of that during the buildup to the Y2K crap,'' Price said. ''What's different now?''

''It's true that we heard it all back then,'' Kurtzman agreed. ''But no one paid it much attention because it didn't fit into the pseudo-religious hysteria that had everybody by the gonads. But when Y2K turned out to be a bust, the 'real millennium' is front-page news again. Many of the doomsayers who were disappointed by the lack of mass death and destruction last New Year's Eve, have taken up the cry again. They can't wait for Armageddon to start.''

''And you think that could be what's behind this?''

''I think we need to take a serious look at it in that vein, yes. I think that if you took a poll of a statistically significant number of millennium freaks, the peace, love and brotherhood troops would be running far behind the kill-them-all-and-let-God-sort-them-out crowd.

Never underestimate the drawing power of death and destruction. And here we have what looks like a high-tech version of the Armageddon trigger. If this plan is carried out, the world as we know it will change over-night, and I'm not sure for the good.

"Which is why I'm going off the reservation again on this one," Brognola said quietly. "You all know the drill, keep it tight and keep me informed of any new information."

WHEN THE BRIEFING broke up, Brognola asked Price to hang back.

"What is it?" she asked when the room was clear.

"There's another aspect to this that concerns me," he told her, "and I wanted to run it by you before I mentioned it to Aaron."

Price was intrigued. It wasn't like him to hold anything back. "What's that?"

"It might sound a little crazy, but I also want him to take a hard look into Grant Betancourt's involvement in those UN projects."

"Do you know him?"

"I've met him once or twice in the Oval Office, and I know more about him than I want to."

"And?"

Brognola got a strange look on his face. "The 'and' is that he's almost the last man on Earth I'd ever expect to find funding any kind of work at a religious site."

"What do you mean?"

"Well, you know how some people come completely

unglued when certain subjects are mentioned, usually related to race or politics?''

She nodded.

"Betancourt's that way about religion, any religion. One of the Man's staffers once accidentally invited him to a National Prayer Breakfast, and he threatened to completely pull his financial support from the President's campaign. The two of them have been friends since college, so you know how that went over. The staffer was transferred immediately and the rift was smoothed over, but that's Betancourt's usual reaction to anything that has any connection to religion.

"Then—'' Brognola smiled as he thought back "—you know the collection of so-called religious leaders who hang around Capitol Hill trying to get their faces in front of a camera? Well, Betancourt won't even be in the same room with one of them. Once, when he was testifying in front of the Armed Forces Committee about one of his contracts, a celebrated televangelist came in to deliver a benediction and he walked out. When asked about it later, he said that his religion prohibits him from any contact with priests and preachers. When someone asked which religion that was, he looked his questioner in the face and said that it was none of his goddamned business.''

Price laughed.

"So, when I learn that he's funding these heavily religious projects, my alarm bells go off. But that's not something I can even mention to the President. With the history those two have, as far as the Man's concerned, Grant Betancourt is beyond reproach."

"So," she asked, "what will we do if we find out that he's connected somehow with Rainbow Dawn?"

"I'll be damned if I know." Brognola looked sincerely puzzled. "I do know, though, that it will take more than some casual connection we can dig up to convince the Man to listen to us."

"One thing I know," Price said, "is that I want to call Katz in on this now. If this escalates quickly, I want him on top of it so we can react."

"I was just going to mention that," Brognola said. "Can you get hold of him?"

"I think I can have him here by tomorrow, if not this afternoon."

BARBARA PRICE WAS in her office when the comm center called to tell her that Yakov Katzenelenbogen was at the front gate of the farm. Of all the SOG warriors, the ex-Israeli commando was the most knowledgeable about the area that was threatened this time. Also, even though Katz wasn't what one would call an overly religious man, he had an ancestral tie to one of the targets.

A person didn't have to be Jewish to feel the call of Jerusalem, but when her or she was, a person felt a connection to the ancient stones almost on a DNA level. Plus, if this turned out to be what it seemed, his connections with Mossad and the other clandestine operatives in Israel could prove essential in pulling this off without turning it into a circus.

She walked outside to greet him when he stepped out of his SUV. "I'm really glad you're here, Katz."

Katz smiled. "I thought you liked to have me out from under your feet."

She laughed. "Not this time. The situation we're looking into this time needs your personal touch."

"My old stomping grounds?"

"In spades."

"What's the story?"

"Let's get a couple cups of coffee and take them to the War Room."

"That bad?"

"Much worse."

WHEN PRICE FINISHED briefing Katzenelenbogen, the Israeli shook his head. "That's the damnedest thing I've ever heard. It's straight out of a made-for-TV movie. But, if this guy's trying to bring on a millennial Armageddon, I can't think of a better way to do it. The Jews will blame the Arabs, the Arabs will blame the Jews and the West and the Catholics will blame both of them. The entire Middle East will go up in flames, and there's no telling where it will end."

The old soldier's eyes turned hard. "And there's also no telling what the world will look like when it's finally over. As you know, I don't have much time for religion, any of them. But for millions of people, their faith is the most important thing in their lives. And without their spiritual centers to worship at, I don't know what they will do. Some will just curl up and die, but others will lash out. I think that it would unleash an endless cycle of bloodshed.''

"Like the ones that have been going on for how many years?" she asked rhetorically.

He nodded. "You know, I'm the first to jump up and denounce crimes committed in the name of one God or another. God must weep endlessly when he sees what so many of us have done to our brothers and sisters in His name. And I have to admit that the faith of my own heritage has been as guilty of mass murder as the rest.''

Price gave him a serious look. "I've never seen this side of you, Katz. I didn't know that you were a religious scholar.''

"Not as much a religious scholar as a historical scholar," he replied. "My profession sent me to the history books to try to understand why men have slaughtered one another with such gusto for so many centuries. What I found was that for the last two thousand years, too much of the answer has been solely because of religion.''

He shook his head. "For some reason, anytime a man thinks that he has God on his side, he becomes blind to the rest of humanity. He can kill without a second thought if he thinks that God approves of it. God knows that I've killed my share of Arabs and other Muslims as well as more than a few Christians and even some Jews.''

He locked eyes with her. "But never have I killed

anyone in the name of God. The men I have killed died because they were the enemy.''

He took a deep breath. ''If this plan is as you say it is, whoever is behind it must be stopped and, if needs be, he must be eliminated. And not so we can protect the men who kill in the name of their religions. He has to be stopped because humanity still needs something to believe in and a place to go where they can believe it. That's essential for civilization.''

He pushed himself out of his chair. ''But enough of this for the moment. I need to talk to Aaron.''

''You'll find him in his new kingdom.''

CHAPTER TWELVE

Stony Man Farm, Virginia

Yakov Katzenelenbogen got a bit disoriented when he went down to the farm's old computer room to take the tram to the new Annex. He had never seen the room so empty. It had always looked crowded before, but now that it only harbored a few neat stacks of supplies, he realized just how small it actually was. That they had operated out of the room for as long as they had was a wonderment. The new facility should make his job, as well as everyone else's, a lot easier.

Once the leader of Phoenix Force, Katz had retired from the field to become the tactical operations officer for SOG. Though he was no longer a combatant in the field, he was still on-call for any mission that required his particular skill sets. But his main job now was to support the teams in the field.

It took no time at all for the electric car to whisk him through the tunnel to the Annex. When he stepped through the blast door into the new computer room, he was almost blinded by the modern lighting. As his eyes quickly adjusted, he took in the new cyberfacility.

The bank of mainframe computers dominated one wall, but no longer were their power and data-link cables taped to the floor or strung along the walls. Hunt Wethers's and Akira Tokaido's workstations were against the opposite wall under an impressive array of giant flat-screen monitors. A huge, clear glass world situation map dominated the other end of the room.

In the middle of the room was the throne where Aaron Kurtzman ruled over his new cyberkingdom. Unlike the newer-than-new look to everything else, this area looked like it had been magically transported from the old farm house.

"Damn, Bear," Katz said. "You look lost in here. I can actually see the floor around your workstation."

Kurtzman looked up from his screen. "Katz, about damned time you got back here."

"Barbara told me."

"Did she give you the details?"

"Let me get a cup, and you can make sure she didn't leave anything out."

Katz looked around the room hoping against hope not to see a particular disreputable coffeepot. To his despair, it was there and he shuddered.

"Katz!" Tokaido called out from the other end of the room. "Stop! You don't need to drink that. We have a real coffeepot of our own now."

"Thanks, Akira." Katz grinned. "I haven't been

back long enough to be able to choke down Bear's brew yet.''

"Pussy," Kurtzman accused.

"It's doctor's orders," Katz explained. "He wants me to cut back on my daily intake of hot battery acid."

Kurtzman shook his head. "And all this time I thought that you were a real man."

Katz laughed.

AFTER KURTZMAN had gone through every bit of hard evidence he had accumulated on the Project, he paused and said, "Then there's a gut element to this, as well. There's a new undercurrent in popular culture that I think fits right in with this."

Katz smiled. "I try my best not to keep in touch with what passes for popular culture in your country, Aaron. You know that. It's bad for my digestion."

"You have to know your enemy," Kurtzman admonished him.

"But I do," Katz said. "And that's why I pay as little attention to the mindless crap on your television as I can get away with and still live in this country."

"This, though," Kurtzman said as he reached out and hit a button, "isn't the usual crap. Were it not for the messenger, the message would almost make sense."

One of the big screens lit up showing a TV stage with an animated, big-chested, blond woman holding court in front of a huge studio audience. Mellanie Mitchell was wearing another one of her tighter-than-skin ensembles, this one cut almost to the nipples of her breasts, riding high in a push-up bra.

"Nice dress," Katz said approvingly.

"T and A always draws them in," Kurtzman said as he hit the volume control. "But listen to the message."

Mitchell reached out and took what looked like a letter from a large pile. "…And this is yet another one of these pathetic letters I get so often. This writer hopes that I will burn in hell, but will be reborn each day so the burning will continue for eternity. He signs it 'A man who has God in his heart.'"

She threw the letter back on the pile, tossed her hair and filled her lungs most impressively. "I don't know about you, but I find that very sad. I think that the time has come for all people to stop hating their neighbors in the name of whatever God they happen to worship. Hate is hate and hiding behind God when you hate does not make it right. We are about to enter a new millennium and we have a chance to finally bring peace to the world after two thousand years of almost constant conflict. But peace begins with us, each of us."

"She's good," Katz said, "and she's got good material to work with."

"You should see her ratings," Kurtzman said. "They're through the roof and would-be sponsors are going on a waiting list in hopes of being picked up."

"I'm a bit surprised at that," Katz replied. "Usually, American companies are so gun-shy that they steer clear of controversial shows like this."

"Well, she's careful never to mention denominations

or names. She just keeps hitting on the message that
the world would be a better place if everyone would
stop using God's name to kill their neighbor. Then, she
hints that something is coming down the pike that will
make that easier to do than it's ever been before and
that's the part that bothers me.''

"Who's behind her show?" Katz asked.

"We don't know yet."

"I want to know as soon as you do."

"And," Kurtzman said, hitting another series of keys
that brought up a map of the world with red icons dot-
ting it, "if Mellanie Moonbeam wasn't enough, we've
had a rash of religious 'appearances' lately. Catholic
countries are getting visits from the Virgin Mary as you
would expect. But we've also had various Muslim
saints and martyrs appearing in the Middle East with
the same message."

"Which is?"

"That the faithful have been suckered for far too
long and it's time to dump the entire program and get
real."

Katz shook his head. "That's not going to go down
too well with most of that audience."

"What's amazing this time is that the people who
witness these appearances aren't the old standbys we
usually see, in that they're not newly nubile virgins or
village idiots having seizures. These apparitions are being seen by everyone who isn't blind."

"Holograms?" Katz asked.

"That's what I'm thinking."

"How about the Israelis? Have they seen any apparitions?"

"Not that have been reported."

"I'm not surprised. They don't have a tradition of that kind of revelation. If they want to get fired up about God, they study the book again and find something new."

Katz studied the map for a moment. "I need a hard copy of that map and any reports you have of these sightings. Also, have you done hard copies of that TV program?"

"Sure have."

"Good, I want to start studying the message that's going out and try to figure out why they're doing this."

"Beyond preparing the faithful for the end of the world as they know it, you mean?"

Katz shook his head. "It can't be that simple."

"But what if it is?"

WHEN HAL BROGNOLA arrived at the farm that evening, he had a worried look on his face. To keep up the appearance that nothing special was going on with SOG, he'd been sticking close to his D.C. office.

"I think the Man's on to us," he told Barbara Price.

"Why?" she asked. "What did he say?"

"He didn't come right out and ask me," Brognola explained, "but he was rather curious about what the action teams were doing. And, as you well know, he rarely thinks of us unless he has a problem somewhere."

"What do you think's making him curious?" Price asked. "We haven't made the national news on CNN or anything like that. So far, it's all been pretty low-key."

"Well, I think that's partly my fault," Brognola admitted. "I should have had you look into those so-called UN-sponsored teams more thoroughly before I took Aaron's information to him. If I'd seen Grant Betancourt's name associated with them then, I might not have pressed for permission to look into them so hard."

"You think that this Betancourt is trying to get him to call us off?"

"That's hard to tell," he said. "But one of the things we haven't developed yet is the exact relationship between him and Rainbow Dawn. And, as I said before, he's the last guy in the world I'd ever expect to find in bed with a cult. But it's just too big a coincidence for him to be funding those projects without knowing who's behind them. He's much too smart to make a mistake like that."

"Katz is back," she informed him. "Let me get him in here and let's pick his brain."

"Good idea," he said. "I'm tired and my brain is overdue for a lube, oil and filter."

"HOW DO YOU LIKE the Annex?" Brognola said in greeting to his tactical operations officer.

"That subway ride is a bit of a bother," Katz said.

"But I really like the new setup. We finally have a place to conduct a war if we need to."

"I don't have a war for you yet, but the Armageddon business looks like a bull market."

"What now?"

"Well," Brognola started. "I think that I might have raised the President's suspicions when I took Aaron's concerns to him and asked permission to look into them. All I can say is that at that time I didn't know Betancourt's involvement."

Katz digested Brognola's report before asking, "Do you think that Betancourt is close enough to the Man that he would have told him about us?"

"I don't think so," Brognola said. "As a politician, over the years he's pretty well had it hammered into him that loose lips sink ships. The SOG access list is shorter now than it's ever been, and I'm doing everything I can to keep it that way."

"But you said that Betancourt is one of his oldest friends."

"That's true," Brognola replied. "And it goes deeper than that. They were roommates back in their undergraduate days, and apparently they dated the same girl for quite a while without it getting in the road of their friendship."

"What happened to her?"

"I've never heard," Brognola replied.

"What about Betancourt, did he get married later as well?"

"To be honest with you, I haven't a clue. Like I said,

I loathe the man and I've never wanted to know anything about him beyond what was forced on me."

"The first rule of war is to know your enemy," Katz reminded him.

"Let me see what I can find," Price said as she clicked on the computer in front of her. "If this guy's doing what we think he is, we need to start profiling him and I'd like to start with his marital status. You can tell a lot about a man by who he's sleeping with."

"Or what."

"Grant Betancourt's only part of our problem," Brognola said. "The other half is the UN."

"Now what?" Katz asked.

"The UN has somehow become concerned about the security of the Cultural Heritage teams in Vatican City and Jerusalem."

"What does that mean?"

"I don't know the extent of it yet. But all information relating to those projects has suddenly become classified. They're also talking about sending in special UN security units to aid both the Vatican and the Israelis."

"That will damn near guarantee that something goes wrong," Katz snorted.

"I'm afraid that 'something' will be Armageddon if we don't find a way to stop it."

"I want to put Phoenix Force on standby," Katz said, "and get David in here. If we do have to take action, I want him to be in on the planning stages."

"Do it."

"What do you want me to tell the guys in L.A.?" Price asked. "They've been in a holding pattern and Carl's starting to get restless."

"Tell them to just maintain surveillance for now, until we can get this sorted out."

Los Angeles, California

IN THE RAINBOW DAWN headquarters, Miller was going over the latest batch of intelligence reports from his field teams and the Phoenix office.

The rental car that had been left on the street after the carjacking attempt had been traced to Rudy Reyes as expected. The rental agency wasn't happy about the condition it had been returned in and was looking for the elusive Mr. Reyes to discuss the damage. Posing as an LAPD officer, one of Miller's men had been able to get a copy of the rental agreement and the credit-card slip. The Visa number had been traced to an offshore account, which could mean a number of things.

The survivors of the carjacking incident hadn't been able to get tag numbers for the other two cars. But they had been able to provide basic descriptions for two of the three men in Reyes's covering team. Those descriptions, as well as a lobby security-camera photo of Reyes, were being worked up in the Phoenix headquarters, but nothing had come of it yet.

Miller was confident, though, that he would get a handle on those men. Security Plus was one of the nation's best civilian intelligence-gathering operations.

Grant Betancourt hadn't gotten to where he was by not knowing his competition cold. From the very beginning, he had used both human and cybersleuths to dig as deeply into his opponents' worlds as he could. When he made a move on someone, he knew their finances, their resources, the personality of the man making the decisions and his future plans.

Since Betancourt Industries was now one of the nation's biggest defense contractors, he also had his cybertentacles deep into all levels of the government. The fact that one of his subsidiaries had created the security software that guarded most of the nation's secrets made that child's play.

Miller was confident that it wouldn't take the Phoenix office very long to give him the information he needed. And, when he had it, he had the action teams necessary to make this problem go away quickly. In the meantime, he'd have his men start making foot patrols in the neighborhood of the Rainbow Dawn building.

CHAPTER THIRTEEN

Stony Man Farm, Virginia

The atmosphere in the War Room was tense when the Stony Man crew assembled. No one had expected to be involved with such a mission, and they didn't have a well-developed game plan. They were completely winging it this time.

Aaron Kurtzman and Hunt Wethers represented the cybernetics staff and Cowboy Kissinger the logistical. Buck Greene was on hand in case the mission would have any local security fallout. Barbara Price and Yakov Katzenelenbogen would present the situation and their proposed ops plan.

Katz took the podium first this time and laid out his notes. "Okay," he said, "here's the drill. We have come across information indicating that...."

WHEN PRICE FINISHED her presentation, Katz stood again. "The main problem," he said, "is that if we take this on, we'll be sending in small teams with no backup against pretty good local security forces. Then, of course, going in completely on our own means that if we screw up, we'll have no back door. If we get caught, we'll be headline news. More than likely, in the resulting furor, this organization will cease to exist and most of us will spend the rest of our natural lives in jail."

Katz scanned the faces at the table. "This is gut-check time, people. Before we take this thing any further, each of us has to decide if we're willing to put it all on the line for something that isn't really our business and that no one has asked us to get involved with."

He turned to Brognola. "And for something that won't affect the security of the United States to any appreciable degree one way or the other. Sure, the unrest that most certainly will result if this plot is carried out will have fallout that might affect us to some extent that can't be calculated at this time. But, in a worst-case scenario, few Americans will die from these actions unless they happen to be in Rome or Jerusalem when it goes down.

"So, what will it be?"

"I can't speak for Carl," McCarter said, "but I'm up. I don't think we can stand by and let something like this happen, and I know my people will all concur."

Price looked up. "Let's do it."

Wethers and Kurtzman looked at each other and nodded. "We're on," Kurtzman said.

"It doesn't make any difference to me one way or

the other," Greene said. "Until I'm told to do otherwise, my job is to insure the security of this place. Unless the President sends troops against us, it doesn't really matter to me."

He smiled. "Then, of course, things will get real interesting around the old farm."

The only person at the table who hadn't spoken yet was Brognola, and Katz turned to him.

"Hal?" he said. "This is going to affect you more than any of us, because this time you'll have an active part to play in the mission. Your job will be to keep the President off our backs while we're going up against the locals and probably the UN."

Brognola took a deep breath. "Let's do it."

"Okay," Katz said. "That was the easy part. Now, how in the hell are we going to do this?"

BROGNOLA MADE the call to Able Team's hotel because he wanted to talk to Lyons and Bolan himself. After briefing them on the situation as the farm knew it, Lyons didn't even have to be asked. "We're in," he said.

"What's the plan?" Bolan asked.

"I need Carl and the guys to leave for the Rome mission right away. Katz is going to Jerusalem with half of Phoenix Force, and David will take the other half to Saudi Arabia."

"What do you want me to do?"

"Actually, I'd like you to stay in L.A. and keep working that end of it."

"I think that can be arranged," the Executioner said

evenly. "I may need Aaron to work up a heavy-duty cover, but I can handle it."

"I was hoping you'd say that. I hate to leave you without backup on the ground, but this is going down fast and we have to move on it before it gets away from us."

"And you're going to wing it without official sanction again."

Brognola laughed. "You picked up on that."

"Some things never change, but I can handle things here just fine. The only thing we haven't been able to break open yet," Bolan added, "is where Givens suddenly got his army. They're professional hardmen, not cult groupies with guns. Even though it looks like he's the man behind everything that went down here, I have a feeling that someone else is backing his plays."

"So do I, and Aaron agrees with me," Brognola said. "The problem is that while we have a suspect, we can't put a finger on him yet."

"Who do you think it is?"

"A defense contractor named Grant Betancourt."

"The guy behind Betancourt Industries?"

"That's him."

"You know what that means, don't you?"

"Yes, I do," Brognola said. "It means that the nation's largest defense conglomerate is being run by a guy who may not be the straightest arrow in the world. But he's also the President's closest friend."

"Wonderful."

"That's why we're having to do this one on the sly. I can't bring in the Man."

"I understand."

Israel

EVERY SUMMER, an army of archaeologists and their unpaid helpers descended on the timeless city of Jerusalem to try to wrest secrets from its ancient stones. Even with all the archaeological work that had been done in the Holy City since the mid-1800s, the site had been inhabited since the Neolithic period and there were secrets aplenty left for those who were willing to spend the time looking for them.

Many of those archaeologists were fervently looking for physical evidence that God had actually had something to do with the city's history. Every year the media released reports that some rock had been found that might have been touched by an ancient personage connected to the deity. What made that one rock different from a thousand others just like it was rarely scientific, but Jerusalem wasn't a scientific place. It was a place of faith.

Along with these academic seekers of the unprovable, thousands and thousands of tourists flew in every day to look for a nonspecialist's version of the same thing. For those who considered religion to play a serious role in their lives, Jerusalem wasn't just a vacation site. They came to try to get closer to God, under any one of three names.

Though this annual invasion made the small city a unique form of hell on earth for the local population, it also was their major source of income. Fleecing the gullible while spinning tall tales of times long past was a major occupation for a large percentage of the population of Jerusalem. Whether Jewish, Christian or Muslim, they all lined up to fight for their share of the tourist trade. If you wanted to see where Abraham, Jesus or Muhammad did such and such, there were hundreds of guides ready to tell you what you wanted to hear and show you what you wanted to see, and it had been that way for at least sixteen hundred years.

That the accuracy and veracity of what these guides said was in serious historical question, didn't matter in the slightest to most of the tourists. They had come for a religious experience and that was what they got. They got even more than they could have dreamed when they ventured into the endless warrens of dusty shops in the old city. These places purported to sell everything from splinters of the true cross to fragments of pottery actually used in Solomon's palace. Maybe even from a cup the legendary king had drunk from.

As the seekers and swindlers alike sought their dreams among the ancient stones, others prepared to bring these dreams to an abrupt end.

THE TEN MEN and women of the Geo-Tech mapping team didn't look at all out of place among the other foreign scientists working in the city. They wore the same mixture of shorts, blue jeans and sneakers and that was de rigueur for the field-team set. What was different about them was that they were short on shovels and trowels and long on complicated-looking scientific equipment in big black boxes and computers.

They were also long on security. Hard-eyed, submachine-gun-toting Israeli soldiers had met the team at the airport and they wouldn't leave them until their work was completed. As with almost everything that happened in Jerusalem, there were those who didn't want to see this team do their job. Also, Geo-Tech was introducing a rather large quantity of easily transportable nuclear materials that required around-the-clock security.

There was a fine irony in the fact that bitter religious battles were the reason that the Geo-Tech team had been invited to electronically map Jerusalem, the most-examined archaeological site in the world. With religion driving most of the excavations, religion was also the force behind the repeated attempts to bring an end to them. In particular, the ultraorthodox Jews saw any excavation in or around the city as being a possible desecration of holy ground. Their objections centered around a religious prohibition against disturbing Jewish graves no matter how old they were. And, with the long role Jerusalem had played in the history of the Jewish people, almost anyplace in the city was a potential grave site. Bones didn't have to be found at a dig to spark an Orthodox protest.

When the Orthodox Jews weren't trying to block the excavations, the Muslim population was. Particularly anytime a dig took place too close to what the Jews called Temple Mount and the Arabs the Dome of the Rock. Since the Jews wanted to know everything they possibly could about their long-vanished temple, and the Muslims wanted the Dome left undefiled, there could be no meeting of the minds.

Not wanting to shut down all archaeological research, the Israeli government had turned to Geo-Tech for a solution. The mapping project had been designed to take a noninvasive look at what lay under the modern city. Neutrino radiation mapping would act like a medical CAT scan and would create a layer-by-layer electronic image of the buried ruins.

Since the city had been continuously inhabited for at least four thousand years, there was much to see under the modern levels. As each new conqueror had destroyed the city, the rubble had been flattened and built over again. When the mapping was completed, theoretically every man-made object right down to items the size of a soup can would have been mapped. The worked stones and foundations of ancient buildings, filled-in well shafts, tunnels in the bedrock and graves would be recorded to within a millimeter. Then, the various religious authorities would be able to fight over the recorded images instead of grabbing stones and taking it to the streets.

It was a well-intentioned project, and it would greatly expand the historical knowledge of the city. It would also be the last scientific expedition at the site for the next five hundred years or so. As soon as the mapping was completed, the nuclear materials that had been used to create the ground-penetrating scans would be gathered together and made to react in a very special way.

When this rather unorthodox bomb went off, very little physical damage would result. Just something in the order of a thousand-pound high explosive bomb burst. What would happen, though, was that every living thing within two miles of ground zero in the ancient city would receive a fatal dose of radiation. Children and the elderly among the affected would start dying within six hours of exposure. Hardier individuals might make it for another day or so, but none of them would survive longer than that.

That in itself would be an unimaginable horror, but for the faithful, that wouldn't be the worst of it. For the next five hundred years, Jerusalem and the area immediately around it would be completely uninhabitable to all forms of life. To attempt to visit those holy grounds would be to commit suicide.

Ever since the fireballs over Hiroshima and Nagasaki had ended World War II, doomsayers had wailed nonstop about the horrors of nuclear war. The sheer amount of ink and paper that had been devoted to this hysteria could swamp the Pacific Ocean. In the Western World, the public was so propagandized about nuclear weapons that the facts were almost impossible to learn.

No one ever stopped to think that while both Hiroshima and Nagasaki had been flattened by the first nuclear weapons used in war, the cities hadn't been rendered uninhabitable. The survivors of those two fireballs still lived at ground zero, as did their children, grandchildren and great-grandchildren. The hysterical horrors that were forecast for the aftermath of a nuclear detonation simply hadn't come to pass. And for one simple reason: the ground hadn't been poisoned by residual radiation.

Both the Fat Man and Little Boy bombs used over Japan had been simple fission devices and they had been detonated in the air over their targets. The fireballs had touched the ground and the pulverized material that had been sucked up into them had returned to earth as radioactive fallout. But it had been short-lived radiation.

All the postwar hysteria about nuclear winter and great glassy craters where cities once stood had diverted pubic attention from the real horror of nuclear weapons. Hardly anyone was aware that it was possible to erase life down to the bacterial level in a large area without damaging much of anything on the ground.

The first method to accomplish that was through the use of neutron bombs. These were specially designed nuclear weapons that were detonated high in the sky and produced a massive, but short-lived burst of hard radiation measured in microseconds. These weapons killed life, but they didn't irradiate everything else because that would render the targets useless to the attacker as they wouldn't be able to be occupied.

There were many kinds of nuclear radiation, though. The radiation that would be produced by the Jerusalem bomb would not only kill like a neutron bomb, but would also render the stones and soil of the city as killingly radioactive as the ruins of Chernobyl.

For the next five hundred years or so, Jerusalem would remain a wasteland, approachable only by someone wearing a full nuclear contamination suit, and even then only for short periods of time. Not only would this close off Jerusalem to both the Jews and the Christians, it would also have an effect on the Muslims of the world. The third most holy site in Islam was the Dome of the Rock, and it would also be rendered out of bounds along with the rest of the city.

For the first time in thousands of years, the religious fervor the city generated would finally start to dissipate and peace would finally reign. The force of arms had been tried and had failed, endless talking and political wrangling had failed even worse, but the application of modern science wouldn't fail.

By the time the next millennium rolled around, the pile of stones once known as Jerusalem would be only an interesting footnote in a history book.

CHAPTER FOURTEEN

Stony Man Farm, Virginia

Now that the action teams were being deployed, Aaron Kurtzman shifted into phase two. In the best of all possible worlds, he would have done that before the teams were dispatched, but there had been no time.

This was one of the strangest missions they had undertaken in a long time, a situation where his high-tech toys would be of little, if any, use to the men in the field. The Stony Man warriors knew where their targets were, and they knew what the opposition was going to do. Few questions were left that needed answers, except of course, how they were going to do whatever it was they decided to do. And that was a decision he could not help them with.

There was one thing he could do while he waited for the situation to develop and it was something that should be part of every mission plan, an order of battle on the enemy. He had been so focused on the plot itself and the men behind it that he hadn't taken the time to work up any background information on the people who were doing the dirty work for Givens and Betancourt. Since the action teams were so thin on the ground and had so much stacked against them, even the good guys, maybe a little insight into the personal histories of these wackos might help even the odds.

This kind of work was one of Hunt Wethers' specialties, so he would enlist his help. Without having a hard timetable for the planned events, they had to work fast.

Los Angeles, California

MACK BOLAN DIDN'T mind having Able Team pull out to go to Rome. The overseas part of this current situation held little interest for him. He had come to California to find out why a young woman had been murdered, and there was no doubt in his mind that she had been. Nor was there any doubt that the leader of Rainbow Dawn, Roy Givens, had ordered her death because she had learned of his bizarre plot to destroy Vatican City, Jerusalem and Mecca.

That anyone could even conceive of such a thing, much less try to put it into action, was almost beyond comprehension, but Bolan didn't care why Givens was doing it. Understanding individual pathology wasn't one of his concerns. With Phoenix Force and Able Team targeted against the overseas manifestations of Givens's insanity, he was free to deal with the man himself. And deal with him he would. He would also deal with the nest of vipers Givens had created, Rainbow Dawn.

He doubted that many of the Dawners were aware of what their leader was doing. A secret like that couldn't be trusted to more than a chosen few. And, for that reason, he would give them a chance to change their allegiance to Givens. Should any of them decide that they wanted to die for him, however, he would give them that opportunity as well. As for the men of Givens's security force, they had already fully declared their intentions by attempting to ambush Rosario Blancanales. If they came into his sight, they would go down immediately with no quarter given.

Taking on this task alone also didn't bother him. He had worked by himself long before he had hooked up with Hal Brognola to form SOG, and he kept his hand in the solo business in between Stony Man missions. He chose his missions carefully, and the one thing that always drew his attention to any particular act of wrongdoing was the deaths of innocents. Givens had killed or ordered the deaths of Jennifer Wayne, her father and her Dawner boyfriend.

Those acts had been the work of pure evil, and Bolan had little tolerance for evil.

NOW THAT Able Team had moved out, Bolan didn't need to keep the hotel suite they had been using as their base camp. For the kind of work he was going to do, he needed to be a little less obvious.

After checking out a couple of sites, Bolan chose a

small motel in the downtown area. It was conveniently close to his primary target, but still far enough away that no one should accidentally stumble on him coming or going. Taking the end room on the second floor of one of the wings, he quickly settled in, installing a few security monitors. Before Able Team had departed, he had relieved Schwarz of most of his gadgets. He had also helped himself to all of the hardware and ammunition he thought he might need.

There were two ways that he could conduct this operation. He could wait for the farm crew to develop leads for him, or he could go out and rattle a few cages himself and see what kind of rats scattered for cover. Even though his instincts were to follow the latter course, he decided to have a talk with Kurtzman and get his input before making his first move. The computer wizard was bound to have a hunch or two that would be more accurate than most people's hard information.

A call on his scrambler phone put him in contact with the farm's computer room. "Kurtzman," the voice on the speaker snapped.

"Bear, it's Striker," he replied. "I wanted to check in and let you know where I am."

Kurtzman's voice warmed. "How's L.A.?"

"SOS."

Kurtzman laughed.

After Bolan gave him his motel address and room number, he got to the purpose for the call. "I wanted to get your latest input on the Rainbow Dawners."

"I have one thing I think will be very helpful," Kurtzman replied. "Akira dug up a set of the original builder's blueprints for their headquarters building, and they might help, should you decide to take your inquiries directly to the source, as it were."

"You can count on that."

Kurtzman chuckled. "I thought you might feel that way. Beyond that, we haven't come up with anything of much use. The communications intercepts aren't revealing much beyond the fact that the security is being provided by a firm in Phoenix called Security Plus. They're a legit outfit and specialize in high-profile executive security. What they're doing guarding a scumbag like Givens, we don't know yet."

"I guess I'd better find out then," Bolan said.

"I'll call you as soon as we get anything new."

"And I'll pass on what I learn."

Los Angeles, California

ROY GIVENS WAS relieved when Miller reported that whoever had been monitoring them had apparently departed. "All their surveillance gear has been moved out," the security man said, "and the room is completely clean."

"Does that mean that they're gone and things can go back to normal around here?"

"It could. It could also mean that they've finished with that stage of their surveillance and have moved on to something else."

"But what?" Givens asked. "It's supposed to be over now. With Hoop dead, there's no possible way anyone can connect me with that girl's death."

"For making a real stupid move, you did luck out there," Miller admitted.

Givens was so used to taking crap from Miller, he didn't even bother making a pro forma protest. "And," Givens continued, "whoever that Reyes guy was really working for, those candid photos I gave him should shut them up for good. They know that I have the original negatives and can make more copies anytime I want."

"You have the bit maps," Miller automatically corrected him. "They're computer constructs, and it's not exactly like running down to an instant photo shop and waiting an hour for the prints."

"Whatever," Givens snapped. He was a little tired of being told how much he didn't know about the array of computer gear Miller had brought with him. He could use it well enough to do what he needed to do. "If they keep trying to hound me, I can make that girl look real bad. I could leak a few of the better shots to one of the tabloids and start a real shit storm for them."

"That is something you will not do," Miller said coldly. "The Phoenix office wants the public to completely forget Miss Jennifer Wayne, and that means that you'd better forget her as well."

"But what do I do if it starts up again?"

"If there are more attempts against you, you mean?" Miller asked. "That's simple. You do what you should have done in the first place. Keep your fucking hands off it and leave it to the professionals.''

"But you weren't here then," Givens protested.

"But I am now." Miller smiled. "And, for your protection, this building is completely secure now. You will not leave it for any reason, nor will your top assistants. Everyone stays here until I say differently."

"But what about Mellanie's show?" Givens asked. "I have a producer and several assistants who have to be at the studio when the shows are taped."

"They can go, but they'll be escorted by my men. And I'm sending a team to secure that building as well. I can't believe how half-assed this entire operation has been, but that's over for the duration."

Miller smirked. "You can zone out here to your heart's content with your space cadets and even get caught up on your nookie now that little Jennifer's gone. But you'll do it in this building and nowhere else."

"But," Givens said, "I need to go home and get some things from my house."

"I have a squad covering your property, so you don't have to worry about it. You give me a list of what you need, and I'll have it collected and delivered. I'm not joking when I say that you're staying here. Even if you have a heart attack while you're humping one of your cuties, the doctor is coming here. You aren't going to him.

"And," Miller added, leaning closer to him, "you'd better get that in your head. My people have been instructed to shoot your kneecaps out to prevent you from leaving."

"But what's the big deal?" Givens wailed. "I don't understand."

"You don't have to understand, dammit! All you have to do is what you're told."

That was becoming the story of Givens's life, and he didn't like it one bit. But he knew better than to cross Betancourt's chief guard dog.

Stony Man Farm, Virginia

WHEN BARBARA PRICE met Hal Brognola on the chopper pad, he looked as she expected him to, harassed and worried. "You know," he said, shaking his head, "I've got to come up with another scam to get out of the office before too much longer. Telling the Man that I'm coming down here because the new gear in the Annex isn't working has gotten old. He asked me to look into the contractors and get back to him on what the hell's going on."

Barbara Price didn't smile. When your own side was checking up on you, a person had to be careful. "How about taking a leave?"

"If I did that, I'd have to come up with a detailed itinerary and numbers where he could contact me, the whole nine yards."

"Maybe we can invent a crisis somewhere."

"We've got enough of a damned crisis already, and the problem with that is that we can't control the media.

There's no way we could get CNN to back us on something like that."

"How about I dispatch Akira to your D.C. office to set up a mini–command post so you can keep in direct touch? With our new satcom gear, we can easily set up a dedicated channel for you and continuously feed it like we do when we're working in the War Room."

"That might not be a bad idea. It's either that or I have to start taking real long lunch hours."

"I know it's only ninety miles," she said. "But with travel time back and forth to the chopper, it wouldn't leave you much time on the ground here."

"Let's go with the command post idea," Brognola said. "I'll invent a job title and issue the ID and passes he'll need to clear security in the building. He can be doing some kind of statistical analysis of domestic terrorism or something like that."

"That ought to cover him."

"And, speaking of domestic terrorism, have you heard from Striker?"

"Just a quick check in after he moved to a new address. He's still working up a plan to infiltrate the Rainbow Dawn building."

"Has he said anything about following up on the Betancourt end of it?"

"Not yet," she replied. "He's still focused on settling accounts with Roy Givens."

As far as Brognola was concerned, in the larger scheme of things, Givens and his followers were small change. But, with the evidence connecting him to the girl's death as well as the other cover-up "accidents" and the attempts on Blancanales, he knew Bolan would stay on that until he had concluded his business with Givens. And it was hard for him to find fault with that.

If the attention was always focused on the big sharks, a lot of little barracudas ranged free. Someone needed to pay for what had gone down in L.A., and he was confident that the Executioner would collect the debt.

"I'll leave it at that for now."

"I don't think you have any choice," Price gently reminded him.

Brognola laughed. "You've got that right."

Los Angeles, California

FOR HIS FIRST MOVE on his own, Bolan decided to make a walk-by recon of the Dawners' building. He had done a drive-by with Able Team, but he wanted to get close on the ground. First, though, he did a map recon from the blueprints Kurtzman had faxed him.

The Dawners' building looked to be typical seventies Southern California construction, an eight-story square box. It looked impressive enough, but it wouldn't be around for many more years. As he had seen before, the building had only two points of entry on the first floor, through either the lobby or the fire door in the rear. That was good for keeping out unwelcome visitors, but it would also keep those who were inside trapped in, and that might come in handy for him when he made his move.

The single-story basement was half utilities and storage area and half an underground parking structure. The parking structure was the most likely place for an intruder to use in an attempt to infiltrate the building. And, for that reason, he could count on it being well-guarded. Therefore, it wasn't his first choice entry point.

It wasn't too likely that Givens had modified the utility area when he took over the building. As long as the heat, water and air-conditioning systems worked, there would have been no need to do anything to it. There might have been a few upgrades, but the building was new enough that nothing serious should have been done. And, since the blueprints showed all of the hook-ups to the city's utility tunnels, that looked like his best approach route.

CHAPTER FIFTEEN

Los Angeles, California

Bolan found that confirming his blueprint recon of the Dawners building with a foot recon wasn't going to be as easy as he had thought. After parking his BMW a block away and approaching on foot, he spotted the walking plainclothes security patrol half a block away. In that part of L.A., no one wore sports coats and ties this time of year unless they had something to hide, like a shoulder rig or a holster at the small of the back. A second pair of armed guards, but in black uniforms, stood on either side of the building's main entrance as if it were an open bank vault.

Nonetheless, he decided to see what kind of opposition these gunmen presented and crossed at the light to their side of the street. The minute he reached the sidewalk, he found himself the subject of intense scrutiny. Both the plainclothes patrol and the two door guards locked eyes on him. When Bolan headed north on the sidewalk, the two plainclothes men fell in a dozen steps behind him.

Moving like a man with somewhere to go, Bolan passed the entrance and glanced at it as if he wondered why the guards were there. He let his eyes slide past them to check out the lobby inside in a casual glance, and found it to be what he expected. Two more guards were posted inside. Approaching the corner of the building, he next passed the entrance to the subterranean parking lot. Again, there were two black uniformed guards by the ticket stall, and the moveable barrier blocking the entrance was a steel beam.

Whoever was running that security force knew how to seal off a building. They had everything in place but snipers on the rooftop.

At the corner of the block, Bolan broke off his recon and continued on his way. Nothing was going to be accomplished by bumping heads with those people. At least not now.

Back at his BMW, the soldier decided to make a penetration of Roy Givens's house. He'd given it a drive-by when he first arrived in L.A., but now he wanted to see what he could find inside. Considering the level of security he'd encountered at his headquarters, he was interested in seeing if it extended to his residence.

ON HIS DRIVE-BY of Givens's house, Bolan spotted a dark, late-model Buick sedan parked in the driveway. It looked to be a twin to the one that had been used to cut off Blancanales' car when the attempt had been made on him. Not unexpectedly, this was further confirmation that Givens had been behind that hit. Proceeding halfway down the block, Bolan parked the vehicle and got out.

It was helpful that Givens had the corner lot. It was even more helpful that this was a "no power poles" neighborhood. The junction box for the electrical power to his house was mounted high on the masonry wall around the lot. It was also convenient that the box was at a far corner of the lot where the wall was partially concealed by the neighbor's trees and shrubbery.

Dressed in workman's clothing and carrying a nylon bag, Bolan walked up to the power box, cut the lock and looked inside. Since this was an older house, it was easy to see where newer wires had been connected. They would be the power leads for a security system and maybe direct Internet access. It was also easy to cut them.

Closing the power box, he used a small mirror on an extendable shaft to check the grounds inside the wall. When he saw the way was clear, he closed the bag and stashed it out of sight.

Reaching up with his gloved hands, he pulled himself onto the top of the wall and dropped onto the other side. Keeping low, he hurried across the open expanse of lawn to the cover of the detached garage. From there, he watched the house, but didn't see any movement at the windows.

It was a short distance to the back patio door by the pool. As was so often the case, he found that the sliding glass door didn't have a positive security lock, only a simple key lock. He had it open and was through the door in twenty seconds.

Inside, the house was dim with the curtains drawn. He paused for a few seconds to allow his eyes to adjust before he started to check the ground floor. A quick sweep of the rooms showed them to be clear. And, with the exception of a couple of paper coffee cups on the counter, it looked as if no one had been there for a few days.

Hearing a muffled noise from the upper floor, he drew his Desert Eagle and headed for the stairwell that led upstairs. If the noise came from a house sitter, he or she wasn't leaving much sign of their stay.

He was just approaching the stairwell, his rubber-soled boots silent against the thick carpet, when he caught a flash of movement at the top of the stairs and saw a gun. He dived for cover as a single shot rang out.

Shooting before asking questions wasn't the act of a house sitter, not even in L.A., so Bolan wasn't going to give the gunman a second chance.

When the gunman moved into the open to see if he had scored, the Desert Eagle thundered. The .44 Magnum slug entered the man's head above his right eye and exploded out the back of his skull.

The hammering of a 9 mm subgun from the top of the stairs told Bolan that the man had a partner. But that partner also had a bad habit of shooting before he had a clear target.

Instead of making a suicidal rush up the stairs, Bolan

moved back into the shadows, staying out of the direct line of sight of the gunman, and waited. Human nature being what it was, he didn't have long to wait.

The gunman hugged the wall as he came down the stairs slowly one step at a time. His MAC-10 minisubgun was at the ready as he peered into the darkened hall at the bottom of the stairs.

Bolan had taken a cushion from a chair and as soon as he could see the lower body of the gunman, he tossed it away from him. The gunman heard it hit the floor and stepped into full view, sending a spray of 9 mm rounds in the direction of the sound. Bolan aimed the Desert Eagle and fired a single round. The gunman tumbled down the stairs, a .44 Magnum slug through his heart.

Stepping around the body, Bolan rushed the stairs and found the upper landing empty. In the first room he checked, he saw more empty paper coffee cups and a half-filled ashtray. The two gunmen had been in here, the master bedroom. And, from the number of boxes, both full and half-packed, they had been collecting Roy Givens's belongings. It looked as if Givens was moving out for a while. The amount of clothing and shoes being packed made that almost a certainty. And he didn't need an address written on the boxes to know where he had holed up.

If he wanted Givens, he was going to have to go to the Rainbow Dawn headquarters to get him. But that was fine with him. Givens's security people had just moved themselves up on his list of things to do. When it came time for him to settle with Givens, he would deal with them as well.

Bolan made a quick sweep through the upper floor, but found little of interest. In what had to be Givens's office, the dust patterns on his desk showed that his computer had already been removed as well as any important records it might have contained.

Leaving the bodies behind, he let himself back out the patio door. Locking it behind him, he crossed the lawn and disappeared over the wall.

Vatican City

THOUGH IT WAS completely surrounded by one of Europe's largest cities, Vatican City was a medieval enclave built upon what had been a cemetery in ancient Rome, and made into an independent ministate of some 108 acres in 1929. Had it been located in the United States, the Holy City wouldn't have been big enough to make an even halfway decent theme park. But, because of the Catholic Church's influence, the Vatican had power that went well beyond its modest physical size.

At one time, the entire Christian world had been ruled from this small, walled compound. A shrewd mixture of politics and the force of arms had held most of Europe in its thrall for centuries. That had been a time when proud kings had crawled on their knees to get the Pope's blessing for their crowns. It had also been a time when a large percentage of the wealth of the Western World had been funneled into Rome.

That age was long past, and today the Vatican had been reduced to dealing with purely spiritual matters. Even so, it was one of the top tourist draws in Italy. Hordes of visitors, both the devout and the merely curious, couldn't help but be impressed to see what hundreds of years of unimaginable wealth had been able to accomplish in such a small area. The stunning museums, art collections and opulent architecture were among the most remarkable in the Western World and gave the visitor a vivid glimpse into times long since past.

One of the few remaining symbols of the political power the Vatican had once imposed upon the Western World was the 100-man Swiss Guard. Drawn from the Catholic cantons of Switzerland, these serious young men were the modern incarnation of the hardened warriors who had fought and bled for hundreds of years for the papacy.

The Swiss guardsmen in their gaudy yellow-and-purple uniforms designed by Michelangelo might have looked like refugees from a Renaissance circus, but they didn't clown around. On public view they were armed with gleaming fifteenth century–style halberds, but the best modern small arms that money could buy were never far away. In a world where many of the church's bitterest enemies were also the world's most accomplished terrorists, they could take few chances. Their job was never easy because they guarded against not only the Church's declared foes, but also against those of the faithful who were overcome by their faith.

This perennial problem had reached a fevered pitch during the last few months leading up to Y2K, when hundreds of thousands had gathered in St. Peter's Square to fearfully await the dawn of the new millennium. The Swiss Guard had successfully protected its employers during that time, but just when the guardsmen thought they could relax, the world of the faithful erupted again. A series of "miraculous appearances" throughout the Catholic world was sending thousands of fervent believers to the Vatican again. Any time religious emotions were aroused, the Swiss guardsmen had to be on their toes.

WHEN THE MEN AND WOMEN bound for the Vatican Library had arrived in Rome, their fingerprints had been run through Interpol before their photo ID tags were issued. After having survived several Y2K security threats, some of which hadn't been announced to the press to keep copycats at bay, the Church was taking no chances even with a UN-sponsored team. The bomb that had been planted in St. Peter's Basilica had been big enough to bring the monumental building crashing down had it detonated.

But once the team members had been cleared, their equipment was delivered and they went to work setting it up. The decontamination chamber was brought in sections into an empty room in the basement of the main library and assembled on-site. Since the Church wasn't big on chemical engineers, no one noticed that it was a rather massive item even considering that it was designed to treat a hundred books at a time. Additionally, no one noticed the amount of chemicals that came with it, nor what they were. But then, even the average chemical engineer wouldn't have seen anything unusual about them, either.

Once the decontamination chamber was set up, the archives team started the process of treating the millions of books and manuscripts contained in the Vatican Library. Everything from fragments of ancient Egyptian papyrus scrolls to the more than one thousand years' worth of Church records and archives were scheduled to go through the chemical process that would preserve them for hundreds of more years.

Some of these manuscripts were so theologically sensitive that no one outside the church had ever been allowed to see them. Particularly those documents that detailed the early history of the church. These were escorted by handpicked priests to the treatment area. There, they were signed over to the conservation team, and the priests departed.

One category of items, however, was never let out of the sight of a pair of hard-eyed priests from the Congregation of the Doctrine of the Faith, not even when they were being treated. Not long before, their office had been known as the Holy Inquisition, and it had been responsible for what the Church called "the repression of heresy." These records were considered more than top secret because it was difficult to talk to political leaders about peace if that era of Church history became too well-known.

The treatment of the ancient documents wasn't a scam. It was intended to preserve them for the next five hundred years, and that was about as long as it would take before humans would ever see them again. When the decontamination chamber was turned to its primary purpose, a persistent nerve gas generator, it would be at least five hundred years before anyone would be able to occupy the Vatican again.

THE PARTICULAR formulation of nerve gas that had been chosen for this job was code-named Agent Violet. It had been developed during the cold war to counter CBR protective gear the Soviet Bloc had issued extensively to its troops. Along with being a persistent nerve agent that killed on even microscopic contact, the gas included a compound that ate both synthetic and natural rubber protective gear. In the end, Agent Violet had never been produced in the United States because of the treaties banning chemical warfare that had been signed in the eighties. But the data on the tests that had been conducted hadn't been destroyed.

Grant Betancourt had come across the formula for this gas when he had acquired a small chemical company that had been involved in Defense Department contracts back in the seventies. When this particular contract came to his attention, he immediately saw the nerve agent's possibilities. Creating a small organization inside one of his larger defense-related companies, he continued the research clandestinely. The results had turned out greater than he had expected. Agent Violet was a chemical warfare dream—or nightmare, depending on which side of it a person ended up on.

When Betancourt was putting together his plans for the Project, he decided to use his nerve gas to neutralize Vatican City. It was a center of religious fanaticism and deserved to be destroyed, but where the other two targets were surrounded by desert, Vatican City was surrounded by a vital modern city. In addition, it was a repository of architecture, art and literature unmatched in the Western World. Even though most of the art and literature was religious in nature, it was a vital part of Western history and deserved to be preserved.

And that was where Agent Violet would come in.

Once the gas generator was running, there would be no way to get to it to shut it down. Men in protective clothing wouldn't be able to go in and turn it off because their suits would fail long before they reached the machine. The smallest hole in their protective suit would result in almost instant death. To further protect the machine, a series of booby traps would be set up in case robotic devices were sent in to try to disable the generator.

The only way to protect the public of Rome would be to permanently evacuate an area around Vatican City and erect an impermeable barrier to keep the gas in and the people out. The Vatican could finally become a real museum exhibit, but one that could only be seen from afar.

The Catholic Church would most likely survive this catastrophe, but it would no longer have the weight of history behind it that was incarnated by Vatican City. There might still be a pope or two elected afterward, but it wouldn't be the same thing. With vivid proof that Vatican City and all those who lived within it, including the Holy Father, had been struck down, the armor of the ages would crumble.

To those who would say that the destruction had been done by the hand of man, it could always be countered by asking why hadn't God protected his own? If the pope hadn't been able to save his own life through prayer, what chance would the average sinner have?

It would be a strong message, and one that Grant Betancourt was counting on to make a real difference to the future of the world. One way or the other, rational thinking had to triumph if humankind was to develop to its full potential.

CHAPTER SIXTEEN

Rome, Italy

Rosario Blancanales looked resplendent in his clerical collar and black suit when he stepped out of the bedroom of Able Team's hotel suite in Rome. In a city full of Catholic priests, his Hispanic looks allowed him to blend in almost without notice. He was a little taller and more buff than the average priest on the street, but priests did come in various sizes.

"Are you sure you're going to be able to get away with this?" Gadgets Schwarz asked.

Once more Blancanales had taken the point position. And, even though he was going into the place they were trying to save, Schwarz was nervous. Playing a priest wasn't the same as playing a drug lord or an insurance investigator.

Blancanales shrugged. "Why not? I was raised in the Church and I know the drill."

"What if someone wants you to bless them?" Schwarz asked.

Blancanales got a solemn look on his face and raised

his right hand with his first two fingers and thumb extended. "In the name of the Father, the Son and the Holy Spirit, amen."

He dropped his hand and smiled. "I won't take confessions, though. That would be a little too much.

"But," he added, patting his briefcase, "I'm not here to give guidance to sinners. I'm a Catholic scholar here to do research for the possible beatification of a Mexican nun, Sister Maria Catherine, who was martyred during the French occupation of Mexico in 1863. She's a little-known martyr, but one who personified—"

"Okay, okay," Lyons said, butting in. "You've got the rap down, Pol. How about the paperwork?"

"Well, it carries the signature of the archbishop of Mexico City and it lists me as Father Juan Marcelles, so it should fly."

Lyons shook his head. "I'm not even going to ask how the hell you came up with all of this so fast."

"I have friends and family in the business." Blancanales smiled.

WHILE BLANCANALES presented himself to the chief archivist of the Vatican Library, Lyons and Schwarz took a guided tour of the "Architectural Gems of the Vatican." They had studied their maps of the 108-acre-walled compound, but there was nothing like a visual recon to fix the images in their minds. If and when they went in, it was more than likely they would be keeping to the underground passageways. But they needed to

JUDGMENT IN BLOOD 173

know what the surface buildings looked like and where the entrances to the subterranean levels were located.

Both of them had armed themselves with a thick guidebook and made notes as the tour guide talked incessantly in three languages about the history of the individual buildings and the politics that had gone into their creation. At the end of the three hours, they had seen all they needed to see for an initial recon.

"We just got a lesson in not judging a book by its cover today," Schwarz said as he and Lyons got into their rental to drive back to the hotel. "Their security setup isn't as half-assed as it looks. Those walls might look quaint to the tourists, but they aren't going to be easy to get over, and that's saying nothing about defeating the sensors I know they've got hidden away."

Schwarz shook his head. "And the Swiss Guard in their funny uniforms might look ridiculous, but they've got hard eyes."

"You got that right," Lyons agreed. "And they also have semiautomatic pistols tucked underneath their pretty little uniforms."

"I wouldn't be surprised if those lockers in their guard posts contain even more serious hardware than a 9 mm SIG-Sauer."

"I'm liking this setup less and less," Lyons said.

"Maybe Pol will have better luck."

"If he doesn't, we're screwed."

WHEN FATHER JUAN Marcelles presented himself to the chief archivist of the Vatican Library, Monsignor Xavier Penelli, he found the librarian to be straight out of central casting. The man was thin, in his late sixties or early seventies, balding, wore wire-rimed glasses and had a faint air of mustiness about him as if he, too, were made of ancient parchment.

"Would it be easier if we spoke in Spanish?" Penelli graciously asked.

"English is fine, Father," Blancanales replied. "I went to college in the States."

"So did I," the Italian replied. "Notre Dame."

"I only made it to Gonzaga."

"That's a good school, too."

"I enjoyed my time there."

"I see that you want to look into the archives for material relating to Sister Maria Catherine," the librarian said as he quickly read the letter of introduction.

"She's a favorite of the archbishop, and he's very anxious to complete his petition to the Holy Father for her beatification."

"I can understand that," Penelli said. "I have long felt that the Church needs more Latin American saints, and Sister Maria Catherine would be a wonderful candidate. Her faith is an inspiration to all of us."

Penelli noticed the expression on Blancanales's face and smiled. "You are surprised that I know of her, Father. I majored in Latin American politics of the nineteenth century and wrote my thesis on the French experience in Mexico. It's an obscure period, I know, but it interested me. Two Catholic nations colliding in the Western Hemisphere. In a way, it was a replay of the Napoleonic conquest of Spain, but fortunately, it wasn't so tragic.''

Blancanales started to sweat. He hadn't expected an Italian priest to be familiar with an obscure Mexican martyr who had died more than 150 years earlier.

"Please excuse me," Penelli said, spreading his hands in an expressive gesture. "I do get carried away on the subject, and you aren't here for a lecture on a history that I'm sure you know far better than I. You're here to get into the archives, so I had better have Father Diego show you where to go.''

Blancanales was happy to get off a topic that was bound to trip him up. He did know a little about the French invasion and occupation of Mexico, but only in the broadest outline.

Penelli quickly filled out a file card and handed Blancanales a plastic clip-on pass from a box on his desk. "This will get you into all of the sections of the general archives. Should there be anything you might need from the restricted-access areas, just come and talk to me and I'll arrange for a special pass.''

"Thank you."

"Thank *you* for trying to see that a nun is given the honor she so richly deserves. I'll pray that the Holy Father will look upon your work with favor.''

Blancanales almost felt guilty about what he was doing, but maybe someday someone else would do the research that the good sister deserved. "I hope so, too.''

IT WAS NO TRICK at all for Blancanales to find where
the Vatican archives team had set up its conservation
lab. Hand-lettered signs in multiple languages showed
the way at every one of the library's stairwells. He just
followed the signs down into the basement.

In the building's vast subterranean level, a large
chamber had been cleared out and turned over to the
conservation team. There was no way he could tell how
old this room was, but it could easily go back to the
days of ancient Rome. The fresh coat of white paint
covering the ancient stones looked completely out of
place. It did, though, throw the light around and made
it look a little less like the dungeon that it was.

IT TOOK EVERYTHING Dr. Patrick Renfro, Ph.D., had to
keep from laughing every time a black-robed priest entered his makeshift lab and saw his equipment. They
always stopped and stared as if they had never seen
anything from this century before. Their minds were as
musty and moldy as the books and manuscripts stacked
on the carts they pushed.

Renfro didn't know that he was actually working
for Grant Betancourt. In fact, he had never even heard
of the man. He had been chosen from Rainbow Dawn
and trained for this mission because of his visceral ha-
tred of the Catholic Church and everything that it stood
for. This would be the first time in his career as a chemical engineer that he was going to be able to do something this satisfying. Being able to strike a blow at the
Church that had all but destroyed his life as well as the

lives of his family was better than being crowned the king of the world.

"Excuse me," Blancanales said as he walked around the corner into the lab.

The man in the white lab coat turned to face him and Blancanales saw that he was going to have to turn on the charm. This guy looked like he'd been sucking lemons since childhood and his body language showed that he didn't suffer intruders in his domain.

"Monsignor Penelli sent me down here, but I think I'm lost," Blancanales said. "I'm looking for the register of the books that are being treated down here."

"The register is being kept by one of the priests," the lab man said. "You'll find him at the top of the stairs at the end of the hall."

"Thanks."

"No problem."

Blancanales look a long appreciative look around him. "This is quite an operation you've got here."

"You're an American," the lab man stated.

"Mexican, actually," Blancanales stepped forward with his hand out. "Father Juan Marcelles. But I spent a lot of time in the States, and I was educated there."

Renfro reluctantly shook hands. "Dr. Patrick Renfro, Reactive Technology."

"You know, Doctor," Blancanales said, watching as two of the lab assistants opened the door of the stainless-steel container and brought out a rack of books that had been treated. "After your group is done here, I'm going to talk to my archbishop about trying to contract you to treat the material in our archives in Mexico City. We have thousands of items there from the early years of the Spanish Conquest that not even the Vatican has copies of. Recently, we have tried to start a conservation program of our own. But—'' he shrugged apologetically ''—it's very simplistic compared to what I see here. In fact, when I look at what you're doing, it's hard to even call what we're doing conservation. But we are in Mexico City, not the States.''

Renfro smiled to himself. Of course it would be simplistic. What else could it possibly be in Mexico City? Of all the Catholic nations in the Western Hemisphere, Mexico had the least excuse for being what it was today. At one time, Mexico City had been the most civilized place in the entire New World. It had had the New World's first university, trading banks with contacts in both Europe and the Far East, wide, paved boulevards and street lighting. All of this had been at a time when Washington, D.C., had been little more than a cow pasture by a river with a couple dozen buildings and mud streets.

That had been a century and a half ago. Today, superstition and political corruption made Mexico City a cancerous lesion that devoured anything that Mexico might have to offer to the rest of the world.

''I don't have anything to do with the scheduling end of our work,'' Renfro said. ''But I can give you the number of the contract guy in our home office.''

''That's great,'' Blancanales said. ''And, if you don't mind, could I look around for a while? I'll stay out of your way, but I'd like to see the process so I can describe it in detail to the archbishop.''

Blancanales winked conspiratorially. "He's somewhat, I guess I would have to say, set in his ways? He's not really a man of this century, and sometimes it's rather difficult to convince him that a modern technique can have any value to the Church. He came from a small village in the mountains and is a dyed-in-the-wool technophobe."

"I understand that completely," Renfro said, and he did.

He had almost pulled out of this project when one of the Vatican's flunkies had insisted on blessing the decon chamber to chase away the demons before allowing it to be started up. He had absented himself from that particular barbaric ritual so he wouldn't laugh out loud as water that had been prayed over was sprinkled on the mirror-polished stainless steel. He had, however, firmly insisted that no "holy" water be sprinkled on the interior surfaces.

Nonetheless, Renfro wasn't wildly happy at having an American-educated Mexican hanging around. Even though this man was a priest, he'd apparently been exposed to enough rational American culture that he would be considerably less gullible than the local shamans. At least he would be able to have some understanding of what was going on.

"I'm sure I'll be able to accommodate you," Renfro lied, "but it will have to be at a later time. We're a small team, and we're all too busy now for me to be able to spare anyone to escort you. But, as this project starts to wind down, I'm sure we'll have some slack time."

"That's great. I'm going to be here for several months, so I can keep checking back with you."

"Do that," Renfro said as he glanced at his watch. "Now if you will excuse me, Father, I have to see to my duties."

"Certainly, Doctor."

THAT EVENING, Lyons, Schwarz and Blancanales went over the tapes that had been made of the images Blancanales's lapel video camera had picked up during the day. The bug was too small to include an audio pickup, but the video wasn't bad for a camera the size of a pencil eraser.

"That's as far I was able to get into the lab," Blancanales said as he concluded his show-and-tell. "Just a foot inside the door. But at least I got some good shots of that decontamination container and, as you can see, that thing's not small."

"Actually, it's a chemical reactor," Schwarz said. "And it's that big because of the double construction of the walls. They're designed to contain the heat and pressure of a chemical reaction without exploding. And, as I'm sure you noticed, it's made of stainless steel. That thing's going to be there for centuries."

"Now that Renfro's met me," Blancanales said, "I'm going to have to make sure that he doesn't see me down there too often. I have a distinct feeling that he's not too big on priests, or the Church, for that matter. He's one of the most condescending bastards I've ever met and about the last guy I'd expect to see working on a project like that."

"Not if he's planning to destroy Vatican City," Lyons pointed out. "For that kind of mission you almost have to have a guy who hates the Church."

Schwarz ran the tape back to take another look at the route down to the lab. "I want to get in there and see if I can plant bugs in some out-of-the-way places. I also want to try and find where they're storing the chemicals for phase two of this drill."

"You're never going to make it in there as a priest," Blancanales cautioned. "Because of the sensitive nature of much of the books and manuscripts that're being treated, the security in that building's tighter than the proverbial nun's knickers."

"I was thinking of doing a Ninja on it."

"Only if you just make an initial recon," Lyons said. "Not a full-bore intrusion. I just want you to test the defenses and, if you get a chance, plant a few bugs. Be ready to pull out at the first sign of trouble. I don't think the Swiss Guard will shoot first, but we can't afford for them to put the grab on you, either. If we have to call Hal to get your ass out of a Rome jail, it'll get back to the White House in a flash and we'll all be in the shit."

"What do you think we're in now, chocolate?"

CHAPTER SEVENTEEN

Jerusalem, Israel

Yakov Katzenelenbogen felt a wave of nostalgia sweep over him as the taxi that had picked him up at the airport approached the ancient city. He was Jewish, and as such he felt a strong connection to the city. In reality, though, he had no idea when, or even if, any ancestor of his had ever lived there in ancient times. Regardless of his religious heritage, it was possible that none of his people had until fairly recent times.

For all he knew, his earliest "Jewish" ancestors could have been Greeks, Egyptians or even Romans who had converted to the worship of one god. Equally, they could have been Persians, Syrians or a dozen other Middle Eastern peoples. There had been a time when Judaism had welcomed converts as the Christians were later to do.

He was traveling on his legitimate Israeli passport, which had first been issued right after the modern state of Israel had been formed. He had been a kid, then, but he'd soon been swept up in the struggle of the young nation. Before his part in that struggle was over, he had given a son, half an arm and buckets of blood to his homeland. This time, though, if he wasn't successful, he might give his life.

To help him with this critical mission, he had brought two members of Phoenix Force with him— T. J. Hawkins and Gary Manning. Both of them could fade into the background as tourists, and no one would notice them while he tried to contact men he knew from his days with Mossad. Some of those men were old friends and some old enemies. But they were men he could trust with his life, as well as the lives of everyone in Jerusalem.

The biggest challenge wasn't going to be taking out the bad guys; they could be eliminated in a single, brief hit. But, to get to them, they were probably first going to have to go through a layer of UN guards before even getting to the Israeli soldiers. The UN guards, particularly if they were drawn from one of the Irish or Canadian regiments, would be difficult enough to tackle, but it was doable. It was the Israelis that worried Katz.

As a veteran of Israel's armed forces and the country's intelligence service, he knew exactly how good both were. Man for man, they were as good as it could get. It was ironic that on a mission to save Jerusalem, they couldn't openly engage Israeli help. The Israelis were hypersensitive about anything that had to do with Jerusalem. They were only too aware that it was a flash point like no other in the world. Even a small spark in this triple-sacred city could blow up and inflame the entire Middle East.

The three Stony Man commandos were staying at separate locations. Katz chose a small B and B run by a Muslim couple because he knew the owners would catch his Israeli-accented Arabic and leave him completely alone. After depositing his luggage, he hailed a cab on the street outside and headed back for the airport. Kissinger had forwarded their mission pack, and he needed to secure the hardware as soon as possible.

HAWKINS WASN'T what anyone would ever call a religious man. However, as a home-grown Southerner, he was fully aware of the sentiments that were so much a part of his native culture. As a kid, he had been dragged to enough tent meetings and Sunday sermons to have the rap down cold.

After checking into his modest hotel, his first stop was at a sidewalk kiosk that featured racks of religious books and guides. After looking them over, he chose a gaudy tome entitled *A Christian's Guide to the City of the Lord.* It was big enough to be obvious, and carrying it around would automatically tag him as a Christian pilgrim. That would give him the cover for his interest in what the mapping team was doing.

Armed with his book, he headed out to make his initial recon.

GARY MANNING WAS traveling on a Canadian passport with enough credentials to establish that he was a geological engineer. That went well with his blaster's background, and he could talk the talk well enough not to draw attention to himself as he tried to get close to the members of the mapping team. It also called for him to take a room in a better hotel than the one Hawkins was stuck in. Engineers were paid well, so it would look funny if he tried to go on the cheap.

He, too, went into his hotel's bookstore and searched the racks until he found what he was looking for. His book, *The Stones of Jerusalem,* was a little more specialized than Hawkins's popularized reading material. It was an architectural history of the region, and included every building foundation, tunnel and cave that had been discovered in more than a hundred years of digging. Just the thing for a geological engineer.

With his book in hand, he headed out to recon an area where he knew the mapping team would be working.

AS WITH ANYTHING NEW and unusual that occurred in or around Jerusalem, the Geo-Tech mapping team immediately became controversial. Though their technique had been designed to be noninvasive so as to mollify religious sensibilities, that was a little too much to ask in a place like Jerusalem. This was a city where any change to the status quo, however small, had to be cleared through a religious committee. It was true that the mapping project had been approved by this committee, but what men had decided, men could undecide. Only God's works were permanent.

When the first article about the team appeared in the newspapers, protesters started to gather before the day was out. The first protesters were fundamentalist Christians, many of them tourists, who believed that anything with the word "nuclear" or "radiation" connected with it was the work of Satan and a sign of the coming Apocalypse. Not to be outdone, Muslims soon joined in by linking the mapping equipment to the nuclear weapons of the Great Satan, the United States of America.

Most of the time, that kind of response was pure Middle Eastern paranoia, born from a total lack of understanding of modern technology. It was a fine irony that this time the protesters had it dead right. For once, there was a reason for their fears, but they were completely unaware of it. Even had they known, they still wouldn't have understood what was happening.

WARREN BRIDGER, the Geo-Tech vice president in charge of the Jerusalem operation, was disgusted at the throng of demonstrators surrounding his work site. The company had been assured by authorities at the highest levels that this wouldn't occur. Geo-Tech wasn't going to make much more than expenses on this gig, but that wasn't why they were doing it. If this demonstration of the new technique was successful, they could name their own price for future jobs. They could also announce the stock offering and he would finally get the payoff for the years of long hours he had given to get the company off the ground.

If this demonstration hit *CNN Headline News*, Geo-Tech was going to take it on the chin. So far, all the advance publicity about the project had been favorable—an American company going into a world-renowned trouble spot and easing tensions through the application of good old-fashioned Yankee know-how. It made great press, but not as good as a TV newsbreak showing Israeli riot cops busting heads.

The second-in-command of the mapping team, Dave Tolly, wasn't at all surprised at the demonstration. It was exactly what he expected from religious wackos, and this place was wall-to-wall with them. Tolly was the man who would push the button when the time finally came, and he couldn't wait to do it. The sooner these freaks were put down, the better it would be for the entire world.

Bridger turned to Tolly. "What are we going to do, Dave?"

Tolly smiled thinly. "What I'd like to do is turn the army loose and get this shit cleared away."

Bridger quickly checked to make sure that no one had overheard. "Dammit, Dave, you can't say things like that. I warned you before, and I just can't have it. You know we have a lot riding on this project, and if anyone finds out that we're not being 'sensitive' to the local religious concerns, it'll kill us."

"I know." Tolly shrugged. "But don't you really want to take a gun to those assholes?"

"What I want to do," Bridger said, "is to finish this

job and go back and enjoy the bonus we're all going to get when the stock goes public."

Tolly smiled. His bonus would be seeing, from a long distance of course, this entire city dead and everyone in it rotting.

"I'm cool, Warren," Tolly said. "And I'm with you 110 percent. And you're right, the sooner we're done here, the better I'll like it."

HAWKINS STOOD OFF to the side of the demonstration in front of the Geo-Tech work site and watched the proceedings. At first, the Christians and Muslims kept to their own groups. But as the police moved in to contain the crowd, they started mingling. It was like one of the oldest sayings in the Middle East—"The enemy of my enemy is my friend." Bringing religious harmony by the proper employment of riot cops could only happen in a place like this.

When the police showed up, some of the fainter hearts, almost all of them Christian tourists, started moving toward the rear.

Hawkins had his eye on one young female tourist, an American by the looks of her clothing, who was having trouble deciding if she'd had enough excitement for the day. Her eyes were glittering as she snapped a series of pictures of the demonstrators and their signs. He knew that she intended to show those back home to prove that she had actually stood up for whatever it was she thought she was standing up for. She had no idea that she was about to get her head split and her lungs full of tear gas.

That kind of naiveté usually was its own reward. But Hawkins had a weakness for redheads, even very young and very stupid ones. He moved closer to her to be on hand when the shit hit the fan.

The process of separating the sheep from the lions was going along just fine until someone, a local from his clothing, got bored with the process. Finding a sizable rock along the curb, he sidearmed it at the closest cop. The rock bounced harmlessly off the man's riot shield, but that was the signal for the attack to begin.

The Jerusalem riot police were some of the most experienced in the world. To them, it was more than just a dangerous job, it was a profession they took great pride in. They knew that they were the first line of defense in the most volatile city in the world.

The redhead got a whiff of tear gas and started to gag. In her panic, she stumbled when she turned and fell to the cobblestones. That was Hawkins's cue. Taking a last deep breath of clean air, he moved in to rescue her.

By the time he closed with the woman, the party was mostly over. The self-righteous were quickly learning that one's personal religious convictions weren't armor against gas or near-unbreakable carbon-fiber riot batons. For most of the Christians, what had been a strangely exciting religious experience was turning to a raw panic like nothing they had ever known.

The locals, though, were made of sterner stuff, and they had played this game many times before.

The cops also knew the game and knew who they had to concentrate on. For the most part, they ignored the crying, wailing Christians and focused on the rock throwers. If, however, they stumbled upon a gassed Christian in their path, they weren't above giving the person a whack in passing to motivate his or her withdrawal from the playing field.

Hawkins's redhead had gotten to her hands and knees just in time to get flattened by a panicked fat man in shorts and a John Deere cap. When she went down the second time, she hit her head and lay still.

Hawkins was over her in an instant, protecting her with his body. When a local saw an opportunity to kick a foreigner on the ground, he stepped up and raised his foot. Hawkins took that opportunity to practice his patented soccer-penalty goal kick that ended with the toe of his boot in the crotch of the local. That cleared a zone around the woman, so Hawkins scooped her up in his arms and hurried out of the area.

A riot cop appeared out of the smoke, his baton raised, but when he saw that Hawkins was carrying a wounded woman, he refrained and sought another target.

As soon as he cleared the gas cloud, Hawkins spotted a water fountain. By this time, the woman was regaining consciousness but he held her tightly and said, "It's all right, I'm taking you to safety."

She wrapped her arms around his neck and sobbed.

After helping the woman wash her face in the fountain, Hawkins suggested that they find a café somewhere to get a soft drink. Two hours later, he knew almost everything there was to know about Sarah Jenkins and had told her just as much as he wanted of his cover story.

When he said that he had to leave to join up with a tour he had signed up for, she left him with her hotel phone and room numbers and her heartfelt thanks for having been rescued. That was expressed with a hug of Christian brotherhood and a brief pass of her lips over his cheek accompanied by a blush.

CHAPTER EIGHTEEN

Saudi Arabia

David McCarter watched the sun come up from his hotel room balcony in Riyadh.

He had been in Saudi Arabia more than once, but never in a role exactly like this. Part of the problem was that he still didn't know what role he, Rafael Encizo and Calvin James were going to be able to play. They had to go to Mecca, and it was off-limits to infidels. The holy city was not to be seen with profane eyes.

In a strike mission anywhere else in the Middle East, the three of them would drop in, do the job and be extracted. Piece of cake. This wasn't going to be that kind of mission. Exactly what kind of mission it would be, however, had yet to be determined. Pulling off a small-team assault in Saudi Arabia was a real problem. Ever since the Gulf War, the Saudis had beefed up their armed forces, including their unique national guard.

The Saudi national guard wasn't analogous to the American National Guard. It was more like a combination of a national army and a national police force. In their gun jeeps and pickup trucks with air-conditioned cabs, the guard roamed the desert like the Texas Rangers of the Wild West. And, like the Rangers, they were the law. Everything from border infiltrators to camel thieves fell under their jurisdiction, and they were everywhere, all the time.

There was no way that they would be able to infiltrate the 450 miles to Mecca by vehicle. Both the roads leading to the holy city as well as the vast expanses of desert were well patrolled by the national guard. Getting past them wasn't so much a matter of skill as it would be sheer luck, and you couldn't plan a military operation on luck. The roll of the dice by the gods of war was always a factor in any operation, but it wasn't one that you could count on.

A chopper insertion was equally impossible because the Saudi air force had the best AWACS systems in this part of the world thanks to the United States. Nothing bigger than a buzzard that traversed Saudi airspace went unnoticed for very long. And, since the Gulf War, the Saudi F-15s and F-16s were on ramp alert with war shots hanging on their missile racks and responded to the AWACS sightings by shooting first and asking questions of the wreckage later. That system had recently been tested and it had worked as advertised.

Even if the strike plan was still in the air, the recon of the site wasn't. Even though Mecca was off-limits to unbelievers, he and James carried ID and documentation from the UN Cultural Heritage Commission that was sponsoring this "job," and that should get them in close enough to get a look at what they would be facing when, and if, they could figure out a way to get in.

IN THE HOLY CITY of Mecca, Betancourt's specific target was the sacred shrine known as the Kaaba in the center of the city. This was believed to be the remains of a giant meteorite that had struck the earth thousands of years ago. Long held to be sacred by the peoples of the Arabian peninsula, it was the place where the prophet Muhammad had received the revelation from God that had sent him out into the desert to create Islam.

This rock was the very center of the Islamic world and the place every Muslim was required to bow and pray toward five times a day. No matter where in the world they were, Muslims were expected to know where Mecca was in relationship to where they lived so they could make their prayers. Every male Muslim was also expected to make a pilgrimage to this sacred place at least once in his lifetime to worship at the shrine.

The enclosure hiding the sacred stone was in the middle of a huge plaza that was surrounded on all sides by a two-story building. On the interior sides, the structure featured a pillared portico on both floors that looked out onto the sacred rock. It was under this porticoed structure that Gold Star Construction was tunneling to create a new subterranean level that would be used to provide services for the millions of pilgrims who visited the site every year.

Betancourt's plan was to detonate the largest fuel air explosion that had ever been created in this newly excavated area under the sacred compound. The blast's effect would be equal to that of a fair-sized nuclear detonation, somewhere on the order of two kilotons, and it would completely eradicate the Kaaba as well as the sacred compound. Nothing would be left but dust and a rather large hole in the ground.

All traces of the rock that so many had worshiped for thousands of years even before the prophet, and untold millions since then, would have ceased to exist and Islam would no longer have its primary focal point. It was true that there would still be Medina, the prophet's birthplace, and Islam's second most important holy place. But that would be it. Jerusalem, the third holiest city in the Islamic hierarchy, would also have been rendered deadly to visitors.

To Betancourt, the best part was that the destruction of the Kaaba would cause the Muslim world to go completely crazy. Of the three religions, he saw Islam as the most repressive and the most regressive as well as the most volatile. All too many Muslim clerics wanted to take their followers back to the eighth century, not forward to the twenty-first. This would give them their chance to regress en masse back to their Golden Age when they had hacked a barbaric empire out of the civilizations they had invaded and crushed.

In their rage at this destruction, they would explode,

strike out, and would have to be put down by modern armed forces. The body count would be high and that suited him just fine. The fewer fanatics who were left when this was all over meant that there would be fewer problems bringing the region into the modern world.

THE NEXT MORNING, David McCarter, playing the role of a British delegate to the United Nations, and Calvin James as a Caribbean diplomat, boarded a chartered helicopter in Riyadh for the 450-mile flight west to the holy city of Mecca. After flying over miles of sand, McCarter was glad to see signs of habitation below as they approached the city high on the ridge of mountains that bordered the Red Sea.

As UN Representatives, McCarter and James rated a VIP escort, and they got the personal welcome of a minor prince of the Saudi royal house, Prince Khalid Al Saud. Since the 1930s, the House of Al Saud had followed a tradition of sending its sons to the West to get their educations. Those who sought technical training usually went to universities in the United States while those who would follow political or military careers were educated in the UK. As a result, English was almost always the second language in the royal family.

"You understand, of course," the prince said smoothly after the introductions had been made, "that I cannot give you a tour of the Kaaba."

"Certainly, Your Highness," McCarter answered. "That wasn't at all expected. Our mandate is just to look in on the construction work and report its progress to the commission. It is very kind of you to go out of your way to do this for us.''

''Not at all,'' the prince replied as he led them to an air-conditioned Mercedes limo.

UNLIKE IN Jerusalem and the Vatican, no UN security element watched over the work at the Muslim shrine, nor would there be one. As the keepers of the holiest place in all of Islam, the Saudi royal house couldn't risk allowing armed infidels in. They were under constant scrutiny by the other Arab states to insure that they properly preserved the sanctity of the holy site. In 1979, they had let their guard down and the Grand Mosque in the heart of Mecca had been captured by fundamentalist Shiites following a self-proclaimed Mahdi. The revolt had been firmly put down, but blood had been shed in the sacred enclosure.

That incident had put the house of Al Saud in a bad light throughout the Muslim world and as a result, they were under constant criticism, particularly by the radical Muslim elements who accused the Saudis of having become corrupted through their extensive contacts with the West.

As it was, it had taken special dispensation for McCarter and James to even be allowed in the outer compound. The Gold Star Construction team had been granted special permission as well so it could do its excavating work. The rock that was being removed wasn't being blasted or jackhammered, which would have disturbed this ancient abode of holiness. Instead, the underground passages were being cut by the largest industrial lasers that had ever been built.

After being cut loose, the rock was being removed by a small fleet of propane-powered carriers small enough to fit in the underground passages, and they, too, were quiet. Even though it was being done by infidels, the work was a lot quieter than it would have been if conventional methods had been used, even pick and hammer.

At the shrine, Prince Khalid led his guests into the porticoed hall to the room that had been set up for the office of Gold Star Construction. Curtains had been erected between the pillars of the inner breezeway to protect the Kaaba from the defiling gaze of the nonbelievers. Stern-faced guards armed with H&K assault rifles were posted every dozen feet or so to make sure that an infidel wasn't overcome with curiosity and trying to sneak a peak.

In the office, McCarter and James were presented to Bud Bolger, the foreman of the Gold Star team. Except for the most humble temporary mud huts thrown up by the poorest of the poor, almost every modern structure in the entire country had been built by foreign labor.

Most often, these laborers were from other Islamic countries, so there would be no problem of religious pollution. However, the state of technology in most Islamic nations meant that any job involving high-tech methods or materials required bringing in nonbelievers to do the work. And this particular job required using American men and machines.

Bolger hated showing people around, but the prince had told him do to it, so he had no choice. He had a briefing ready and the Saudis offered tea and refreshments while the American used large-scale drawings to explain what they were doing. At the end, he asked if there were any questions.

"Your, er, laborers are all Americans, are they not?" McCarter asked with just the right amount of upper-class British indolence and disdain for the "working classes" in his tone.

"I guess you could say that," Bolger replied. "And so are my geological engineers, my architects, my laser technicians and all the rest of my crew. Even the, how did you say it...laborers?"

He locked eyes with McCarter. "My crew are all one hundred percent Americans because no one else in the world can do what we do. Certainly not any of you—" he paused and smiled boldly "—you-row-peons."

McCarter smiled. This guy was pure Yank and probably a strong union man to boot. He wouldn't be in on any plot to blow up this place, it would offend his sense of doing a job well. That meant that the bombers were hidden in his crew and would have to be dug out.

"Which, of course," McCarter said brightly, "is why your firm was chosen to handle such a delicate job as this. You Americans do seem to, er...excel in certain types of technical endeavors."

Bolger didn't break a smile. "Don't we just. And now, if you gentlemen are done wasting my time, I have a job I need to see to."

"Of course, of course."

As Bolger walked out, a workman in a hard hat and a sweaty shirt walked in. "Bud said that if you want to see the work site I have to show it to you."

"Quite," McCarter said.

RAFAEL ENCIZO ENJOYED the cool air of the lounge in the Riyadh Hilton hotel, the hangout for many of the foreign construction workers who cycled in and out of Saudi. This, and one or two oil company rooming houses, were the only places in this town where a man could get a beer without risking arrest and deportation, if not worse.

Of all the things a religion could prohibit, alcohol had to be the worst. A prohibition against sexual activity wasn't hard to get around—you just did it in an out-of-town motel and made sure that no one saw you going in or out. But it was hard to brew beer without someone noticing. Which was why Encizo was in this bar. If a foreigner working anywhere near Riyadh wanted a beer, this was where he had to go to get it.

So far, judging by the insignia worn on their shirts and baseball caps, he had seen men from well over a dozen of the construction firms under contract in Saudi Arabia, but none from Gold Star. That was odd, because he knew damned good and well that anyone who was caught trying to smuggle booze into Mecca would be summarily executed. The bottle would be produced and the trial would be over. The guilty party's head would be separated from his body before the day was out.

So, Gold Star had hired either a crew of nondrinkers, which wasn't likely, or he would just have to wait a little longer. Either way, hanging out here sure beat the hell out of being stuck anywhere else in this country.

Signaling to the waiter, he ordered another Budweiser. This wasn't the time to be caught indulging himself in a foreign beer when the cooler was still full of Bud and Miller. In this crowd, only when all the American beer was gone could he drink foreign without attracting attention.

"WE SAW THE PROPANE storage tank," McCarter reported to Encizo that night, "and the bloody thing's big enough to blow up half the country. It's got to hold a million gallons at least and I don't have the slightest idea how the hell they got it there."

"Where is it?"

"It's parked right outside the compound with lines running down into the work area to refuel their vehicles."

"So it's easy to get at."

"If you can get across the desert without running into the Saudi national guard and, when you get to Mecca, if you can keep from being spotted by the temple guards, yes. In fact, you can walk right up to it and give it a bloody great thump. Getting to it is going to be the problem. And, of course, there's the small matter of getting away when we're done."

"So what do you think?"

The Briton shook his head. "I'll be well buggered if I know."

"We have to do something, David," Encizo said. "We can't allow this to take place."

McCarter got up, walked to the window and looked out over the night lights of Riyadh. Many of them were mercury vapor lights that gave a golden hue to the buildings, making them look like sets for an *Arabian Nights* movie. "You know, I never thought I'd end up here."

"What do you mean?"

McCarter turned back. "I mean that this is a bloody suicide mission. And, even if we can somehow prevent this attempt, there's no guarantee that the next 'UN-sponsored' team that comes in won't have another plan to blow up that place. I'm not really sure that we'll be able to change what seems to be the inevitable.

"But," he said, "even so, we'll try as we always do. I just hope that the results will be worth the price."

CHAPTER NINETEEN

Phoenix, Arizona

Grant Betancourt went over the reports from his Vatican, Jerusalem and Saudi Arabia action teams. In Rome and Mecca, the Project was progressing more or less per schedule now that everyone was on-site. He didn't have to read the Geo-Tech reports to know what was going on in Israel. All he had to do was turn on the TV and watch it all in living color on CNN.

He had tried to have Roy Givens warn Dave Tolly about the dangers of putting out too much Geo-Tech publicity before their work was completed. But the way the Project was set up, the cutouts were much too deep for Tolly to have any direct influence on Geo-Tech's management, particularly on Warren Bridger. For this mission, he had to trust the six men Givens had been able to plant on the ten-person team. In a crisis, the four outsiders, three of whom were women, could be sacrificed along with Bridger.

Bridger was an executive VP with Geo-Tech and the CEO-owner had insisted on sending him along as a PR stunt more than anything else. He was getting a first-hand look at what self-promoting publicity in a place like Jerusalem had gotten him and maybe he would keep his mouth shut now.

To make sure that he did, Betancourt hit his speed dial for one of the smaller financial houses he worked with. With his personal wealth as extensive as it was, he invested through several houses, and it was well-known that he was always on the lookout for the up-and-comers in the high-tech markets. That kept the old-line firms on their toes and still gave the new guys hope. The company he was calling was handling Geo-Tech's initial stock offering, and they had been pushing hard to get him to make a significant investment in the company. A subtle warning from him should be enough to get Bridger pulled out or at least muzzled.

"Bradley," Betancourt said when the phone was picked up, "Grant Betancourt here."

"What can I do for you, Mr. Betancourt?" Bradley Rivers had learned right off the bat not to waste Grant Betancourt's time with pleasantries when he called. His job was solely to listen to what the man had to say and to answer the occasional question if asked.

"Look, I've been watching CNN and it looks to me like Geo-Tech has really stepped on their foreskins over there in Jerusalem. I'd been giving some serious thought to getting on board with their initial offering. You know that I like to encourage high-tech start-ups. But frankly, Bradley, I'm concerned now."

Rivers felt his world crashing down around him and

his expected commissions falling after it. If Betancourt bailed out, the big man would take much of the high-tech investing community with him, and he'd be left with his Johnson in his hand. His company had put a great deal of time and money into promoting Geo-Tech, and the stock had to take off for them to get their return on the investment.

"If they don't know better than to run their mouths off and create this kind of local reaction, I'm not sure that I want to risk getting involved. If this incident doesn't put an end to them, they're going to be working in other politically or religiously sensitive areas in the future, and it's obvious to me that they don't have a clue about dealing with people. Cutting-edge technology and fresh ideas are all fine and good, and as you know, I like to see that, but people skills are never going to go out of style."

Rivers hadn't yet been asked a question, but he knew what kind of answer Betancourt was looking for.

"You're one hundred percent correct, Mr. Betancourt," he said. "I was shocked myself when I saw the coverage. As Geo-Tech's house for their initial offering, I was going to call their president and talk to him today. My gut is if they can't get this turned around over there ASAP, they need to find someone else to handle their stock. As it is, it's looking too risky for our investors and we couldn't recommend it in good faith."

"Let me know what they say," Betancourt replied.

"Will do, sir."

Betancourt put the phone down and smiled. Sometimes it was so easy that it wasn't even fun. That should take care of that situation and, with the Rome project running along nicely, that left only the Saudi project that needed his attention. It was slightly behind schedule, but he had been assured that it was only temporary.

Something about a pending UN inspection of the work site had thrown them off schedule a bit. Since he had the UN running interference for him, he had to expect that sort of thing. And it also gave him added layers of cover. When the hammer fell, he would be among the first to ask the UN what had gone wrong.

SINCE IT HAD BEEN the height of the tourist season when the Geo-Tech mapping team had arrived, it hadn't been able to find quarters for everyone in the same hotel. Warren Bridger and the three women were in one hotel close to the Christian Quarter, while Dave Tolly and his five Dawners were in another hotel on the other side of town closer to the north of the Muslim Quarter.

Tolly was sleeping when the phone rang. "Yeah?"

"It's Warren," Bridger said. "I need to talk to you over here ASAP."

"Damn, Warren, it's almost midnight. Can't it wait till morning?"

"I'm sorry, but I have to talk to you right away and I can't do it over the phone. We don't know who's listening in."

"Okay, okay," Tolly said. "Just let me get dressed and I'll try to find a cab."

"Make it as fast as you can, please."

WHEN DAVE TOLLY arrived at the hotel, Warren Bridger looked like he'd been hit by a truck. "You won't believe the call I just got from Bill."

Tolly could believe anything that came from Bill Webster, the Geo-Tech CEO. For a brilliant engineer, the man was a basket case when it came to dealing with anything that couldn't be expressed with mathematics. "What good news did Wild Bill have for us this time?"

Bridger got a strange look on his face. "The good news, I guess you'd say, is that I'm going back to the States tomorrow and you're taking over the team."

Tolly was taken completely aback at that news. That wasn't in the playbook he was working from. "What in the hell are you talking about, man?"

"Bill's blaming me for the riot at the site today," Bridger said. "He thinks I must have shot my mouth off about the nuclear materials and scared the locals. I offered to fax him copies of the press releases so he could see what I'd said for himself, but he wasn't interested. He says that the investors are panicking and the only way he can save the company is to get me the hell out of here."

"Damn, Warren," Tolly said. "Do you think it would help if I talked to him and explained that the wackos around here don't need any excuse to riot? I mean, I've never seen a place like this in my life."

"It's already past that." Bridger shook his head. "He has me booked on the first plane out of here in the morning and if I'm not on it, I'm fired."

"I don't know what to say."

"The only thing I can say," Bridger stated, "is that you'd better make damned sure that you don't start another fucking riot."

"I'll try not to." Tolly hid a smile. "Do you want me to take you to the airport in the morning?"

"No, thanks. I'll just slink out of here on my own."

Now THAT Dave Tolly was the man in charge of the Geo-Tech mapping team, Frank Cross, the engineer in charge of the equipment, had been promoted to second-in-command. Cross was another one-time student who had been the recipient of a Betancourt Industries scholarship. After graduation, he had taken a job at Geo-Tech and risen in the company.

"Dave," Cross said, looking around at the hard-eyed, gun-toting UN security force that had been at their work site when they had showed up that morning, "is this really necessary?"

"I know what you mean," Tolly replied, "but with the riot yesterday, the home office thinks it is and so does the damned UN. I've been given assurances, though, that they'll keep out of our way while we're working."

Cross shook his head. "It's just that with the Israelis

all over us already, man, having these guys on top of that might make things a little complicated. And you know they understand English.''

The UN security unit that had shown up overnight was an Irish infantry regiment.

''We'll just ignore them,'' Tolly said, ''and try to get this thing back on schedule. We lost most of the day yesterday, and I'd like to get back on track. With Wild Bill on the warpath, I don't want to piss him off any more than he already is. I can't get sent home, too.''

''I guess. But I sure don't like having those guys hanging around so close.''

''We can work around them,'' Tolly stated. ''But tell the others not to talk too much when they're around.''

''You want me to tell the women, too?''

''No,'' Tolly said abruptly. ''We're going to have to watch ourselves around them even more now.''

''I wish the hell you could get them sent home, too.''

''So do I,'' Tolly said, ''but we're stuck with them.''

''It's just that it's going to get tight on D Day, and I don't want to have to worry about keeping them out of the way while we get set up.''

''Don't worry,'' Tolly said. ''I can handle them.''

THE MORNING after the riot, Yakov Katzenelenbogen, Gary Manning and T. J. Hawkins met for breakfast in a small café well away from their respective hotels. Though they had no reason to think that they were being watched, taking extra security precautions now might pay off before the mission was over.

"I think we have ourselves the kind of problem my old granddaddy would have called a ball buster," Hawkins said as he sucked down his coffee. "The Israeli cops were going to be difficult enough, but now we have a bunch of Irish bastards to deal with as well."

Manning looked properly offended. "The Irish Rangers aren't all bastards," he said. "With them, that distinction's reserved exclusively for their regimental sergeant major and the quarter-master sergeant."

"They sure as hell aren't cupcakes, even if they're wearing the blue beret. Somebody's taking this thing seriously, and they don't even know why."

"Security is always taken real seriously in this town," Katz explained. "I don't know who suggested having the Irish back the locals, but you're right. Having them on board does make this even more difficult for us."

"Before the riot started," Manning said, "I got close enough to get a quick look at the mapping team's gear, and everything I saw was real portable. That means that they can hide it damned near anywhere they want. They aren't going to need a large cavern or something like that to set up their bomb. They'll be able to put it where they want it, clear out of town and detonate it."

"How did your attempt to get in touch with your old contacts go?" Hawkins asked Katz.

"The man I wanted to see," Katz reported, "is no longer available. He may even be dead for all I know, because I couldn't really ask around. I had planned on telling him exactly what was going on to try to get his feedback and ideas. But, obviously, that won't be possible now.''

"Is there anyone else you think you can bring in?" Manning asked.

Katz shook his head. "I'm not sure. You saw part of the reason why I'm stuck yesterday. Rioting over the most trivial things has gotten so out of hand that it's dominating city politics almost to the exclusion of anything else. Common sense has no place in it anymore, if it ever did.''

"I'm not sure I follow you," Hawkins said.

"Well," Katz said, "look at it this way. Anyone I talk to about this is going to automatically filter what I tell him through his own religious background before thinking rationally about it. Since this project was proposed by the Jews, the Christians and Muslims are automatically opposed to it. Any opposition coming from either of those two camps will, as you saw yesterday, be met with force. Then, with the UN sanction, the secular Israelis aren't going to see a problem no matter who brings it up.''

"So what in the hell are we going to do then?" Hawkins asked.

"I'll be damned if I know," he said. "I really don't. All we can do is keep real close tabs on that mapping team and try to find out when they plan to be done. D Day will follow very shortly after they leave the city.

They can't risk having their bomb found after they put it in place."

"Maybe we can pull a snatch on them so they can't leave." Hawkins suggested. "They're not likely to detonate the bomb while they're still here."

Katz smiled in spite of himself. "I wouldn't be too sure of that, T.J. You forget where you are. This city can make otherwise very rational people do some very irrational things. This is probably the only city in the world that has a psych ward in the city reserved exclusively for the religiously insane—most of the inmates are tourists. The locals call it the 'Jerusalem Disease' and every year dozens of otherwise sane people completely lose contact with reality and do something irrational enough to get arrested. The idea of a suicide bomb squad, even made up of American scientists, is so common here that it hardly bears mentioning."

He leaned across the table. "The real problem is that we don't have the slightest idea why this action is being taken. We jumped in so quickly to try to stop it, we didn't get much beyond learning that a madman was trying to destroy religious centers. We didn't spend too much time asking why he would want to do that or what he would gain from it. Kidnapping the team is a good idea, but if they're suicidal fanatics, it won't matter. They'll be willing to die with the rest of the city if it will further their cause."

"I guess that we'd better get learning everything we can about them."

"I already have Aaron working on that end of it, but

it's coming in slowly. So far, none of the team has much more on their records than a speeding ticket or two. Since religious affiliation isn't a matter of public record in the States, it's hard to look into that.''

"I saw a couple of women on the team," Hawkins said. "Maybe I can try to get close to one of them and do the old face-to-face and belly-to-belly."

"Not a chance, T.J.," Manning replied. "That's my job this time. I'm the engineering type around here, and I'm sure that I'll speak their language better than you."

Hawkins laughed out loud. "In your dreams."

CHAPTER TWENTY

Jerusalem

If Gary Manning was going to work his charm, he had to get as close as he could to the Geo-Tech work site, which meant dealing with not only the Israeli riot cops but with the Irish Rangers in the UN blue berets as well. Fortunately, he knew a lot about the famed rifle regiment and could thicken his accent enough to pass as a Canadian of Irish decent.

After strolling up, he edged closer and closer to the roped-off site trying to get a better look at Geo-Tech's gear until he almost ran into one of the Rangers.

"Top o' the morning, rifleman," Manning said in as thick of an accent as he could muster.

"So you're Irish are you now?" the rifleman replied.

"That's what me Da claims." Manning grinned. "But me Ma might argue with the old man. She always fancied a man in uniform, she did."

The Irishman cracked a small smile.

"Me Da was away with the Royal Engineers in Germany and she worked in the local NAAFI."

The rifleman's smile grew wider. That was the oldest story in the world, but it was a rare man indeed who would own up to being a bastard.

Manning peered past the soldier. "Is this that bunch of Yanks that's making a geological map of this old pile of stones?"

"That it is."

"How did you get the honor of guarding a bunch o' Yanks?"

"You'd have to ask the bloody RSM that one," the trooper said. "Me mates and meself, we was enjoying ourselves in Bosnia yesterday we were, when Staff yelled at us to grab our kits, and here we are."

The sergeant in charge of the security detail noticed that Manning was talking to one of his troopers and stormed over, the hobnails on the bottom of his combat boots clattering on the cobblestones.

"Murphy!" he snapped.

The Ranger snapped to attention. "Sergeant!"

"You!" The sergeant stuck his face an inch away from Manning's. "No talking to my men. They're on duty."

"And a very fine duty it is, Sergeant. We Irish love looking after the bloody Yanks, don't we now?"

"Look, Paddy," the sergeant growled, not into playing old home-sod games with anyone today. His orders were to secure the area against any and all, rioting or not, and his stripes were on the block if anything happened. "Piss off."

Manning looked insulted. "You sound more like an SAS man in Belfast than a Ranger, boyo."

The Ranger sergeant's eyes tightened, but he wasn't going to let himself get sucked in.

"Just go away, Paddy," he said, "before I have to call in the officer. He's a bloody Rupert and gets all out of sorts when I interrupt his tea, and he's always bloody drinking his bloody tea."

"Is there a problem, Captain?" one of the Americans asked, walking over.

"I'm no bloody officer," the sergeant snapped. "I'm a bloody sergeant, and this man doesn't want to move on."

"Dylan Fergeson," Manning said by way of introduction. "I'm a mining engineer from British Columbia, and I was just curious about your equipment. If I understand what was written in the paper about it, it's the sort of thing that might be real useful in my line of work."

"I'm sorry," the American replied, his face set. "But I'm under strict orders from the home office not to allow civilians in. Insurance problems, I'm sure you understand."

Manning did, and he also understood that he wasn't going to get a foot closer than he was now. More than that, he understood the two Israeli cops who were walking toward him with their riot batons in their hands.

"Well, good luck to all here," he said. "And you, too, Sergeant."

"Bugger off," the sergeant growled.

T. J. HAWKINS WAS SEATED in a sidewalk café across the street from the Geo-Tech site when Manning made his attempt to get in closer. As he expected, his teammate was turned back. It would be his turn to try something next, but he had no idea how in the hell he was going to work it. But that seemed to be the theme there so far.

The only thing he had done right in this town so far was his dinner date with Sarah Jenkins, the young woman he had rescued from the riot. It had been really low-key, but not for lack of trying on her part. He had played dumb, though, and had been able to keep her out of his bed without making her feel too rejected.

Instead, he had regaled her with tales of the archaeology of the city and of his interest in the team that was working to make the electronic map. He told her the legend of the Lost Ark of the Covenant and the belief, held by some, that it was hidden in a cavern under the Dome of the Rock. When she hadn't known the significance of that edifice, he had launched into the history of the Second Temple, its destruction by the Romans and the later Muslim Conquest when the site had been given over to Islam.

Like all too many American tourists, she wasn't really cognizant of the history of the city she was visiting and was completely entranced. When the evening was over, she had gone back to her room with her virtue intact, but with her interest in the man she knew as Bill Davis burning brightly. She had never met anyone quite like him and fully intended to make a point of seeing him again.

HAWKINS ORDERED his coffee of the hour to pay for sitting at his table when he heard a woman call out. "Bill, Bill Davis."

When he looked up, he saw a smiling Sarah Jenkins walking toward him. Under her arm was a copy of the archaeology guide book he had recommended.

"Hi, Sarah." He stood and pulled out a chair. "What are you doing here?"

"I'm so glad I ran into you," she said breathlessly. The fact that she had staked out the two Geo-Tech work sites since right after first light had a lot to do with it.

"God works in mysterious ways." Hawkins grinned. "Can I offer you something to drink, a coffee or an orange juice?"

"A juice please."

As Hawkins waved down the waiter, Jenkins got to the secondary reason she had tracked him down. "You won't believe it, Bill, but the women who work for that mapping team you were telling me about are staying in my hotel. I ran into two of them at breakfast, and we talked about their work."

The woman was right, he didn't believe it, but he also knew that she wasn't involved with Geo-Tech in any way. Unbelievable or not, though, this might be the opening that had eluded them so far.

"What did they have to say about their work?" he asked.

"Oh," she gushed, "you were right, it's the most interesting thing I've ever heard of. I didn't know that archaeology could be so exciting. I asked them about that chamber where the Lost Ark is supposed to be, but they didn't want to talk about it too much. They said that with all the controversy about their work, even if they found it, they wouldn't be able to do anything about it."

"That's a fact," he replied. "The riot you got caught up in yesterday is nothing compared to what would happen if they tried to do something like that. The Muslims claim that site all the way to the center of the earth."

She sighed. "You would think that in a city as blessed as this, people would get along better. I just don't understand it, I really don't."

Which put her in the distinct majority, Hawkins mused. No one understood.

"The best part," she said, is that they offered to let me visit them on the job this afternoon and see what they were doing. Isn't that exciting, I mean—"

"They did what?" Hawkins had a hard time keeping in character and not coming out of his chair.

"Today at three o'clock," she explained. "Susan said that I could come and look at what they're doing. I think it's going to be so exciting."

"Do you think she'd mind too much if I tagged along?" Hawkins leaned forward, smiled with the full force of his Southern charm and let his accent soften. He did everything but bat his eyes at her. "I mean, I won't get in the way or anything like that, but I'd just love to see what they're doing, too."

"Oh, I...I don't see why not." Sarah suddenly felt flushed.

"Great." He grinned. "And I know a great place where we can have a little lunch while we're waiting. I know you'll love it, it's so quiet and out of the way. It kind of reminds me of the little garden restaurants in Charleston."

"Oh...that sounds nice," she said.

"Great," he said as he pushed back his chair. "If you will excuse me for a moment, I need to go to the men's room and then we can walk to our restaurant. It's not far."

"KATZ," Hawkins radioed over the com link, "it's T.J. I need you to grab one of our Minicams and meet me at a restaurant in the Muslim Quarter called the Silver Garden."

"What's going down?" Katz asked.

"I just wrangled an invite to visit the Geo-Tech work site."

Katz shook his head. Manning's failure this morning had been expected, but disheartening anyway. Leave it to Hawkins to pull off something like this. "How the hell did you manage to do that?"

"It's complicated," he said, "so I'll explain it later. But, I need you at the restaurant within the hour so you can hand the camera off to me. Do you think you can get it there in time?"

"I should be able to."

"Look, I can't risk a cell phone or com link contact, so I'll keep an eye out for you and catch you when you go to the men's room, okay?"

"I'm leaving now."

THE SILVER GARDEN WAS everything Hawkins had said it was, but the decor was more ancient Egyptian than it was antebellum South. But since Sarah had never been to Charleston or anywhere even close to it, it could have been an exact copy of the Planter's Club for all she knew. The minute she walked into the atrium, she fell in love with the place. Her companion had a lot to do with that, though. Hawkins could have taken her to the city dump and she would have loved it.

Not only was the decor Arabic, so was the menu, and Hawkins helped her through it by ordering tea, salads and stuffed pita sandwiches for both of them.

"This is all so good," Jenkins said as she dived into her tomato, cucumber, onion and goat cheese salad. "My tour is one of those all-inclusive things, and the hotel always serves us American food."

Hawkins laughed. "Their version of stateside food you mean. Man, most of those guys do things to a poor old hamburger that would make Ronald McDonald want to cut his wrists. I mean, it's not necessary to leave the lettuce out in the sun for two days before putting in on top of the patty. And the mayo. I don't even want to think of where they get the mayo. Then there's the patty itself..."

She laughed happily. This was the best time she'd ever had in her entire life, and certainly the most fun she'd ever had in the company of a man. If she'd known that there were men like him in the world, she'd have come to Jerusalem years before.

KATZ ALMOST stopped short when he walked into the Silver Garden and saw Hawkins keeping a pretty young redhead enthralled with one of his tales. The woman was laughing, her eyes sparkling as she reached out to touch his arm. What in the hell was Hawkins thinking? The world was about to come to an end and he was trying to get laid?

He composed himself and walked past the table on the way to the washrooms in the back. He didn't have to wait very long before Hawkins joined him.

Hawkins correctly read the look on Katz's face and forestalled his biting comment. "Cool it, Katz," he said. "She's my ticket to visiting Geo-Tech at three."

"T.J., you're not James Bond here. We can't afford to have some woman—"

"Her name's Sarah," Hawkins said evenly, "and if you have a better way to get in close to Geo-Tech, how about sharing with me? From what I saw this morning when Gary tried, you don't get in there without an invite."

"Okay, okay. Look, I'm sorry, but you're endangering her."

"She's in Jerusalem, so she's endangered already," Hawkins pointed out. The only way to save her is to save everyone. Do you have the camera?"

"Here." Katz handed over what looked like a thick, fancy ballpoint pen.

Hawkins clipped it in his shirt pocket. "I'll be in touch."

HAND IN HAND, Hawkins and Sarah Jenkins strolled to the Geo-Tech work site on the boundary of the Jewish and Muslim quarters for their appointment with Susan Brown. When they met the first line of security, Jenkins told the Irish guard that they were expected and handed him Brown's business card. The soldier escorted them through the line and told the first American he saw that Dr. Brown had a visitor.

Doctor Susan Brown turned out to be an outdoors type in her late thirties, tall, rail thin, with the permanent dark tan and the squint lines around the eyes appropriate to a geological engineer. She raised an eyebrow when she saw Hawkins with Sarah, but didn't comment as he introduced himself.

"Bill is so interested in your work," Jenkins gushed. "He's the one who told me about the Ark and everything about the temple and all that."

"I really do appreciate this, ma'am." Hawkins grinned boyishly. "Or should I call you Doctor?"

What a charmer, Brown thought, no wonder Sarah was smitten with him. "Susan will do."

CHAPTER TWENTY-ONE

Jerusalem

When Dave Tolly saw Susan Brown walk up with two civilians in tow, he would have killed her on the spot if he'd had a gun. "Dr. Brown," he called out as they came closer, "May I speak to you for a moment?"

Brown had a smirk on her face when she walked up. "What is it, Dave?"

"What in the hell are those two civilians doing here?" he snapped. "I sure as hell didn't authorize any visitors. You know what the UN officer said about doing that. It's an open invitation to a bomb attack."

"The woman is staying in my hotel," she explained. "We got to talking over breakfast and since she was interested in our work, I invited her to see what we're doing. I think the guy's her summer lover. Anyway, he likes archaeology so I invited him, too."

"Goddammit, woman," Tolly almost growled, "what in hell is wrong with you? We have people trying to kill us here, and you invite strangers into our work site?"

Brown enjoyed tweaking this little bastard immensely, which was more than half of the reason why she had extended the invitation in the first place. She had known that he would go ballistic and foam at the mouth.

"The blue berets patted them down for anything more dangerous than a guidebook. I know that *A Christian's Guide to the City of the Lord* can be more than a little dull, but I don't think that anyone's been killed with it yet. The guards even thumbed through the pages to make sure a bomb wasn't hidden inside."

"Mr. Webster is going to hear about this," Tolly threatened.

Brown smiled broadly. "Why don't you call him right now, Dave? And, while you're at it, you can tell Wild Bill that he can kiss my bony ass if he doesn't like the work I'm doing. I knew him when he didn't have a pot to piss in or a window to throw it out of, and he still hasn't wised-up. He pulled out that simple bastard Bridger and replaced him with an even simpler one, but I don't think he can replace me that easily. There's not another neutrino scanner operator anywhere this side of the pond."

Tolly realized that Brown had just called him a simple bastard, but he also knew that the dyke bitch had him in a real jam. It would be impossible to replace her in time to complete the project.

"Have it your way," he warned. "But if your guests fuck this up, I'll see that you never work again."

"That's nice, Dave." She smiled widely. "And in

return, I promise to break your fucking face if you give me any more of your shit.''

Tolly stood there as she walked away, wishing even more than ever that he had a gun. But he would have the last word no matter what.

HAWKINS HAD FOLLOWED the conversation intently, trying to get as much of it as he could on tape. The pen hiding the Minicam was clipped into the binding of his guidebook and, with it under his arm, it was easy to aim and shoot. How much it could pick up that far away was another matter.

''Your boss didn't seem too happy about us being here,'' he offered when Brown joined them. ''Maybe we should leave and come back another time.''

''Dave?'' Brown inclined her head in the direction of the retreating Tolly. ''He's not really my boss, and you're my guests today so you get the full tour.''

''Sounds great.''

''You just let me know if I get too technical.''

''No problem.'' Hawkins sounded enthusiastic. ''I like it technical. The Discovery Channel is my favorite entertainment.''

Brown shuddered inwardly. At least it wasn't a televangelist, she thought.

AFTER DROPPING OFF the Minicam with Hawkins, Katz went to Manning's room where a minielectronic command post had been set up. The camera was transmitting to a remote receiver close to the site, which was retransmitting the images to the hotel.

"He's good with that thing," Manning noted as he watched Hawkins slowly pan his camera from left to right across each piece of equipment he was shown. He lingered on data plates, company logos and anything else that might ID the gear and its capabilities. If any of it could be used to set off a bomb, the farm should be able to identify it.

"I just hope that he ditches the girl," Katz muttered as he watched the black-and-white images. "We're too thin on the ground as it is to risk her learning anything."

"You're not saying that T.J. talks in his sleep are you?" Manning grinned.

"Dammit, Gary. You know what I mean."

Manning laughed. "The end of the world's coming, Katz. Maybe he's just feeling the tug of the old DNA. You know how that works."

"He can do it after we're done here."

"I think that's the problem. There may not be an after."

BY THE END OF HIS TOUR, Hawkins had seen every piece of equipment Geo-Tech had at this site and none of it had looked like it could be turned into a nuclear bomb. Not that he was an expert on nukes. Maybe Kurtzman and Kissinger could make something of it because he sure as hell couldn't.

"I can't tell you how much I have enjoyed this Su-

san.'' Hawkins extended his hand and Brown shook it.
''This was just fantastic. I'd really like to do something
for you in return, so I was wondering if you could join
Sarah and I at dinner tonight?''

Brown looked at Jenkins and saw the way she was
looking at her man. ''I don't know...''

''Oh please, Susan,'' Jenkins pleaded. Anything that
Hawkins wanted to do was more than all right with her.

''Sure,'' Brown said, more than willing to help one
of the sisterhood. ''That sounds like fun.''

''Great,'' Hawkins said. ''I'll tell you what, this is
buffet night at the King David, and you've never seen
a buffet until you see the spread they put together there.
Why don't I meet both of you in the lobby at, say,
eight? It's not formal, but if you ladies will get dressed
up, so will I. And, after that, I know a great nightclub
where they play almost-quiet music. It's a great place
for conversation.''

''I'll be there,'' Brown promised. After all it would
be good to have an excuse to put on a dress and be
noticed as a woman for a change, instead of an engineer. In a place like that, maybe she could even get
lucky. She was a little overdue.

''YOUR'E GOING to love her, Gary,'' Hawkins said as
he got ready for his date. ''She's an outdoors type,
damned near as tall as you are and looks like she can
hold her own in a Ranger snake pit.''

''Just what I need, a female Ranger.'' Manning

shook his head, wondering why he'd allowed himself to get sucked into this.

"But you two have so much in common," Hawkins said. "Like you said this morning, you'll speak the same language."

After explaining his spur-of-the-moment plan to Katz, he had talked Manning into going along with it and the pair of them had made a recon of the King David. If this worked, they might have their in.

THE WAITER HAD just brought the two women their predinner drinks when T.J. Hawkins looked over at the bar and spotted Gary Manning sitting in a well-lighted spot.

"I'll be damned," Hawkins said. "That's my old buddy Roger Railing over at the bar. I'd recognize his ugly puss anywhere. I wonder what he's doing here?"

Susan followed Hawkins's gaze and saw a rugged-looking man sitting by himself. He was well-dressed, but had that look of someone who was used to working outdoors. "Where do you know him from, Bill?"

"He's a mining engineer, and we used to work together in Canada."

"I didn't know that you'd worked in Canada," Jenkins said.

"I've been around. I wonder what Roger's doing here."

"Why don't you invite him over?" Brown suggested. "He looks like he could use some dinner." Having a dinner companion would also keep her from being a third wheel.

"You wouldn't mind?" Hawkins asked.

"Not at all."

"I think you'll find that he's a real nice guy."

"Roger, old Buddy," Hawkins said as he walked up to the bar. "What in hell are you doing here?"

Manning looked surprised and grinned as he shook Hawkins's hand. "Bill, I could ask you the same. As they say, it's a small world."

"Look—" Hawkins gestured over to the table where the women sat watching "—if you're by yourself, come on over and have dinner with us."

"I don't want to impose."

"Not at all." Hawkins took his arm. "We need a fourth."

MANNING TURNED OUT to be a great dinner companion and kept everyone enthralled with tales of engineering derring-do in the frozen north. That, combined with excellent food, made it a nice evening.

After desert, Hawkins suggested that Manning and Brown join them on a moonlit walk around the city walls before they stopped by the night spot he had mentioned.

"No, you two go ahead. I have to get up early." Brown begged off. "And don't worry, I can find my own way back to the hotel."

"If you'd like," Manning offered, "I can drive you home or I can get you a cab."

"Let me buy you a drink," she suggested, nodding toward the bar, "and we'll talk about it."

"That's fair." He grinned.

THEY WERE into their second drink when Katz walked up to the bar. "Roger," he said. "How nice to run into you."

Manning turned to his date and said. "Susan, I'd like you to meet an old friend of mine, Ari Landau. Ari, this is Dr. Susan Brown from Geo-Tech."

"Oh, yes," Katz said as he seated himself beside the woman. "The company that is doing the archeology mapping job. I know about you."

"It seems that everyone in this town does," she said. "But not everyone likes us."

"That's because of the nuclear material Geo-Tech imported. There are those who fear it."

"But that's not realistic." This was an old story to Brown, the locals going freaky every time someone mentioned anything atomic. "If there was anything wrong with the nuclear source material, I'd know about it. I'm the neutrino specialist on the team."

"Did you inventory all of the nuclear material when it arrived here?" Katz asked.

"No," she said. "I didn't arrive with the rest of the team. I was delayed wrapping up my last job. By the time I got here, everything was set up and I just got to work."

"Do you know where the source material is stored?"

She hesitated. "Yes, but I don't have access to it."

"Why is that?" Katz asked.

"Well," she said, "Dave Tolly, he's the guy in charge of the team now, said that he has to be person-ally responsible for it. Something about Israeli govern-ment regulations."

"Dr. Brown," Katz said, "can I be candid?"

"Of course."

"An irregularity regarding Geo-Tech has come to my attention. I'm trying to track down its validity, and you can help us a great deal with our investigations."

That official phrasing struck the woman as being a bit odd. In fact, this whole day, starting with her meeting Sarah Jenkins and the invitation to dinner, was starting to look just a little too convenient. It was right out of a cold war spy novel. She was beginning to think that she had been set up, but for what she had no idea.

"May I see some identification?" she asked Katz.

Katz dug out his Mossad photo ID card and handed it over. "I don't know if you read Hebrew, but it says that I work for Shin Bet, the Israeli secret service."

The photo matched, but that was all she could read. Handing it back, she looked at Manning, "Where's yours?"

He produced an ID saying that he was a Justice Department special agent named Roger Railing.

"Am I in some kind of trouble?"

"No, you're not," Manning said quickly.

"But I don't understand. You're saying that Geo-Tech is involved in some kind of wrongdoing?"

"That's what we don't know yet," he said. "All we know is that they imported a large amount of nuclear material to be used on this project, and we're concerned about it."

"Why doesn't someone take a look at it, then? That sounds simple enough to me."

"Normally, that would take care of it, yes," Katz

said. "But this is an unusual situation here. We have reason to believe that this material might be intended for another use entirely."

"Such as?" she asked. Then she remembered what they were talking about and that Mossad was one of the world's premier counterterrorist organizations. If that material got into the wrong hands, and in the Middle East that usually meant Arab hands, it might be dangerous.

"That's what we don't know yet," Katz said. "And that's why we went through this elaborate subterfuge to get a chance to talk to you alone."

She looked Manning up and down, "Well, at least you're not a cheapskate. I did get dinner and a couple of drinks out of it. But I guess it all goes on the old government expense report, doesn't it?"

"Susan..."

"How about Dr. Brown until you tell me what in the hell is really going on here?"

"Dr. Brown," Katz said, "believe me, we are no danger to you in any way. The company you are working for, though, may be. As I am sure you are aware, your nuclear source material can be manipulated in such a way that it will generate a sustained burst of hard radiation, right?"

"Yes." She frowned. "But the source material is matrixed, and there are safety locks. Everyone who uses neutrino generators knows how to keep that from happening."

Manning locked eyes with her. "What if they don't want it not to happen?"

Brown suddenly felt very small. If someone purposefully did override the safety locks, there was a chance that the generator could heat up enough to go into a small, subcritical-mass fusion reaction very similar to a nuclear power plant core meltdown. And, instead of releasing harmless neutrinos, it would send hard radiation into the very earth, killing everything in sight for hundreds of yards.

"Chernobyl," she stated quietly.

"That's what we're afraid of," Katz replied.

"But you must warn the people," she said.

"That's where this gets real troublesome," Manning said.

"But, I don't understand."

Brown realized that she had said that several times in the past few minutes, but it was true. If this was a real threat, why were two men talking to her about it in a bar? Why wasn't it headline news?

Katz and Manning exchanged glances. "If you would like, Doctor," Katz said, "I have a satcom link in my hotel room that will let you talk to a high-ranking American official in Washington. I think he can convince you that we aren't madmen and that we need your help. In fact, everyone in the city needs your help."

Something about the man calmed her. "That won't be necessary," she said. "What can I do?"

CHAPTER TWENTY-TWO

Vatican City

The stone walls around Vatican City dated back to 852 A.D., and they hadn't been built for show. A few years before their construction, a raiding army of Saracens had taken Rome and sacked it. The walls had been constructed shortly thereafter to insure that the Vatican would be safe from the next invading army that stormed through town. Rome itself had fallen on such hard times that it was completely indefensible, but the papal see was small enough that it could be defended.

Today, as then, the walls served as the first line of defense for the papal guardsmen because they limited visitors to the three entrances where they could be more easily controlled. That was, of course, most critical after dark. The night guard shift wasn't as big on the flashy Renaissance uniforms as were the day-shift troops. Once the tourists had gone back to their hotels, except for the guards at the main posts by St. Peter's, the Swiss Guard got into more modern gear. Their standard night kit included firearms instead of halberds, two-way radios and flashlights.

Since modern roads followed the outline of the fortress, the walls were brightly lit by both streetlights and spotlights. In the States, that might have been a problem for Able Team, but not in Rome. In Rome, it was expected that streetlights were subject to power outages and burnouts. No one would even notice if a section of the wall suddenly went dark.

To make sure, though, Carl Lyons and Gadgets Schwarz sabotaged the lights along a hundred-yard section of the northwest wall and the Viale Vaticano right before dusk fell. While they worked at their sabotage, Rosario Blancanales, wearing his priest's garb, strolled around the area as if he were out to take the evening air. If anyone noticed the two workmen messing with the power poles, having the priest around made it okay. No one would dare do anything bad in front of a priest.

After cutting the power, the trio disappeared to wait out the night.

THE WEATHER and the cycle of the moon were both cooperating when Able Team returned to the section of darkened wall later that night. As Schwarz moved into position for his climb, Lyons donned night-vision goggles and scoped out the wall and the rooftops that overlooked his planned route.

"I don't see anyone with low-vision gear or sniper rifles on the rooftops," he informed Schwarz over the team com link.

"Roger, I'm going for it now."

For the incursion, Schwarz wasn't wearing his usual night combat clothes and face paint. Even unarmed as he was, being caught in that gear would get him questioned as a terrorist for sure. Instead, he was in the typical European burglar's costume of sneakers, dark pants, black pullover and black wool cap. It was also a common enough clothing for laborers and seamen, so he could try to pass himself off as a drunken late-night tourist. Trying to explain away some of the things in his bag might be a little more difficult, but if he got spotted, he'd ditch the bag and pretend the com link was a CD player headset.

For this climb, he had brought nothing more high tech than a padded grappling hook and a rope. To scale a medieval wall, nothing worked as well as medieval equipment. Once the hook was set on the top of the wall, Schwarz went up the sloping face hand over hand. Slipping between the battlements, he crouched in the dark to survey his surroundings through his NVGs.

The top of the wall was wide enough to march men five abreast, but it was empty. The rope and grapple wouldn't be needed for a descent down the inside face of the wall. Untold centuries earlier, someone had conveniently built stone steps that led into the gardens below. Almost half the compound inside the walls were the papal gardens and a man could hide very well in them.

"I'm on top," Schwarz radioed to Lyons, "and I can't see any sensors, so I'm going in now."

"Roger," Lyons replied.

Taking one last look at the ground between him and the library building, Schwarz took off his night-vision goggles and clipped them to the rope. Being caught with them was a big no-no. Keeping to the shadows of the battlements, he made his way to the stairs and down to the ground.

It was a short distance to the western entrance of the building, but he didn't have to get close to see that it was guarded. That didn't come as a big surprise, with centuries' worth of secrets hidden in that library, he had expected guards. Even so, he worked his way around to the east entrance to check it as well.

"Both entrances are posted with stationary guards," he reported to Lyons. "I'm going to have to go directly to the underground route."

Before the first Christian churches were built on this site, the Vatican had been a cemetery for the noble families of old Rome. By the time the Christians came, most of the massive tombs had fallen into disrepair, and the new rulers had felt no compunction about finishing their destruction. To lessen the work that this entailed, the tombs had their roofs torn down and the rubble was used to fill in the walls. In fact, the basilica of St. Peter had been built right on top of the largest of those old tombs.

Under this landfill, though, remained the durable paved roads the ancient Roman engineers had laid down between the tombs. Since it would be well over a thousand years before Christians would learn to build such roads again, they soon found a use for those they had once buried. As more buildings went up on Vatican hill, many of these ancient underground roads were uncovered. Walls were built along their traces and then roofed over to create instant tunnels from one building to the next. In some cases the old tombs were turned into dungeons and storage areas. This work continued until modern times when a network of tunnels connected all of the buildings within the 108-acre enclosure and with many outside the walls.

During the build-up to Y2K, an attempt to infiltrate the Vatican via the tunnel network had been foiled at the last moment. To prevent future attempts, the Vatican had ordered that all of the tunnels leading into its territory be blocked by steel-reinforced concrete barriers. While reducing the threat from outside, the barriers also blocked escape from the Vatican compound.

Most of these underground passageways were poorly lit and a map was vital if a newcomer wasn't to get lost. Schwarz had studied the map before setting out and had made a sketch of where he wanted to go. That and a small compass on his watchband should be enough for him to navigate by.

The spot he had picked to attempt his descent into the bowels of the Vatican had been spotted during Lyons and Schwarz's recon in the south end of the Belvedre Courtyard. He was making his way there when a small clink of metal on metal sounded clearly behind him. He froze in the shadows against the wall.

The guardsman seemed to be more intent on the act

of making his rounds than he was on the art of doing a good job of it. He didn't turn his head at all to check the shadows as he passed. He marched a straight line at a measured pace as if he were on parade. Even so, the modern-age uniform for the Swiss warriors apparently also included rubber-soled boots. Schwarz would remember that.

As soon as the guard cleared the courtyard, Schwarz hurried to the light-well grating he planned to use as his personal elevator to the lower levels. As Lyons had reported, the grating on the light-well cover was made of marble, not cast iron, and it slid aside noiselessly. He lowered himself into the hole, and, holding on with one arm, felt around until he found the iron rungs of a ladder sunk in the stone wall of the shaft. Shifting his hold, he dragged the marble cover back in place.

The rungs of the ladder stopped abruptly eight feet above the tunnel floor below him, but he hung by his hand and dropped the last few inches without a sound. The guards weren't the only ones with rubber-soled boots.

The tunnel was dimly lit from an overhead light twenty yards away, but it was enough for him to see that he was alone. Taking an electronic tag from his bag, he tore the cover off the adhesive and placed it out of sight on the shaft of the light well. Now he could find his way to this spot in a hurry.

Taking out his sketch map, he located where he was and clicked on his com link. "I'm in the tunnel," he said softly.

"I've got you," Blancanales reported. Schwarz's bag had been tagged with a locator bug, so they could keep track of him.

Heading north, Schwarz made only one wrong turn in the dark before he found the archives lab Blancanales had visited earlier, but it was occupied. Apparently, the archives team was working twenty-four-hour shifts. On top of the night-shift lab techs, a uniformed, armed guardsman complete with radio was on hand to keep a close eye on the treasures that were going into the decon chamber.

Keeping to the shadows, Schwarz inched as close as he could get while still keeping out of the light. Now that he was seeing the lab without the distortions of the Minicam Blancanales had used for his recon, he realized just how big that chemical reactor was. When that thing got cooking, it would be able to produce a huge amount of gas in a very short time. From the air currents he felt, the interlinking tunnel system would distribute it to the other buildings very quickly.

His video camera was small, but it was better than the microcam Blancanales had used. He decided to redo the video recon so they could study it in detail later.

Backing out into the corridor, he clicked on his com link. "I'm at the lab," he whispered, "but they're working tonight. I'm going to go ahead, though, and start taping. Tell me if the pictures are coming through."

"Roger," Blancanales sent. "Watch your ass."

Back in position, he started taping every foot of the lab he could see.

"I've got good copy," Blancanales told him. "Keep it coming."

After taping everything he could see from his side of the door, he backed into the shadows and carefully crossed to the other side of the opening to get a clear look at the other side of the room. Through an open doorway, he could see that a second room beyond the main lab had also been painted white. He also saw that the stainless-steel piping ran from the decon chamber back into this annex. His bet was that was where the chemical tanks were being stored. He taped what he could get, but there was no way that he was going to get through the lab to take a closer look at the back room.

Backing from the doorway again, he went down the dimly lit tunnel, looking for another way into that back room he had spotted. He had covered thirty yards with no result when he heard noises in the tunnel behind him.

He glanced at his watch and saw that it was coming up on midnight, which was probably time for the changing of the guard. A traditional guard change overlapped the shift going on with the shift coming off and meant that there would be twice as many troops in the area until the swap was complete. That meant twice as many eyes looking for anything out of place in their very ordered miniuniverse. So it was time for him to be gone.

Instead of going back the way he had come, Schwarz continued north in the tunnel. According to his map, there was a branch not too far down that led to the museum picture gallery where a light-well at the end of that building would put him close to the darkened section of the wall.

BACK IN THEIR hotel room, the Able Team trio went over the new images Schwarz had taped.

"The real problem," Blancanales pointed out, "isn't the chemical reactor itself. We can make a commando raid and destroy the damned thing easily enough. Considering how easy it was to get in there, we could probably even get away clean. But that would last only until another one could be brought in and placed under armed guard."

Lyons nodded. That was true enough, and that was what had bothered him about this gig from the very first. How were they going to shut that damned thing down for all time? For them to do that, they had to somehow convince the Swiss Guard that there was a UN-sponsored nerve gas factory hiding in their basement.

But, of course, it wasn't really hiding. Everyone knew where it was, but no one knew *what* it was. Maybe that was the way to deal with it, to expose it for what it was. But that just brought them back to square one again. This was starting to make his head hurt because as long as the UN was involved, there was no way he could see to win.

CHAPTER TWENTY-THREE

Los Angeles, California

Mack Bolan knew better than to fight on his opponent's home turf, but this time it couldn't be helped. The Rainbow Dawners were holed up in their building and, if he wanted them, he was going to have to go in there to get them. That didn't mean, however, that he would have to go in on their terms, nor without making preparations.

Attacking a prepared position, which in modern urban combat terms was what a building was, always favored the defense. Every first year military cadet knew that. But while a position like the Dawners' building with its limited entrances kept attackers at bay, it also trapped the defenders inside. Once he was in, it would be like a fox in the henhouse when the door was locked. The only trick would be getting himself inside without being spotted.

According to the blueprints and his personal recon, there was no way he was going to force his way in through the main entrance. The same went for the parking structure entrance or the rear fire door. That left only the roof or the basement. The roof was his preference, starting at the top and working his way down; clearing the building as he went would be the best tactic. But because he was working solo, that was the least likely option because he would have to involve an outsider to get him there.

That left him the basement option, and he decided to head down there to try to make a recon of the surrounding buildings to see which one would best serve for what he had in mind.

Los Angeles, California

MELLANIE MITCHELL stormed into Roy Givens's office. One of Miller's storm troopers had tried to announce her, but she had brushed him aside with an elbow to the gut and slammed open the door.

Miller was halfway out of his chair with his side arm in his hand before he saw who it was.

"Go back to playing with yourself," she snapped at him as she passed. "It's just me."

Givens was on his feet as well, his guru smile plastered on his face. "Mellanie! How nice to see—"

"Cut the shit," she snapped at him. "I want to know how much longer I'm going to have to put up with those fucking Nazis you sent to the studio."

"Those men," Miller cut in, "work for me, not Givens."

"Then I guess I have to talk to the hired help then,

don't I?'' She half smiled as she let her eyes run up and down him dismissively.

"Miss Mitchell—" he started to say.

"Why don't you just call me 'big-titted bitch' like all the rest of your black-shirts do."

"Miss Mitchell," Miller started again, "if any of my people have been insulting to you, I assure you, I'll take care of it personally."

"Will you take care of it by getting them the hell out of my studio?"

"I'm afraid that's not possible," Miller replied. "For the interim, your security is of utmost importance."

"Is it more important than my continuing the show?"

She turned to Givens. "I'm about ready to tell you to kiss my ass and take my act somewhere else."

"I'm afraid that's not an option," Miller said.

She spun on him. "What did you say to me?"

He smiled before answering. "I said that you will not be allowed to discontinue the show."

"Just a minute, Miller," Givens cut in. "You can't—"

Miller turned to him. "Shut the fuck up and sit down while you still can. This is none of your business."

Mitchell shook her head. "I don't know who's blowing who around here," she told Miller, "and frankly, boys, I really don't care. But my contract's with Roy, not you. So butt out of this."

Miller's eyes grew hard. "I don't think you heard me, you big-titted bitch."

When Mellanie automatically swung at him, Miller took the punch without flinching. But the blow he delivered to her belly in return doubled her over at the waist.

Reaching out, Miller grabbed the sides of her face in one hand and pulled her erect. "I won't mark your face," he said, smiling as he held her jaws as if they were in a vise, "but if I hear one more smart-mouthed crack out of you, I'm going to beat you to within an inch of your life. Got that?"

For the first time in many years, Mellanie Mitchell was afraid of a man, truly afraid. Looking into Miller's eyes was like looking into the face of a mad dog. There was nothing in there she could possibly reach.

"I asked you a question." His voice rose slightly.

"I understand," she said, gasping for breath.

"Good." He released her and pulled back. "Now maybe we can get back to the topic at hand."

"Sit," he pointed at the couch.

She hesitated, but when he started to move toward her, she sat down.

"Now, here's how it's going to be. You and Roy are going to keep your mouths shut until I ask you a question. And, you—" his eyes glittered when he turned on Mellanie "—you are going to do what you are told as well as keeping your mouth shut. And don't even try to think of the alternative. I can assure you that you won't like it if you do."

Satisfied that he had his audience's complete attention, Miller went on. "Things don't have to be any different than they have ever been around this fruit farm, but security will be maintained. I can't afford to have any more slipups, so if everyone just does their job, everything will be fine. Roy can inspire the sweet young things with the wisdom of the ages in his one-on-one sessions. And you, Miss Mellanie, can continue to share your bountiful charms and insightful visions with your national audience.

"It's all very simple. And my job is to keep it that way."

Mitchell realized that when Miller smiled it was all with his mouth and it never reached his eyes.

"Now," he said, "if the two of you will excuse me, I have a job to do."

Mitchell and Givens watched him leave the room, then sat for several minutes without saying a word.

"Good God," she whispered, breaking the silence first. "What junkyard did you find him in?"

"Don't say that," Givens hissed as his gaze darted around to the corners of the room.

"Are we being taped?"

When Givens laid a finger against his lips, she understood. "Well," she said, keeping her voice light, "this has certainly been enlightening. I'd really like to stay and chat, Roy, but I need to get back to the studio and work on the next show. You know how it is. The work never ends."

She got to her feet and headed for the door. "I'll catch you later."

She halfway expected to find one of Miller's Nazis

waiting outside the door for her, but the corridor was empty all the way to the elevator. If she could get out of this place, she might get a chance to run.

ON THE ELEVATOR ride to the first floor, she glanced up at the roof of the car and saw the video camera for the first time. When the door opened on the first floor, she also saw the camera covering the bank of elevators. For a place of restful contemplation, Big Brother was watching.

When she entered the lobby, she saw that two of Miller's dogs in civilian clothes had spotted her. She knew that she couldn't outrun them, but she walked faster, hoping to cross the lobby and get outside before they could catch up with her. Her hopes were dashed when a uniformed guard at the door moved over to block it, speaking into his lapel mike.

"Okay, boys." She spun to face the two plainclothes men. "What's the deal?"

"We're your new personal security team, Miss Mitchell," one of the men said. "I'm Troy and my partner's Rick."

"I don't need personal security."

"Miller says that you do," Troy said firmly.

This was neither the time nor the place to get into this, so she smiled and said, "Okay, boys, looks like we're stuck with each other. Let's go."

When she headed for her car in the staff parking lot, Troy took her arm. "We're using a company car this time."

"What about my car?"

"One of us will drive it over to your house later this evening."

"But there's some stuff in it I need to use this afternoon."

"I'll have it delivered to the studio then."

Seeing that this was getting her nowhere fast, she capitulated yet again. "Whatever you say, boys."

BOLAN WAS WATCHING the front of the Rainbow Dawn building when he saw the blond woman walk out with a goon on each side. He didn't have a directional mike handy to pick up the conversation, but he didn't need one. It was obvious by the woman's body language that she wasn't happy about her escorts.

It suddenly hit him where he had seen the woman before. Before Able Team had moved on to Rome, Gadgets Schwarz had watched a program called *The New Frontier* every chance he had. And, unless he was mistaken, this woman was Mellanie Mitchell, the star of the show. When he saw that she was being secured in the back of a waiting sedan, he decided to follow and see where they were taking her.

Starting his BMW, he gave the sedan half a block before pulling out into traffic behind it.

RICK DROVE the Buick four-door while Troy sat in back with Mellanie. Rather than pull away from him, she carefully inched closer until their thighs were almost touching. Her movement had hiked her already-short skirt almost up to her crotch, and she slumped in the seat to increase her exposure. It wouldn't be too much longer before he noticed. In fact, it would be impossible for him not to notice. Pheromones would see to that.

There were those times when a woman had to use what she had to get what she wanted. And right now, all she wanted was to get the hell out of that car and hopefully get a half-block head start on these goons.

It was a desperate move, but she was desperate. She didn't know what kind of hold Miller had over Givens, but it was more than apparent that good old Brother Roy was no longer the master of his own destiny. And, if that was the case, neither was she. For far too much of her life, someone else had controlled her. It had taken guts, hard work and luck for her to become her own person. She wasn't about to go back to the old days if there was anything she could do about it.

She didn't have to be a mind reader to know what Miller had in store for her, and she'd kill herself before she became a sex toy again.

BOLAN HAD STARTED to think that he had read that scene in front of the Dawners' building wrong when he saw the woman inch closer to the guard in the back of the sedan. But he still followed because he rarely read someone that wrong. Whatever she was doing, it wasn't what it looked like.

Traffic had gotten thicker and he was only two cars behind the sedan when the woman made her move. Just as the driver was breaking for a light, he saw the woman turn to the man and say something. When Bolan saw him look down, he knew what she was doing. It was the old exposed-crotch trick, and it worked every time.

The man's eyes were fixed when the woman slammed her elbow into the side of his head, bouncing it off the side window. Though the car was still moving, the rear door on her side flew open and she jumped out and rolled on the pavement. The car behind her stood on its brakes and missed her as she got to her feet and started to run in Bolan's direction.

Bolan slid his BMW as close to the curb as he could get and hit the emergency flashers. The driver behind him hit his horn and swerved to miss him as the Executioner stepped out, his sport coat unbuttoned. Ahead of him, the driver of the woman's car opened his door.

The pedestrian traffic on the sidewalk was only moderate, but the woman crashed headlong into a lamppost when she turned to look back over her shoulder.

Seeing the woman go down, the driver of the sedan paused to reach behind his belt when he stepped from the car. Bolan didn't have the sound suppressor fixed to his Beretta, but he didn't hesitate. He drew the weapon and had a clear sight by the time the gunman's piece was leveled.

The Executioner's single shot took the gunman high between the eyes. His head snapped back with the impact of the 9 mm slug, and he collapsed to the ground.

The sound of the shot echoed between the buildings, but few people even bothered to look around for the source. It was only one shot, and in L.A. it took a burst of automatic fire to get anyone's attention.

Bolan holstered his piece, cleared the few steps to the woman, took her arm and pulled her up to her feet. "Come on!" he commanded. "I have a car."

The woman glanced back at the body bleeding into the gutter and shuddered.

"I'll get you out of here."

Bolan shoved her in the driver's-side door and said, "Stay down until we get clear."

Powering away from the curb, Bolan took the first right and kept going for two blocks before taking another right.

"You can sit up now, Miss Mitchell," he said.

The woman pulled herself up and took a good look at her rescuer. "Who are you?"

"I've never met you, but I'm a friend."

"You shot Rick to keep him from shooting me."

"Like I said—" he kept his voice warm "—I'm a friend."

"Okay, friend, can you take me someplace where I can get a drink?" she asked, her voice breaking.

"No problem."

MILLER DIDN'T HAVE Roy Givens to blame this one on, but that didn't mean that he was off the hook, either. The bastard should have warned him that the damned woman would try something like that. Troy had a concussion, Rick was dead from a single shot to the head and Mellanie was in the wind. The Phoenix office was going to have his ass on a plate if he didn't get her back.

At least though, he had lucked out regarding the cops. Rick had been carrying his Security Plus ID when he went down, but Troy had been able to drive the car away before the cops showed up. Standard operating procedure on a Class Zulu situation like that was to clear the area even if it meant leaving the dead behind.

Miller had been able to convince the LAPD that Rick's death and the missing car was the result of a carjacking. Since the car had been a new Buick, the story was believed. Now all he had to do was concoct some kind of story about Mellanie and set up a network to find her. At least it wouldn't be easy for her to hide. She was so well-known that anywhere she showed her face, she'd be recognized, no matter how she tried to disguise herself.

Miller had been on a number of challenging assignments for Security Plus, but he had never seen anything like this in his life. Breaking into top-secret labs in foreign countries and stealing entire experiments was nothing compared to this. Maybe if he knew why he had been called in on this, he would understand what was at stake. Sometimes, the overly tight security at Security Plus wasn't a good thing.

CHAPTER TWENTY-FOUR

Los Angeles, California

Bolan wasn't going to take the woman to his motel until he had a better understanding of her situation with the Dawners. He had saved her life, but that didn't automatically make her one of the good guys. He could, however, put a couple of drinks into her and see if that paid off. He pulled into a cocktail lounge displaying a neon Come On In sign and found the traditional dimly lit table in the back.

Mellanie Mitchell was so shook up that little was said while she slugged down her first bourbon and Bolan signaled for a refill. Halfway through the second, she started to talk.

"Roy's always been a little crazy," she said, "but until all this started about that girl, he's been rationally crazy, if you know what I mean?"

Bolan nodded his understanding to keep her talking.

"I mean, he was able to get his Rainbow Dawn scam going well enough to make a ton of money. So, when he gets hold of me and offers me my own TV show, what am I going to tell him? I'd have been crazy not to have at least given it a try. Dancing for a living gets a little old after a while, and I was starting to hit the wall. I'm not nineteen anymore.''

She smiled, mostly to herself. "Hell, it's been awhile since I was thirty-nine.''

Bolan gave the correct reply. "It happens to all of us.''

"Everything's been going so good," she continued. "I mean, I never thought that the show would do as well as it has. But I've been number one for that time slot in a couple of real important markets for some time now.''

She took another sip. "Then one of the guys working for him brought that poor girl into the inner circle and everything went to hell when she died.''

This was Bolan's cue to get into the conversation. "She didn't just die," he said. "She was killed.''

Mitchell's eyes went wide. "You're kidding!''

"I don't kid about things like that.''

"Oh, no.'' She looked down. "Are you sure?''

"She was murdered by a purposeful overdose of heroin.''

"Oh, Jesus," she said softly. "Poor kid.''

"Did you ever meet her?'' he asked.

"No. I only heard about her after she was dead. I don't spend too much time over at the funny farm. I mean, I get along with most of those people well enough. I have to in order to do my show. But, when I'm around too much peace, love and naiveté it makes me want to act out, you know? Just to see the expressions on their faces."

Bolan grinned. "I understand that. But what happened around there after she died?"

"Well, nothing much happened at first. Then, it was all over the news that she'd been found, and then her father was killed a couple days later. That's when it really started getting weird."

"What do you mean?"

"Roy was running around in a state of panic. There were a lot of meetings that I wasn't in on and then, of course, he called in those security Nazis."

"The guys you were running away from?"

She shuddered. "Yes."

"Do you know where they came from?"

"They call themselves Security Plus, but their leader, who goes by Miller, is straight out of some old World War II Nazi movie."

She closed her eyes briefly. "And his men aren't a hell of a lot better. They took over Rainbow Dawn completely and even Roy is cowed by them, particularly by Miller. It's almost like they're in charge now, not him. Anyway, I went over there today to see if I could get the guards out of my studio, and Miller and I really got into it. I threatened to bail out on the show, and he wasn't going to let me."

She took another sip of her drink. "I don't know what would have happened, mister, if I hadn't gotten out of the car. I don't even know where they were taking me."

Now that Mitchell was on her third drink, her adrenaline level was back down and she was thinking a little more clearly. Setting down her glass, she looked at Bolan. "But enough about me, who the hell are you, a cop?"

Bolan shook his head. "Nope, I'm not a cop. My name's Jim Barnes, and you can say that I'm a friend of Jennifer Wayne's family."

Mitchell knew more about cops than the average citizen, and she also knew a lot about the underworld. If her rescuer wasn't a cop, he was connected. He had that particular look that couldn't be faked. You either had earned it or you didn't have it. And she just remembered that he had shot Rick.

"If you're not a cop, who are you connected with?"

"No one," Bolan replied. "I work for myself."

"For money?" Mitchell understood mercenaries. Women had invented the profession of doing it for money.

"No," he replied, holding her eyes with his. "I do what I do because someone has to do it."

Oh, Jesus, she thought, a true believer. That could be good or it could be bad.

She studied him for a moment. "Why did you rescue me back there?"

"Actually, I was keeping an eye on the Dawners' building when I saw you being taken out. It looked to me like you were under duress so I followed you. When you bailed out of the car, I thought I'd try to help."

"Did you kill Rick, that guy you shot?"

"He was drawing down on you," Bolan said simply.

"And you just drove away."

"Why would I have stayed?"

Mitchell laughed. "I don't know who you are, mister, but you've got balls. And I don't care what you say, you've got to be connected pretty heavily. Even in L.A., it's not every day that you can just step out of a car, shoot someone, and then drive away."

Bolan grinned. "Here you usually shoot as you're driving by without getting out of the car, right?"

She studied him for a long moment. "Look, I know that I probably owe you my life, and I'll pay you in any way I can. But I don't know what to think of you. I'm not Lois Lane, and this isn't a comic book. A bad movie maybe, and I think I need to disappear from here before I find myself in deeper than I already am.

"So, tell me what I owe you. I'll take care of it and be on my way."

Bolan understood her completely and, in her place, he'd be thinking of doing the same thing. "I'm not sure it'll be that easy for you to disappear," he said. "As long as Givens is doing whatever he's doing, I don't think he's going to be happy about having you running loose."

"It's not him I'm worried about," she said. "It's that bastard Miller."

"As far as what you owe me," Bolan said, "I'll settle for a couple hours of your telling me everything you know about Givens, his organization, your TV show and the security force in that building."

She laughed. "I haven't heard that one in a long time, the old 'come up to my room and we'll just talk' routine. Okay, whatever."

"I'd rather do it somewhere out of sight. But, if you want, we can talk in public. It just has to be someplace where we can't be overheard."

"You're serious, aren't you?" she said. "You just want to talk?"

"I'm as serious as death," he answered.

"Okay," she said, making up her mind. "Let's go to your room."

Bolan placed a twenty on the table and escorted her out into the daylight.

MITCHELL HAD NEVER BEEN to this particular motel, but she recognized the room well enough. If she had misjudged this big guy, this might be the last motel room she ever visited. He wasn't a man she'd like to have angry with her, but if he was on the level, he might be her salvation. Even though he looked like he had seen one too many bad roads, there was something in his eyes that was appealing nonetheless.

She had cast her dice and would watch them roll until they hit the side rail.

"Okay," she said, taking a deep breath, "what do you need to know?"

"Basically everything you can tell me about Givens and his setup in that building."

He reached out, grabbed the faxed blueprint of the

Dawner building and placed it in front of her. "This might help."

She shook her head. "If you have this, what do you need me for?"

"You've been in there and I haven't. It's as simple as that. Also, I need information about that Miller guy and his security force."

"Okay, to start with, Givens's office is here." She stabbed a finger down on a corner suite on the fourth floor. "And Miller has his office, I guess you'd say, in the same suite."

"Then..."

"You know," Mitchell said after Bolan had finished quizzing her, "if you're thinking of going into the Dawner building for whatever reason, and I really don't want to know if you're going to do it," she added quickly, "I just happen to have a pass key."

"How did you get that?"

"Back before everything went crazy," she said, "Roy trusted me and gave me a key so I could work on my program materials after hours."

"Have you tried using it lately?"

"Not really," she replied. "Miller keeps one of his thugs in the lobby at all times and he lets me in after hours. You're thinking that the locks have been changed, right?"

"Yeah, I am," he admitted. "It's a common precaution when a new security unit takes over. But it still might come in handy. Do you have it with you?"

"No, it's in my desk at the studio. But I can sneak in and get it for you, no problem."

"I'm not sure that's a good idea," Bolan said. "If Miller's men are willing to shoot you down on the street, they might be waiting for you there."

She laughed. "I can get past those fools. I use the tunnel to the neighboring building that comes out under the main stage. I've been using it a lot lately since the goons showed up. My office is right next to the stage, so I can get in without their seeing me."

"That's fine, but I'm going with you."

"I'll be okay."

"Like you were when you got into that car? They're going to be looking for you."

"Okay."

THEY DROVE to the studio in Bolan's BMW and, following Mitchell's instructions, he parked in the basement of the building across the street.

"A lot of the buildings in this area are set up this way to share parking spaces," she said as she led him to the elevator leading into the basement.

On the bottom floor, the elevator opened into a large storage and utility area with a metal door on the streetside wall. "That's the door over there." She nodded at it. "It usually isn't locked."

The door was open and the tunnel leading under the street was brightly lit. At the far end was another metal door with a No Entrance sign stenciled on it in red.

"That's to keep the winos out," she said as she took a key from her purse and started to unlock the door.

"I'll do that," Bolan said.

"Sure." She handed the key over.

Bolan didn't pull his piece, but his jacket was unbuttoned and he could clear his shoulder holster quicker than most men could make up their minds to fire.

MILLER'S DUTY OFFICER in the Rainbow Dawn building saw the telltale light that indicated the basement door at the studio building across town had been opened.

"Delta," he said into his mike, "this is Base. You just had an intrusion through that basement door of yours. You'd better check it out. It might be Big Tits coming back to clean out her desk."

"Delta, roger," the leader of the four-man security team at the studio said. "If it is, I'll save you some."

The duty officer laughed. "Save enough for all of us."

AS MITCHELL HAD SAID, the door in the studio building opened onto an open area under the sound stage. Since a program wasn't in progress, it looked and sounded deserted.

"My office's over there." She pointed to a row of doors on the far side of the room.

Bolan's eyes swept the backstage area and didn't see any signs of surveillance gear, but it was too easy to hide a video pickup here. Worse than that, he didn't have good fields of fire. "Okay, but this has to be fast."

"I know right where it is."

Bolan stood at the open door of the office while Mitchell went to her cluttered desk and started the search.

"I can't find the damned thing," she said, opening another drawer.

Hearing a faint noise on the other side of the stage, Bolan drew his coat back. "Let's go," he said urgently. "Someone's coming."

"But—"

"Now!" Bolan gritted, as he filled his hand with the 93-R. A quick twist attached the sound suppressor.

He was backing toward the basement door, covering his front when the roar of a large-caliber handgun sounded from his left.

Dropping into a crouching turn, Bolan tracked and sent a short burst at a man in a black uniform with a nickel-plated handgun in his hand. Wanna-bes always went for the customized hardware with the overly sensitive triggers. They were okay for static target practice, if you went in for that kind of thing, but in a combat situation, the light pull could betray you.

The guard had had him cold. But, in his excitement, he'd jerked the trigger and now he'd never get a chance to correct that flaw in his shooting style. The Beretta's slugs hammered into the man's chest. He went down without a sound.

"Is there a side door?" Bolan asked.

"To the left and all the way to the back."

That was too far away to make an escape. He had

allowed himself to get boxed in by a floor plan, and now he would have to shoot his way out. "Get back in your office and lay on the floor against the inside wall."

As she hesitated, another guard moved in from the other side. Bolan didn't wait, but tripped off another snap burst that sawed him across the abdomen.

As he turned back to Mitchell, a third guard appeared from the corner where the first one had been. Bolan and the guard fired at the same time, but at different targets.

Bolan's 3-round burst walked a short distance across the guard's black shirt, leaving a trail of 9 mm holes. The custom .45 slipped from the guard's fingers as he went down.

The guard's single shot had also connected. A patch of red had appeared to the left between Mitchell's breasts. Her eyes went wide as if she were puzzled, and she made a little "oh" sound as she slumped to the floor.

Bolan didn't bother to check her pulse. He knew the location of the human heart as well as any cardiac surgeon, and she'd been hit with a .45 slug.

With the woman dead, there was nothing left for him to do but run. This wasn't the first time in his career he had been forced to cut his losses, nor, he knew, would it be the last. Those who were responsible for this would be called to judgment, only not right now.

CHAPTER TWENTY-FIVE

Los Angeles, California

After closing the studio's basement door and entering the tunnel, Bolan paused to fire a single 9 mm slug into the lock. That should slow any pursuers long enough for him to get back to the parking structure.

Holstering the Beretta, he sprinted the short distance through the tunnel to the elevator, and rode up to the parking level. Sliding into the driver's seat of his BMW, he fired it up, engaged first gear and calmly drove out onto the street. He was less than two blocks away when he saw the first of the LAPD cars racing toward the studio building with their sirens roaring. The ambulances and SWAT team vans would be following closely behind.

Stony Man Farm, Virginia

AARON KURTZMAN had one of the TV screens surrounding his workstation on autopilot, as he called it. It was connected to a computer program that scanned over a hundred broadcast and cable channels at cyberspeed, searching for key words and phrases. When it tripped on one of them, it sent the TV programming live to Kurtzman's workstation, as well as recording it for later study.

He was working on developing more background on the personnel of the UN teams when the TV set clicked on to L.A.'s Channel 7. Jo-Anne Winters was in the station's Crisis Desk, with every hair in place and her face set in the professional look she wore for everything from a car chase on I-5 to the end of the world.

"We have a breaking story from downtown," she said. "Miss Mellanie Mitchell, star of the popular *New Frontier* show, was killed in an apparent assassination in her studio less than an hour ago. According to the building security spokesman, Miss Mitchell was in her office when an intruder broke into the building this afternoon and suddenly started to fire. She, as well as three of the security guards who responded to the attack, were killed."

The screen switched to a building, with cop cars and a pair of ambulances in front, that had to be the studio.

"Miss Mitchell's highly rated program was a mixture of New Age, humanist and millennialist programming delivered with her own unique flamboyance and enthusiasm. According to a network spokesperson, she routinely received death threats, most of them from fundamentalist groups. One of her most vocal critics has been the Reverend Billy Jo Mann of the Greater Glory

Kingdom Church and we go now to Jill Swanson on location for an interview with him.''

The silver-haired Pastor Mann was posed in the parking lot of his church so the glass-and-chrome palace of his vanity would dominate the background of the shot. In his summer-weight suit with the dark shirt and white tie, he looked like a retired Mafia Don who had just arrived in town from wintering in Miami.

''Pastor Mann,'' the reporter said, shoving a microphone into his face, ''we have received word at Channel 7 that Mellanie Mitchell has been gunned down in her studio. You have been a vocal critic of her program since its inception. Do you have a comment on her death?''

''I can assure you,'' he intoned solemnly, ''that no one from the Greater Glory Kingdom Church had anything to do with Miss Mitchell's death. However, I must say that I'm not sorry that she has gone to the fire of God's judgment. At a time when Christ's Glory Kingdom is coming closer with every passing minute, she was preaching the very word of Satan.''

The preacher dramatically stuck one finger up into the sky. ''God will not be mocked, He will not. The glorious kingdom of His son, our lord and savior, will reign supreme and all those who speak against it will burn in the eternal flame of Holy Justice.''

The remote camera panned back to Swanson, who had dropped the professional reporter face for a look of personal revulsion as if she had just brushed up against a giant slug. ''There you have the Reverend

Billy Jo Mann's response to this senseless killing. Back to you Jo-Anne.''

Kurtzman's hand snaked out to stab the intercom button. "Barb, there's something's going down in L.A., I'm flashing the video over to you."

Price watched the tape clip through twice before getting back to Kurtzman. "Have we heard from Striker lately?" she asked.

"Not today," he replied. "But, if he was involved in this, he may be keeping low for the time being."

"Keep on this and break in if anything new comes on."

"Will do."

Phoenix, Arizona

GRANT BETANCOURT also wasn't sorry to hear that Mellanie Mitchell had been killed. After going over Miller's report of her outburst in Givens's office and her breaking away from her escort, it was obvious that her usefulness had come to an end. Her TV show, however, wouldn't die with her. In fact, now that she had been martyred in the cause of rational thinking, the show would be reborn with even better ratings than before.

It would be easy to find another blond bimbo with big breasts to take her place, but this time, she would have an armed escort on every show. The apparent threat of danger would send the ratings through the roof. Talk about the battle between good and evil. On second thought, maybe the next star should be a smaller woman, five two or three, and maybe they could back off on the breasts, too. Make her look vulnerable, but brave, and give her six-foot-plus guards who looked like rejects from a WWF ugly contest. He could have hecklers planted in the studio audience and have the guards react to protect her. He could drive Jerry Springer completely out of business.

And that Bible-thumper who had stuck his bony finger in the air on TV was going to find it jammed up his nose all the way to his brain stem before this was over. In fact, one of the first blows that would be struck in Mellanie's name would be against that obscenity grandiosely titled the Greater Glory Kingdom Church. The self-titled Reverend Billy Jo Slimeball was already under investigation for playing secret games in the dark at his so-called Youth for Glory summer camp. So far, the parents of the young players had been paid off so the kids weren't talking, but two could play that game and he had more money than that scumbag could even comprehend.

The bigger issue, though, and the only one that really concerned him, was the identity of the man who had kept Mellanie from being recaptured on the street and who had apparently accompanied her to the studio. Whoever he was, he was bad news. He had killed Miller's men as easily as if he had been shooting tin cans off fence posts. Someone was focusing on Rainbow Dawn, and Betancourt was convinced more than ever that it was connected with the deaths of the senator and his daughter. The word from his White House sources was that there were no ongoing official investigations into those incidents, but it was obvious that someone was interested.

On the other side of town, Security Plus's home office was processing the security videotapes from the studio right now, and he should have the computer-enhanced clips showing the mystery man within the hour. As far as the LAPD was concerned, the security camera system had, unfortunately, been down for maintenance at the time of the shooting and no tapes were available, and it would stay that way.

Whoever this guy was, this wasn't something he wanted the cops to get involved with any more than they already were. When he learned who this man was, he would have him taken care of, not turned over to the LAPD.

More immediately, though, something had to be done about Roy Givens.

Betancourt didn't need this right now, but he should have expected it. The situation with Givens had never been an equal partnership. The man was only a simple tool of limited use, and it had only gotten worse since the incident with the Wayne girl. Without being paranoid, he could only assume that the mystery man who was attacking Givens's Rainbow Dawn could become a serious threat to him, as well.

Until then, he had felt that it would be impossible for anyone to connect him to the cult leader. But Givens had stupidly allowed his dick to create a situation where he had come under serious suspicion, and whoever was investigating him was good. This meant that Givens had outlived his usefulness.

While Betancourt felt that it would take a miracle for him to be linked with Givens in any manner, the cult leader had been involved with setting up the Project. And he had proved that he couldn't be trusted to keep his mouth shut any more than he could to keep his pants zipped. Like the girl, Givens had earned an accident, but that could wait while he took care of something even more important first.

He had decided that the timetable for Galileo Day, as he had labeled the conclusion of his Project, would have to be put forward. He had wanted to drag it out so it would happen closer to the turn of the real millennium, but it wasn't the timing that was important. He, too, had fallen into the trap of using empty symbolism as if this were going to be some bogus religious ceremony instead of the release of humankind from the bonds of religion. The only important thing was that the targets be taken out, not when it was done.

Three phone calls would move the target day up and he was happy to make them. The sooner the targets were eliminated, the sooner humankind could awaken from the nightmare and start developing its full potential.

Stony Man Farm, Virginia

AARON KURTZMAN picked up his ringing phone. "Kurtzman," he answered.

"You have your TV on?" Bolan asked. After seeing how the Dawners were spinning out the studio shootout, Bolan had made a scrambled call to Stony Man.

"In living color. What's going down?"

"I've had a busy day."

"That's what I figured."

Kurtzman took quick notes as Bolan briefed him on the street rescue and the studio shoot-out. "It sounds like Mr. Givens is losing control of his operation," he said when the Executioner was finished.

"From what Mellanie said," Bolan replied, "it doesn't sound like he's been in control for some time now, and I believe her. If Hal is right about Betancourt being behind all of this, it makes sense that he sent in a team of hardmen to get that part of his operation back under control."

"That would make sense, particularly since I'm developing information tying several of the people on those UN teams to the Dawners. It looks like Givens was involved in much of the recruiting of the action teams for Betancourt's project."

"I'm going in there as soon as I can set up the entrance and the diversion. I don't think that I'll have too much time to go through his records or anything like that. With the local emergency response being what it is, it's just going to be a run-and-gun set up.

"Is there anything you need?"

"I don't know what it would be. Gadgets left his bag of tricks with me when they moved out, so I've got the demo I need. It's going to be pretty simple."

Kurtzman smiled. Only Striker could say that going up against a well-armed security force of more than a dozen men would be routine. "When are you going to kick off?"

"I can't really say. It depends on how much work it's going to be to get into the utilities area of that building and make my preparations."

"I'll let Hal know what's going down."

"Just give him a broad brush," Bolan suggested, "and tell him that I have a handle on it. I don't want to take his mind off the overseas operations. They have the priority."

"Will do." Kurtzman laughed. "He's going crazy enough as it is having to hang around his D.C. office pretending that nothing's going on."

"Switch me over to Barbara so I can fill her in, too."

AFTER TALKING to Price, Bolan put the blue overalls and yellow hard hat he had purchased into his carry-on, as well as a flashlight and selected items from Gadgets Schwarz's stash. Getting into his BMW, he drove over to the parking structure where he had stashed the white utility van he had rented for the week.

After transferring his carry-on to the van, he drove to within a block of the Dawners building and parked on a side street right in front of a manhole cover. Emerging from the van wearing the coveralls and hard hat, he opened the cover and disappeared under the street.

It was a short walk through the utilities tunnel to the

block the Dawners building occupied. The street addresses were marked on the outside of the access doors and the door to the Dawners building was padlocked, but the bolt cutter in his bag made short work of it.

Inside the Dawners' utility room, his first stop was at the bank of elevators. These were the original Otis elevators that had been installed when the building was built in the seventies. They did, however, have the newer-style emergency locks. To engage them, all he had to do was create slack in the steel cables that ran the cars. And that, as McCarter would say, was a piece of cake.

Schwarz had a small roll of linear shaped charge in his goodies bag. There wasn't much of it on the roll, just twenty feet, but it would be enough for his purposes.

This was one of the handiest explosives ever created. At its name implied, linear shaped charge was like a cord, but its cross section was a thick V shape. The V itself was a strong, but flexible metal-filled extruded plastic. The ends of the two arms of the V were coated with a powerful adhesive and the space between them was filled with RDX, rapid detonating explosive. The V shape made the explosive act like a shaped charge, and it could cut through as much as two inches of steel.

At the bottom of the elevator shafts, Bolan located the drive motors that controlled the cables. After measuring the huge pulleys at the ends of the motor shafts, he cut the linear charge cord to length, peeled the plastic off the adhesive and pressed it in place on the inside faces of each of the pulleys. Two of Schwarz's own miniature radio-controlled detonators on each charge completed the job. When he triggered them, the cutting charges would rip through the pulleys, releasing the tension on the cables, which would activate the safety locks freezing the elevators in place.

The second part of his preparations had him working with the building's forced-air ventilation system. As with most buildings of that vintage, fresh air was drawn in from the roof, cooled or heated and then blown at low pressure through all the floors. Exhaust air was returned to the roof by a separate set of low-speed blowers.

Opening the main vent duct, he taped a dozen smoke grenades against the walls, six on each side. He unscrewed the standard detonators on six of the grenades and replaced them with more minidetonators set on det channel two. The other six were rigged with their detonators set on channel three.

Yet another minidetonator, without additional explosive, was attached to the emergency shutdown control. This was designed to cut off the flow of outside air in case of fire to keep the vent system from feeding the flames. The small charge in the detonator itself would trip that system. This was set to det channel four.

As his final modification to the air system, Bolan hardwired the forced-air control to bypass the emergency shutoff feature. He didn't want outside air coming in, but he had to have the main vent system working.

One last stop was at the phone line master junction box. His last detonator and a triple wrap of standard det cord went around the trunk line. Set to channel five, this could cut off outside landline communication and isolate the kill zone.

On the way out, Bolan replaced the padlock on the utility access door with one of his own.

CHAPTER TWENTY-SIX

Saudi Arabia

The construction workers' lounge in the Riyadh Hilton was rocking. Country music blared from the sound set, and someone had put a *Best of Garth Brooks* CD on automatic replay.

Rafael Encizo was about to call it a night when the man he had been waiting for walked in the door and headed for the bar. The man in the Gold Star Construction baseball cap didn't know that the Phoenix force commando was looking for him, but that was all right with Encizo. He watched as the guy paid for a couple of bottles of beer at the bar and looked around for a table before settling down at the one next to him.

That was going to make the contact child's play, Encizo thought. Now he wouldn't have to go through some elaborate game plan out of the tradecraft manual to find a way to start a conversation with him.

Sucking back his beer, he glanced over and pretended to notice the embroidered logo on the man's cap. "Aren't you the guys who're doing that job out in Mecca?" he asked when he caught the man's eye.

The man nodded as he sucked down his cold beer as if he hadn't had one in weeks.

"What's it like working there?" Encizo asked. "I mean, you hear all those wild stories about that place. You know, that there's guards with big swords standing around ready to cut off your head if you spit on the ground and shit like that."

The man took another long draw on his beer. "You hear a lot of bullshit in this country," he said, glad to have someone to talk to. "But the only guards I saw were carrying some kind of assault rifles, and they weren't fucking around."

"That must have made working there a little tense."

"Yep, it sure as hell did, but that's not why I quit today."

Encizo turned his chair to face him. This guy obviously needed to talk, and he was ready to listen. "What happened?"

"We had an accident, and we're lucky that we all didn't die. One of our propane refueling lines sprung a leak, and the gas caught fire. If there hadn't been a fire extinguisher close by, the whole damned place would have gone up."

The man shook his head. "I tried to tell Bud that working around that fucking propane was only going to cause problems. But would he listen to me? Hell, no. On top of that, refueling down in the work site has got to be one of the dumbest things I've ever heard of."

The bottle came up again for another long drag. "Man, we were lucky that it only burned this time and didn't explode. I don't think any of them have any idea just how dangerous that stuff is."

He looked Encizo full in the face. "You ever been around a fuel air explosive?"

"Can't say that I have," Encizo lied as he waved at the waiter for another round for both of them.

"I was in the Air Force during the Gulf War," the worker said. "A crewman on one of those AC-130s. You know, a Spectre gunship?"

Encizo nodded. "Yeah, I saw them on CNN."

"Anyway, toward the end of the air campaign, we went into Southern Iraq with a Herky drop ship to provide fire support for a FAE raid. We had a Wild Weasel Team on station to keep the SAMs off us, so all we had to worry about was the small-caliber Triple A fire, and it wasn't dick."

When the waiter set another beer in front of him, the construction worker paused long enough to wet his whistle before continuing again.

"We were orbiting at about fifteen thousand when the Herky came overhead at twenty thou, rolled that big boy down the rear ramp and cracked the chutes. It's the damnedest thing you've ever seen, man, fifty thousand gallons of propane floating to Earth on three clusters of cargo chutes. We'd been hammering every Arab position that looked like it was worth wasting ammunition on with our forties and the 105. No one was shooting back, so we checked fire to watch the bomb come down."

The man's eyes went out of focus as he remembered. "That damned thing floated down to within, I guess, a few hundred feet of the ground, and all hell broke loose. We weren't expecting that kind of flash, and it blinded us for a few seconds. Just when we could see again, the shock wave damned near tore our wings off and it did rip the drop tanks off the pylons. We had fuel spraying out of the ruptured hookups like it was from a fire hose. The pilot unassed the area immediately and called for a tanker to top him off just so we could get back to the air base."

The man met Encizo's eyes. "After we landed, the plane had to be scrapped. Both wings and the airframe had been damaged so badly that it wasn't worth salvaging."

He shook his head. "That was just a fifty-thousand-gallon explosion and our tank in Mecca holds over a million. It's supposed to be the largest portable propane tank ever built and if that damned thing ever kicks off, these Arabs can kiss their holy city goodbye. Shit, there won't even be any decent-sized rubble left."

"I'm surprised that your boss is letting something like that happen."

"Shit," the man said, "Bud's a good man, a real good man. But he's really got his ass in a sling on this job. He can't hardly do a damned thing without running it through the company contract rep first. He's the actual boss out there, and he's got his gang of ass-kissers who're making it real hard for the rest of us to do our job.''

The man looked up. "You know, I've been on a lot of jobs since I hung up the blue suit, but this is the first time I've ever wished that I was back in the Air Force. At least they knew how to handle explosives.''

"It's funny you should mention that," Encizo said. "I know how strong you union guys are about job safety, so isn't the union rep saying anything about this?''

The man shrugged. "Since we're not at home, the union rep doesn't have a hell of a lot to say about the work-site rules. And I gotta say that most of the guys really don't care, either. We're pulling down three times union scale as well as hardship pay, and that's a bunch of money. Most of the guys are thinking about getting new RVs or paying off their mortgages, and they're willing to take the risk.''

"How would you like to talk to someone who does care?" Encizo ventured to ask.

"What do you mean?''

"Well, I happen to know that there's a couple of UN guys here who're looking into that job because it's being paid for by some kind of UN fund. If there's something wrong going on out there, they're really going to want to know about it.''

"Sure." The man finished his beer. "I'll talk to them. Let's go.''

Encizo laughed and reached for his cell phone.

"First, I need to give them a quick call. And what did you say your name was?"

"Ralph Biggs."

"Nice to meet you, Ralph," Encizo stuck his hand out. "I'm Carlos Evens."

Biggs shook his hand. "Do those UN guys have anything to drink?"

"I'm sure that can be arranged."

Biggs shoved his chair back. "Let's go."

ENCIZO'S PHONE CALL gave McCarter and James time to set the stage for their guest. The main requirement apparently was the booze, and UN diplomats also had a dispensation from the rules of Islam in their hotels.

The VIP suite they were staying in was more than a cut above the other rooms in the hotel, and Biggs looked around in wonder as the introductions were made.

"I understand that you have information about job safety at the Gold Star Construction site in Mecca," McCarter said. "I'd really like to hear about that."

Biggs looked over at the standing bar on the other side of the room. "You wouldn't happen to have something to…?"

James strode forward with a glass, an ice bucket and a bottle. "Would you care for bourbon, Mr. Biggs?"

"So," McCarter said when Biggs was finished with his story, "you say that the crew is taking great risks with their refueling procedures?"

"Damned straight." Biggs swirled the bourbon and ice cubes in his glass. "When you're running propane-powered equipment, you're supposed to refuel a hundred yards off-site."

He shook his head. "Man, if we were back in the States, OSHA would have our balls for what we're doing. All those eco-Nazis who scream about using natural gas vehicles have no idea how dangerous those damned things are."

"How'd you like to talk to someone who can get that situation straightened out real fast?"

Biggs looked over at Encizo. "He said that you guys could do that."

"Actually, we can't," McCarter said smoothly. "But we know how to get this information to the man who can, Prince Khalid of the Saudi royal family. He's the guy who's actually supposed to be overseeing the work. We were there earlier today, and he escorted us to the site. A man named Bud, I believe, gave us a briefing and showed us around."

"That's Bud Bolger, the supervisor," Biggs said. "He's a good man. It's that asshole Dick Rawlins you have to watch out for."

"And he is?"

"He's the company rep."

Biggs shot down the rest of his drink, and James was right on the spot to refill his glass. "Man, I don't know what our management was thinking when they sent him out here of all places."

He looked up at McCarter. "Dick hates Arabs. His

younger sister was killed when that Iraqi Scud missile hit that mess hall here during the war. When I heard him bad-mouthing the locals, I tried to explain that the Saudis are the good guys, but he calls them all ragheads and doesn't care where they're from.''

The three Phoenix force commandos finally had their first lead on the action agent behind this plot. A man with fire in his heart to avenge a loss would be the prefect candidate to lead a mission like this. Now all they had to do was to convince the Saudis to shut down the operation while they still could. Which, of course, was going to be damned near impossible.

''How'd you like to go back there tomorrow and show the prince what the problem is?'' McCarter asked.

Biggs shook his head. ''Damn, that's going to really queer my chances of ever working for Gold Star again.''

''I don't think you'll have to worry about that,'' Encizo said. ''And, even if it does, I can get you a federal job where you can never get fired.''

''Sure.'' He held his glass out again. ''I'll go with you, why the hell not? Maybe I can keep someone from getting killed out there.''

A rather large number of someones, McCarter thought.

Vatican City

UNLIKE THE VAST majority of Americans who went to Italy, Dr. Patrick Renfro of the Vatican archives team didn't find Rome to be charming. As far as he was concerned, it was just another European slum, and he might as well have been in Mexico City or Lima. It was true that the so-called Eternal City was cleaner by several magnitudes and one could at least eat the local food and drink the water without getting a terminal disease.

But, to him, Rome was the center of everything he found the most disgusting about human society. Everywhere he went, he couldn't escape the overwhelming feeling that the black-robed butchers of the Inquisition were watching his every move. It was as bad as being a kid back in Boston in Saint Mary's Academy again.

To keep in touch with what was going on back in the land of the free and the home of those brave enough to think for themselves, he picked up a copy of the overseas edition of *USA Today* every evening when he went back to his hotel room. Reading news from America always helped make the bad taste in his mouth go away so he could sleep.

The story about the assassination of Mellanie Mitchell, and it could only be an assassination, hit him like a blow. She had been a little over the edge and a little too corny sometimes, but he had enjoyed her TV show for what it was. It was fluff, but as a counter to the Bible-thumpers it had been a breath of fresh air, promoting rationality untainted by the pious lies told to enslave the human spirit and the revolting stench of incense.

One of the most difficult things about being in the

Vatican was that he constantly smelled incense. For years, the merest whiff of it had made him want to puke. Even now, if he didn't steel himself, he would gag.

The sidebar accompanying the article that reported the ravings of that white trash preacher who said that he was glad Mellanie was dead maddened him. The fact that the article ended by saying that charges of child molestation had been filed against the pastor did little to mollify him.

At least that scumbag was going to get his, but that was only because he wasn't a protected Catholic priest. The Church had made sure that the man who had preyed on Renfro hadn't had to pay for his crimes. In fact, Renfro was the only one who had paid, first in what had been done to him and secondly by being disowned by his family when he had tried to expose that pedophile priest.

But that was in the past, and he was the one who had the power now. He would finally have his personal vengeance and, at the same time, would also avenge the untold millions who had suffered even worse than he had at the hands of an uncaring Church.

When Renfro was awakened later that night by a phone call from the States, he was overjoyed by what he heard. With D Day put forward, he would be free of the stink of this place even sooner than he had thought. The rest of the books and records that hadn't been treated would just have to take their chances with the vagaries of time and fortune. But, since they were mostly religious garbage anyway, it wouldn't be any great loss if they ceased to exist.

Stony Man Farm, Virginia

AARON KURTZMAN WAS adding the finishing touches to the order of battle he had put together on the people the Stony Man teams were going up against. In each of the target groups, he had found that the opposition fell into two distinct categories. The first were the players, the action men. The second category he was calling fillers, legitimate workers at these sites who didn't know what was really going on.

In the first group were several men who had been awarded Betancourt Industries scholarships. Interestingly enough, almost all of them had, at one time, been heavily involved with conventional religion of one variety or the other, starting at a young age.

In one way, that finding was unexpected. In another, though, it made sense that if these men had been damaged by a rough trip along the path of faith as a child they might want payback. Others seemed to have no personal connection to religion, but had come from families that did. Again, a harsh upbringing at home could also turn a man into a dedicated enemy of everything religious.

What wasn't unexpected was that almost all of these people had cycled through Southern California at one time or another, which gave them possible exposure to Rainbow Dawn. The Dawners' computer records,

JUDGMENT IN BLOOD 289

though, even the classified ones, weren't big on membership lists, so there was no way to check that. Even so, it fit into all the information they had that there was a connection.

It was hard to know how accurate his order of battle was, but it was something that the teams might find useful. There wasn't a hell of a lot more that he and his staff could do to help, and it was bugging him half to death. Modern weapons were being targeted against ancient shrines, but there was little that all of the modern technology he had at his disposal could do to help protect them. Maybe it was fitting that the oldest defense in history, determined men, had been called upon.

Rolling his wheelchair to the fax machine, he loaded his report and punched in three sets of numbers.

CHAPTER TWENTY-SEVEN

Jerusalem, Israel

Dave Tolly didn't like the revised D Day schedule he'd been given. With the mapping project being so closely monitored by the local authorities, any change in their agreed location schedule would have to be discussed for days before he would be allowed to deviate from it. In fact, the way things had gone so far, he was afraid that if he proposed any such change, the whole project would be closed down. Damn these people anyway!

Tolly laughed to himself. You would think that all these God freaks would welcome a chance to go to their respective heavens as soon as possible. If they would just leave him alone to do his job, they'd all be dead and their stupid arguments could finally stop because they'd all be in the fires of hell together.

A bigger problem for him than the Jerusalem government, however, were the security forces, both Israeli and UN, he'd been saddled with. On the one hand, they were all that stood between him and the mobs and, without them, he'd probably be stoned to death. But they, too, wouldn't like him changing his schedule.

But he could probably take care of both of these problems by leaving the bulk of his equipment where it was and moving just what he needed to the new area to set up his surprise.

That way he could say that he wasn't really deviating from the schedule and would split the security forces since they would have to guard both sites.

IN THE STARK LIGHT of day, Dr. Susan Brown wasn't quite sure if she believed the story she had been told the previous night. It was right out of a paperback thriller and, while the men had sure seemed sincere, she wasn't completely convinced now. Grabbing a quick cup of coffee and a roll on the way through the hotel's breakfast buffet, she headed for the site.

When she arrived, she saw Dave Tolly's cronies packing up some of their equipment. "Now what's going on?" she asked.

"I got another message from Wild Bill last night," Tolly said. "He wants me to move up the schedule so we can get out of here a week or so early. It's got something to do with the next job he's got lined up for us."

That would be more than okay with her. She'd had about all of this place that she could stomach. But this just didn't make sense. First and foremost, if they skipped any of the scheduled scanning sites, the resultant work wouldn't be accurate. And without the accuracy they had promised, the entire job would be for nothing and Geo-Tech would gain nothing for having done it.

But if, as Ari Landau and Roger Railing had told her, the only purpose of this job was to have a reason to bring enough nuclear materials together to create a radiation accident, it really wouldn't matter what else the team did or didn't do. And while she had awakened with serious doubts about what she had been told, they were now quickly fading.

"Where are we going?" she asked.

"We're moving over to that site in the Christian Quarter, close to that so-called Tomb of the Holy Sepulchre where the Bible-thumpers say their boss got laid out."

Brown was used to Tolly's total disregard for the religious sensitivities of Jerusalem and his biting scorn for the pilgrims who came to the city. This, though, was a bit over the edge even for him.

Tolly caught the look on her face and asked, "What's the matter, Susan, don't tell me that you believe those fairy tales? You've got a Ph.D. and you should have figured out by now that dead is dead. Those morons who come here are too stupid to figure it out. They think that if they just pray enough and give all their money to some preacher, when they get whacked they'll get to rise from the dead."

His face hardened for a moment. "That's what all my relatives told me when my mom died, but it sure as hell didn't work for her. It's been almost thirty years now, and she's still dead.''

He grinned. ''And that's what's going to happen when these fools die here as well.''

Brown suddenly felt chilled. ''What do you mean by that?''

''Oh,'' Tolly said offhandedly, ''just that with all the riots, the car bombs and all the rest of that crap going on around here, this is a great place to get killed. And, regardless of the Sunday-school stories, they're going to figure out that dying in Jerusalem isn't any different than dying anywhere else. Dead is dead.''

''What can I do to help?'' Susan tried to change the subject.

''Oh, nothing really,'' he said. ''The guys and I have it pretty well under control, so why don't you and the girls take the day off. You know, check out the sights, do a little shopping and I'll see you tomorrow.''

''Tomorrow's the Jewish Sabbath,'' she reminded him. ''We can't work on Saturday.''

''Oh yeah.'' He grinned. ''I forgot. It's God's day, and the bearded old men will stone us to death if we try to do any work. I'll see you Sunday, then. At least the Christians won't try to kill us for doing our job.''

''Sure,'' she said. ''I'll do some shopping. There's a couple of things I've been meaning to pick up for souvenirs.''

After leaving the site, Brown stopped at the first phone booth she found and dialed the number the Mossad agent had written on the back of his card.

"Yes?" Katz answered.

"Mr. Landau," she said, "this is Susan Brown. I need to talk to you and your men."

WHEN BROWN GOT to the hotel, she found all three of the mysterious agents waiting for her. T. J. Hawkins filled a cup of coffee for her as Katz offered her a seat.

"I have to admit," she said, "that when I got up this morning, I thought that I had dreamed our conversation last night. But, when I got to the site, Tolly and his cronies were packing up some of our equipment to move it to a new location."

"What's wrong with that?"

"For one, it blows our planned mapping program. I have to carefully calibrate the scanners based on where I took the last readings, and every location must be scanned in the correct sequence or the results are junk."

She took a deep breath. "And then he started making jokes about dying in Jerusalem being no different than dying anywhere else."

"What do you mean?"

"It's hard to explain, but he went into some rambling monologue about how his mother hadn't risen from the dead after she died even though everyone prayed so much. Then he said that the people here were going to learn that no matter what they'd been told, when they died they would remain dead."

She shuddered. "I'm still not sure if he plans to set off a bomb, but he's sure planning something, and it scares me. I want to help you try to stop him from whatever it is he's doing."

"Before you sign on with us," Katz said, "there's a couple things I have to tell you. First, I'm not connected with the Israeli government. I was some time ago, but not any longer. I'm sorry for the subterfuge, but it was necessary. Second, my men and I usually work for the U.S. government. We're kind of a trouble-shooting team."

"The CIA?"

"No, you've never heard of us before."

"And you said usually. What's different this time?"

"This time, we're here without official sanction."

"I don't understand—"

"It's a long story," Katz replied, "but most of it has to do with the fact that your project is being sponsored by the United Nations. Even if we had irrefutable, concrete evidence of what we think is going on here, it would take weeks, if not months, for the UN to do anything about it. And even then, they would probably do the wrong thing. If we want to stop this, we're going to have to do it on our own."

He leveled his eyes on her. "Which means that if we run afoul of the authorities in any way, we're going to be on our own."

She took a deep breath. "Like I said, I want to go with you."

Katz glanced at both Hawkins and Manning, and both men nodded.

"With that settled," Katz said, putting on his tactical

officer hat, "the question remains as to how we're going to get in there and do whatever it is we're going to do. Even though this guy's building a bomb under their noses, he's still going to have his security troops with him. We're going to have to take their minds off their business long enough to let us slip through."

"I get the job of rabbit this time," Hawkins said. "I'm not much on nuclear technology, so I get the short straw. It's as simple as that."

"How do you want to do it?" Katz asked.

"I was thinking of getting their attention with a few flash-bangs and a couple of well-placed shots."

"You've got to get in close to use flash-bangs," Manning pointed out. "Those riflemen aren't going to let you get away with it."

"Not the way I'm going to do it." Hawkins grinned. "I'm going to use a sling to throw them just like in those Bible stories Brother Jennings used to tell us in Sunday school. This is the City of David, and if it was good enough for him, it's got to be good enough for this old country boy."

Manning knew that when the ex-Ranger started slipping into his Southerner routine that he was preparing to go all-out. The problem was that this time he'd be doing it solo.

Hawkins recognized the look on his teammate's face. "I also took rabbit lessons, and no one is going to catch this ole Southern rabbit."

Los Angeles, California

THE FIRST THING Bolan did when he got back to the Dawners building was to check his earlier work to insure that all of the demo packs were still in place. Seeing them all intact and ready to go, he stripped off his utility-worker coveralls to get down to his black combat suit and took his weapons and assault harness from his bag.

There was too big a risk of being discovered if he used the elevator to reach the eighth floor, but the fire stairs would work just as well. His rubber-soled boots made almost no noise as he took the stairs two at a time, fast enough to limit his exposure, but slow enough that he wouldn't run into company unexpectedly.

AT THE FIRE-ESCAPE landing to the eighth floor, Bolan paused long enough to let his heart rate return to normal. He was in no hurry and could afford the luxury of a brief break. Once he kicked off, he'd be running and gunning until it was over.

Taking the radio detonator from his pocket, he set it to det channel one, armed it and hit the button. No sound reached him where he was, but the light over the exit door flickered as the cutting charges took the elevators off-line.

Next he switched to channel two and fired the first batch of smoke grenades in the vent system. Firing the detonator on channel four cut off the fresh air intake, and channel five severed the phone lines. After switching back to channel three, he stowed the detonator and he started to count down the seconds it would take for the smoke to start appearing.

Cracking the door, he peered out and saw a hallway already filling with white smoke. Snapping his gas mask down over his face, he turned on the air and stepped into the smoke-filled corridor, his Beretta 93-R in one hand and the Desert Eagle in the other. The fire alarms were blaring and the sprinklers were drenching the carpet. The fire department would be arriving soon, so the clock was ticking.

The low-vision goggles in the mask turned the smoky corridor into a glowing green tunnel. The steady feed of air insured that he wouldn't be incapacitated in any way. The smoke wasn't really dangerous, but it was blinding and reduced the oxygen-carrying capability of the lungs by some twenty-five percent, which induced panic. That wouldn't be a factor with him, but it would affect the opposition.

WHEN HE HAD FIRST taken over Rainbow Dawn's security, Miller had been amused to find all the miniature surveillance monitors Givens had scattered around the building. As he would have bet, most of them had been placed in areas like the women's dressing rooms, their exercise rooms and quarters. A few had been real security scanners and covered the lobby, rear door and the approaches to those entrances, but most of them had been devoted to voyeurism.

One of the first things he had done was to completely rework the system. To be sure, he had left a few of the

choicest video pickups in place, but had repositioned
the rest to cover every inch of the hallways and stairwells. He liked to catch a good T and A shot as much
as the next man, but his mission was to watch for intruders.

But even with all his surveillance gear, he was having a difficult time figuring out what in the hell was
going on. The fire alarm had tripped, but as yet he had
no indication of a fire anywhere in the building. The
billowing clouds of smoke looked and smelled more
like a smoke grenade than a real fire, and that meant
trouble.

He had no doubt that he was under attack, but by
whom or what he had no idea. If he had to place a bet
on who it was, though, it would come up being that
guy who had taken Mellanie Mitchell to the studio to
die.

He had dispatched four five-man fire teams to search
the building's eight floors as they cleared out the
Dawners. Another six men were in the lobby shoving
people out the door, but they would be his ready-
reaction team as soon as the other teams made contact.
Everyone was locked and loaded, but so far, they
hadn't spotted the opposition.

With everyone in a panic, his men were being extra
careful not to pop caps on wild-eyed Dawners. The
authorities would be on the scene in minutes, and the
last thing he needed was to have to try to explain the
wrong dead bodies. The hardware was covered, as his
company was a sanctioned private police force, and all

the paperwork had been properly filed to cover their use. Nonetheless, as with any black-shoe LAPD officer, a wrongful shooting would be a real pain in the ass. The Phoenix office didn't like that kind of mistake, and it would go hard on him as well as on the shooter.

"This is Base, report in order," he radioed to his fire teams.

"Alpha, clear," the first team leader responded.

"Bravo, clear."

"Delta, clear."

Miller frowned, where was Charlie Team? "Charlie," he radioed, "this is Base, report."

With Miller concentrating on his men, Roy Givens saw his opening. He had what could be called an overly healthy respect for fire. The fire that had allowed him to change his name and his life had been an accident, but it had taught him the raw power of flame. Every fiber of his body was screaming for him to get out, but Miller had other ideas.

"I swear to God," Miller snarled when he saw Givens inching toward the door, "if you even think of running until this building is completely cleared, I'll put a bullet in your fucking leg. You're supposed to be in charge here, and it doesn't look good for the boss man to shit his pants and bug out."

"But—"

"Just stand over by the window and keep the hell out of my way. If it gets too smoky in here, take a chair, break the glass and stick your head out."

"But it's shatterproof glass," Givens wailed.

Milled turned and fired a 9 mm round into the window. It punched through, leaving a spiderwebbed hole. "Hit it there and it'll break."

Givens slumped back against the wall beside the window, afraid to move.

JUDGMENT AT POCO
Miller sneer and the fire team leader saw the smoke
the... expected to clear... that... the... you

CHAPTER TWENTY-EIGHT

Los Angeles, California

The leader of Miller's Fire Team Charlie wasn't having a good day in the Rainbow Dawn headquarters. The combination of dense smoke and water from the sprinklers made it almost impossible to see more than a couple of yards in any direction. He didn't know how Miller expected him to clear these rooms under these conditions. And, so far, this floor had proved to be empty anyway.

When the team leader saw Bolan emerging from the smoke, he took him for a Dawner space-case stumbling around with his head up his anal cavity.

"Yo, asshole!" he called out, pointing to the exit with his subgun. "Get your ass out of here! Now!"

The team leader blinked to try to see through the smoke and finally saw that the silent figure approaching him was gas-masked and armed. It was the last thing he ever saw.

When Bolan IDed the weapon in the guard's hand, he brought up the Beretta 93-R in one smooth move and triggered a 3-round burst. The trio of 9 mm slugs punched a small triangle in the man's left breast pocket and his heart behind it.

The other four members of Fire Team Charlie saw their leader fall and flattened themselves against the wall. Their subguns were ready, but before they could see a target, they heard a metallic click and saw something drop on the soggy carpet in front of them.

"Grenade!" one of the guards yelled right before the flash-bang went off.

When Bolan appeared through the smoke, both of his hands were spitting flame. Two of the gunmen went down before their eyes could clear.

The two survivors were still seeing spots in front of their eyes, but they blindly fired into the smoke. Unfortunately for them, Bolan wasn't in their line of fire. Two more quick bursts put them down, as well.

MILLER DIDN'T HAVE audio pickups on his surveillance cameras, but, even through the smoke, the muzzle-flashes were distinctive.

"Alpha, Bravo," he radioed to his teams on the sixth and fourth floors, "condition Zulu. Break off and hit the eighth floor. Charlie's got contact."

"Alpha, roger," the first team leader replied. "Can you see who it is?"

"That's a negative, but I've got a body on the floor in the east corridor by room 826."

"Bravo, roger," the second team leader called in.

"It's going to take a few seconds. For some reason the elevators are out."

"Just get up there."

Givens had followed the radio conversation and was alarmed. "What's happening? Who's broken in?"

Miller turned with his pistol in his hand. "If I hear one more word out of you while I'm working, you're going to lose a kneecap."

Givens clamped his mouth shut.

Phoenix, Arizona

GRANT BETANCOURT was working late when he got the call from the CEO of Security Plus on one of his secure phones.

"I just got a call from the situation room, sir. Some kind of attack is taking place at the Rainbow Dawn building in L.A."

"What kind of attack?"

"We don't know yet. But the landlines were cut, and that sent an automatic signal to us."

"How about the radios and cell phones?"

"Nothing there, either."

"Has there been any local response?"

"We don't know at this time."

"Call me the minute you hear anything."

"Will do."

Betancourt didn't need this right now, but he should have expected it. Coming so soon after the studio shoot-out, it had to be the same man, or men, who had gotten involved with Mellanie Mitchell. Regardless of the outcome of this latest incident, he had already decided that Givens had outlived his usefulness. If he somehow survived this attack, he would have to have an unfortunate accident.

AFTER CLEARING the eighth floor, Bolan opened the door to the fire-escape stairs and heard boots pounding up the metal steps from below. With all the fire doors closed, the stairwell was relatively clear of smoke, so he wouldn't have that advantage this time. Holstering his pistols, he swung his slung H&K subgun into position. Taking a concussion grenade from his harness, he pulled the pin, but held the spoon down and waited for the footfalls to get closer.

When he released the spoon, he paused for a single second before lobbing the grenade around the corner. It wasn't a harmless flash-bang, this was a full-sized assault grenade and the close confines of the stairwell increased the effect of the half-pound charge. A man's lungs could collapse if he was too close and took the force in the chest.

Before the blast echoed away, the soldier stepped out and sent a burst of 9 mm autofire down the stairwell.

After ducking back to change magazines, he pivoted out to clear the stairs. Since he was in a hurry, he fired short bursts into the bodies as insurance shots. One guard had only been stunned and tried to bring his piece into action.

Bolan spun and put him back down with a 3-round burst. Now the way was clear.

MILLER FELT the blast of the concussion grenade all the way down on the fourth floor. Whatever was going on up there, it was getting out of hand. He wanted to be up there himself, but he knew that he had to coordinate this rat screw.

"Alpha," he radioed to the team he had sent up to the eighth floor, "talk to me."

"Miller," his radio blared, "this is Larson. I've got real chaos down here in the lobby. These people are going batshit. Half of them don't want to leave because they think they'll be killed if they go outside."

"Goddammit," Miller roared. "Take care of it. Tell them to get moving or you'll start shooting."

ROY GIVENS DIDN'T want to die. He hadn't worked as hard as he had to make himself what he was only to die like a trapped rat. He was rich and powerful and had even richer and more powerful friends. If he could just get out of this room, those friends would set this right. After all he had done for Betancourt, the man wouldn't let him down.

When Miller started to yell on the radio, Givens saw his chance and raced for the door. Catching the movement out of the corner of his eye, Miller drew down and fired in one smooth movement.

The 9 mm slug caught Givens in the back of the head and slammed him sideways against the open door.

"Asshole," Miller muttered.

For a moment, he almost regretted having killed Givens. He usually didn't give in to his impulses like that, but he had this time and that was that. And, with the principal gone, it was time for him to do the smart thing.

"Bravo, this is Base," he radioed. "Where are you?"

"We're still on the fourth floor," the Bravo team leader replied. "The stairs are blocked."

"Join me in the office. We're getting out of here."

WHEN BOLAN FOUND the seventh floor deserted, he started down the stairs, bypassing the sixth floor. By his estimate, he had taken out maybe half of Miller's hard force, and time was running against him. He knew the danger of leaving unknown pockets of opposition behind him, but if he wanted to get to Givens in time, he would have to take the chance.

When he reached the fire door to the fourth floor, he paused to take the radio-controlled detonator out of his side pocket and punch the button to fire det channel three. That released the last group of smoke grenades into the air system to renew the fog of battle.

After giving the ventilation a minute to start spreading the smoke again, Bolan opened the door and headed for Givens's office suite in the middle of the hallway. Through his low-vision goggles, he saw another team of six men coming around the corner at the end of the corridor. And, as with the others, they were armed, which made them targets.

He stepped back against a closed door to see where they were going and saw another dark uniformed figure exit an open door halfway down the hall to join them. When they continued toward him, Bolan leveled his subgun and triggered short bursts, tracking the hardmen individually. The chatter of the subgun scattered the guards. Two went down without moving, but the other five dropped to the floor and returned fire.

With the guards firing blindly into the smoke, Bolan had no trouble keeping out of their line of fire as he picked them off. The enemy fire ended abruptly, and he spotted two survivors running deeper into the smoke to escape the sure death that awaited them if they stayed.

Bolan let the two fleeing guards go unpursued while he looked for Givens. The first door he tried opened into an office suite and, from Mellanie's description, it was Givens's office. He wasn't surprised to see that the body lying in the open door was the leader of Rainbow Dawn.

He'd been shot in the back of the head and, from the look on the cult leader's face, he hadn't known that the shot was coming. Since Bolan hadn't pulled the trigger on him, that meant one of his own people had taken him out.

Bolan didn't need to dispense justice himself to be satisfied. He had set the process in motion, and vengeance for a young woman had resulted. That was justice enough.

The sounds of sirens outside told Bolan that his time had run out. And, with Givens dead, his mission there was completed. The few guards he had left alive would spend a long time trying to explain to the LAPD what had happened there.

RETREATING TO the stairwell, Bolan quickly descended to the utility room. Since he knew that the emergency response would seal off the block around the Dawners building, he had left his van an easy two blocks away through the utility tunnels. Quickly changing back into his coveralls, he stowed his gear in his bag, put on his hard hat and headed into the utility tunnel. He paused long enough to padlock the door to the Dawners building behind him.

Back inside the van, he stripped off his coveralls and put on his windbreaker, covering his 93-R. Starting the van, he pulled out into traffic and worked his way back to within a block of the Dawners' building and parked again.

Playing the part of a curious bystander, he walked up to the police barrier just as the LAPD SWAT teams were deploying from their vans and taking up positions around the front of the building. They weren't ready to charge in against the unknown forces inside. Behind a van in the Dawners' parking lot, he could see technicians guiding a remote robotic vehicle up the front steps of the building. It mounted a TV camera and would recon the lobby for the SWAT team before they went in.

There was an excited conversation among the technicians running the robot, and a four-man medic team in body armor ran up to join the SWAT cops. Apparently the robot had spotted one of the bodies the security force had left behind. Since he hadn't gotten to the lobby, it wasn't one of his.

The SWAT cops made their entrance, secured the lobby and signaled for the medical team to go in. The body came out a few moments later and Bolan took that as his cue. He turned and walked back to his van.

Stony Man Farm, Virginia

BARBARA PRICE WASN'T surprised to get the call from the comm center in the Annex that said Hal Brognola was inbound. As much as he wanted to keep this low profile, there was no way that he could stay away when something like this was going down. Even with everything being fed to Tokaido's mini-CP in his office, it just wasn't the same as being at the farm when the hammer went down.

She met him at the chopper pad and led him directly into the War Room to follow the action. The big flatscreen TV tuned to L.A.'s Channel 7 was running wall-to-wall coverage of the shoot-out.

"Striker just called in," she said, anticipating Brognola's first question. "He said that in the process of clearing the building, he found Givens in his office, dead from a single shot to the back of the head.''

"How about that security chief?" Brognola asked. "What was his name, Miller?"

"We never had a photo of him, so Bolan's not sure if he was in the building. He cleaned out all the guards he could find, but he doesn't know how many of them escaped.''

Knowing how well the Executioner could clean house, he doubted that many of them had lived unless they had dropped their guns and run before he showed up.

"Is Kurtzman keeping track of the LAPD radio traffic on this?"

"He is," Price said. "He's sharing time on an NSA Big Ear bird and is running a real-time intercept on all their radio and landline traffic. As soon as they figure out anything, we'll know it."

Brognola watched the TV coverage for a few moments. A reporter was standing at the rear of an ambulance as another body was loaded. According to the running commentary, that was the fourth one so far. "I guess we can close the book on Roy Givens and his Rainbow Dawn," he said. "If he hadn't panicked and ordered that girl killed, none of this would have ever happened."

"I don't know if the book is closed yet," Price pointed out. "We still have the overseas missions, and those are still iffy. I have reports from all three of our teams, but nothing has been wrapped up yet."

"I'm holding Betancourt directly responsible for those operations," Brognola said. "But, to be honest with you, I don't know when or even if we're ever going to be able to present him with the bill."

"Maybe something will turn up overseas that will help tag him for us."

"Don't bet on it," Brognola growled. "That bastard's slick. The only connection we're going to find will be to Rainbow Dawn."

He glanced down at his watch. "Did Striker say when he'd be due in?"

"He didn't say. He said there were a few things he had to finish up before he could leave."

"Next time he calls, tell him that I'll need a debrief as soon as it's convenient."

Phoenix, Arizona

GRANT BETANCOURT had seen more news broadcasts about Rainbow Dawn than he had ever wanted. But, from what he was hearing, this was the last one he would ever have to watch. Rainbow Dawn was ended and whoever the guy was who had cleaned house in there had saved Betancourt from having to order it done himself. The loss of the dozen or so Security Plus men also wasn't something he'd lose much sleep over.

The thought occurred to him that this exterminator who had involved himself might have been hired by Bowers right before his freeway accident. Since the senator had chaired the Armed Forces Committee, he would have had friends in the Special Operations Command, and they could have connected him with a retired commando who still kept his hand in the game.

That was the only thing that made sense to him, and it would explain how this man had operated—relentlessly and completely unafraid to kill anyone who got in his way. That was a commando's mentality, not a private investigator's. No P.I. would have gone into the Dawners' building alone to hunt down Givens knowing that Miller and his men were guarding him.

His identity really didn't matter anymore. With Givens dead, there was nothing left for this mystery man to follow up. It was over. And that meant that there was no way to connect him to what would be going down in Italy, Israel and Saudi Arabia in the next day or two.

CHAPTER TWENTY-NINE

Mecca, Saudi Arabia

Saudi Prince Khalid looked very concerned when he met the chartered helicopter carrying the two UN representatives at the chopper pad right outside the holy complex. The Briton's phone call had been cryptic, but had carried enough sense of urgency that the prince had heeded it. Anything that threatened the Kaaba had to be taken seriously. Particularly since the as-yet unexplained aerial assault that had occurred several months earlier.

With the two UN men who disembarked from the chopper was a third man, who was introduced as one of their party, and a fourth man the prince thought he recognized as an American from the work crew.

When David McCarter had Ralph Biggs tell his story, the prince immediately took them to the Gold Star office and sent for Bud Bolger.

When Bolger arrived, he pointedly ignored McCarter and James as Biggs repeated his story to him.

"To be honest with you, Ralph," Bolger said, shaking his head when the worker finished, "I'd never really thought anything about that tank as being a danger. If you'd have come to me with this, I'd have gotten it straightened out right away. Rawlins didn't say anything to me about the refueling accident and simply told me that you'd quit the crew, that was it."

"When I talked to Rawlins after that accident," Biggs said, "he told me that if I didn't like the working conditions here, I could take a hike. For some damned reason, he's dead set on doing the refueling the way he set it up. It's almost as if he wants to blow this place up. And, considering that happened to his sister Debbie, I'm not surprised either. He hates this place and everything it stands for."

Bolger looked like he was about to explode. "What in the hell are you talking about, Ralph?"

Biggs shook his head. "If you don't know about it, Bud, then I guess you're the only guy on this whole damned crew who doesn't. Rawlins hates Arabs like you wouldn't believe. His sister was killed in a Scud attack during the Gulf War, and that's damned near all he talks about."

Bolger got a strange look on his face. "Oh, sweet Jesus."

WHEN DICK RAWLINS spotted Ralph Biggs talking to Bolger and the prince in the office, he knew what he was talking to them about. He should have silenced the chickenshit bastard when he had a chance. He wasn't about to let some UN assholes keep him from blowing

JUDGMENT IN BLOOD

this place off the face of the Earth. He had worked his ass off to set this up, and he was going to make it work even if he had to go up in the explosion as well. At least he'd die knowing that he was getting these bastards where they lived. From now on, they'd be praying to a hole in the ground instead of that rock.

Rawlins turned and hurried to the work site. He wasn't alone in his desire to bring destruction to Mecca. Five other men on his crew had similar reasons to want to see as much devastation as possible inflicted on the Arabs.

In the work area, he found three of them together. "Where's Wills and Johnson?" he asked.

"Around the corner, why?"

"Bolger's onto us," he said. "Get them, grab your gear and let's go."

"Where're we going?" one of the men asked.

"We're getting out of here like we planned," Rawlins said. "But we've got to rig that tank first."

WHEN BOLGER LED the prince and the UN men outside, he saw six of his workers and a Gold Star Construction pickup truck by the huge propane tank. He recognized one of them as Dick Rawlins and knew that Biggs had been telling the truth. "Rawlins!" he yelled. "You bastard! Get away from there!"

Bolger's shout was answered by a burst of automatic weapons' fire. Since the two temple guards who accompanied the prince were in front, they took the brunt of the fire and they both went down.

James was walking beside Prince Khalid and took him down with a flying tackle. When the Saudi tried to get up from the sand, James snapped at him in pure American English. "Stay down, dammit. I don't want you to get killed."

"You're not Jamaican," the prince said. "Who are you?"

"Later," James said as he drew his Beretta. "Just stay behind me and keep your royal head down."

Crawling over to one of the dead Saudi temple guards, McCarter grabbed his H&K assault rifle, cracked the bolt to make sure a round was in the chamber and started to look for a target. Rawlins's men were using the propane tank for cover, and he wasn't about to shoot into it. Seeing half a leg sticking out, though, he put a bullet in it. Caught in the open, there was no way the Phoenix Force warriors could retreat or even take cover.

Ralph Biggs was rightfully paranoid about fuel air explosives, but he was also one hundred percent American working man and damned proud of it. He couldn't stand by while his fellow Americans were trying to do something that would bring discredit to him and his country. He decided to take a hand in stopping them and soon found a way to do it.

The prime mover for the propane tank was parked a hundred yards away. It was an eight hundred horsepower diesel rig designed to haul massive oil field equipment from drilling site to drilling site. The tank was mounted on a converted drilling tower trailer, so if he could get hooked up to it, he could pull it into the desert.

Without even thinking, he started to crawl toward it. Once he was out of the direct line of fire, he got up and ran. He had never driven one of these behemoths before, but he had driven 18-wheelers back home. This was a U.S.-made rig, so it shouldn't be all that different.

Since this was Saudi and not the States, when he swung himself up into the driver's seat, he found the keys waiting in the ignition. Switching on the engine, he watched for the fuel pressure to come up before punching the starter and the big turbocharged Cummins diesel coughed into life. Reaching down for the shift lever, he floored the throttle and headed for the tank.

When one of the gunmen saw the tractor coming, he stepped out to level his over-and-under M-16. McCarter had a clear shot and put a bullet in his head. The gunman's dying twitch triggered the grenade launcher, and the 40 mm round arched out over the sand.

Biggs saw the gunman aim at him and turned out of the line of fire. With the power steering, the big rig was more nimble that it looked and the HE grenade missed, blowing a hole in the sand. Turning the tractor's nose away from the tank's trailer, he dropped the transmission into reverse and started backing toward the hitch on the front.

When Rawlins saw the rig heading toward him, he knew what Biggs was trying to do. Roaring in rage, he directed the fire of his remaining men at the tractor while he ran to the device he had been attaching to the fuel valves of the tank when the UN men had shown up.

Making a propane tank blow up wasn't easy, it required a two-part procedure. First, the liquid gas had to be released to expand in the air, and only then could it be ignited. He had made a device that would connect to one of the gas release valves to first vent and then ignite the propane. But he had to remove the hose line that went into the building.

With the workers' attention fixed on Biggs's tractor, a dozen more of the prince's temple guards had gotten into position to bring fire on them from the flank. At a shouted command they opened up with their assault rifles and the fight was over in the first burst. Rawlins was cut down as he worked to free the transfer hoses from the gas valves.

"Cease-fire," McCarter ordered, waving his arms as Encizo and James dashed out to make sure the gas valve hadn't been opened. "Cease-fire!"

"It's okay," Encizo yelled as James waved for Biggs to back up to the trailer. The Phoenix Force commandos held up the trailer's tongue while Biggs slowly backed the tractor's hitch into it.

"That's it," James called out as he dropped the forged tongue ring onto the hitch and locked it.

Encizo opened the passenger's-side door of the tractor cab and swung inside. "Go! Go!"

Biggs dropped the shift lever into first and floored

the throttle. The diesel bellowed black smoke as it took the strain of hauling a million gallons of liquid propane. Seeing an open space between the nearby buildings that led to the desert, he aimed his lethal load into the gap.

He felt that one of the front tires was starting to go flat, probably from the near miss with the grenade, but he kept the rig floored and soon they were traveling at almost fifty miles an hour. As the sand flashed by, Encizo thought that he smelled propane. If he did and the hot engine exhaust set the gas off, they'd hear the bang in Riyadh four hundred miles away.

Ten miles from the edge of Mecca, Encizo saw a sizable depression in the ground off to one side of the track they had been following. "Can you drive into that?" He pointed.

"I think so." Biggs came off the throttle, dropped the shift lever into a lower gear and steered for the low spot. By now the left front tire was completely flat, but the power steering let him control it.

Three minutes later, the top of the million-gallon propane tank was in a depression twenty feet below the surface of the surrounding desert. Biggs and Encizo were briskly walking back toward Mecca.

THE LEADER of the Green Crescent medical team reported that Rawlins and two of the others were dead. Of the three workmen left alive, only one was unwounded, but none of the wounds the other two sustained were serious. They would live to stand trial.

"What will happen to them?" McCarter asked even though he knew the answer.

The prince's eyes were hard. "They will be tried by Islamic law and punished if found guilty."

"How about Bolger and the others who weren't in on the plot?"

"If they had nothing to do with this crime," the prince said, "they will be free to go back to America. You and your friends will be allowed to go free as well, once you tell me who you really are."

"I thought it would be enough," McCarter said carefully, "that we just saved Mecca for future generations."

Khalid studied him for a long moment before nodding. "You have a point."

Vatican City

CARL LYONS and Gadgets Schwarz were continuing their strolls through the grounds of the Vatican while Rosario Blancanales tried to find another way through the tunnels to gain access to the chemicals they felt were stored in the back room of the lab. If he couldn't find a way in, they were simply going to have to make a frontal assault and take their chances.

With a leather-bound book under his arm as a prop, he hurried past the entrance to the conservation lab so he wouldn't be noticed. But there wasn't much activity going on. The hand-lettered sign by the door in Italian and English announced that the chamber was shut down for maintenance. That would explain the lack of activity, but something felt off. Only one man was in the lab, and the door to the back room was closed.

Going back up the stairs to the library, he stepped outside to make a cell-phone call to his teammates.

WHEN BLANCANALES reached the parking lot outside Vatican City, Lyons and Schwarz had cut short their walk and were waiting for him.

"I don't know much about the technology of what they're doing in there," Schwarz said after Blancanales reported what he'd seen, "but I don't see that there's a lot of maintenance involved. All they have to do to treat the books is release the chemicals into the chamber, let the material sit in it for a while and then suck the gas back out. There's not really much involved beyond a few valves and the extraction pumps."

"How about when they convert the chamber to produce the nerve gas?" Lyons asked.

"That's probably going to be a little more complicated," Schwarz agreed. "They'll have to re-rig the scavenger pumps to exhaust into the air instead of into the recovery tanks. But that shouldn't take very long. Then, of course, they'll have to add the intakes for whatever special chemicals they'll be using. Then, it's just set the timer and get the hell out of Dodge."

Blancanales looked up from the pile of faxes that had been waiting for them in their hotel room. "I've been going over the stuff Kurtzman sent us and I've found something that clicks. Until he was in junior high, our man Patrick Renfro went to St. Mary's Academy, an exclusive Catholic school in Boston. Then, in midyear, he transferred to the public schools.''

"How the hell did Kurtzman find out something like that?" Schwarz asked.

"You know the Bear when he gets his teeth into something."

"What do you think it means?" Lyons asked.

"Well, my feeling is that Renfro didn't care much for priests. While there could be several reasons for that, I go for the personal motive. His name is Irish and if he suddenly leaves an expensive Catholic school, more than likely something traumatic happened to him, probably sexual.''

"That's almost a cliché isn't it?" Lyons said.

"Only because it happens," Blancanales replied. "But if it's the case, it gives me an avenue to work on him."

"You're not going to try to play shrink are you?"

Blancanales shrugged. "I'm already playing priest, so why not try confessor and therapist, as well?"

"Because he's likely to shoot you, that's why. If he's freaky about the church, he might not take well to being reminded of why he's that way."

"Ah," Blancanales intoned, "but confession is good for one's soul. And, if 'maintenance' means that they're getting ready to start making gas, the time for confession is now.''

EARLIER THAT DAY, it had been child's play for Blancanales to stop by the chief librarian's office and steal two more high-level security passes from the little wooden box on Monsignor Penelli's desk. The Vatican might have been ancient in political intrigue, but it was very naive when it came to modern security concepts. Using a special pass to control entry to restricted areas was useless when they were so easy to steal.

With the passes prominently displayed, Lyons and Schwarz had no trouble getting into the main library building. The guard saw the badges and didn't give them a second glance. A minute later, Blancanales followed and met them at the stairwell that led into the tunnel complex.

At the bottom of the stairs, Blancanales turned to Lyons and Schwarz. "I'll keep my com link open and if it sounds like he's going to shoot me, take him out with a silencer."

Lyons didn't like this tactic, but he liked a gun battle even less. Even in the tunnels, shots would bring the Swiss Guard.

As before, only one man was in the outer room of the lab. Blancanales couldn't see if anything about the decontamination chamber had been changed, but he hadn't studied it long enough to tell. When the man in the lab noticed him, he walked over.

"We're closed." He pointed to the sign.

"Is Dr. Renfro here?" Blancanales asked.

"He's busy," the man said bluntly.

"Tell Patrick that Father Murphy from St. Mary's

Academy in Boston is here to see him. He'll want to see me."

The man looked puzzled, but went through the lab into the second room and closed the door behind him. When Renfro came out, his face was tense. "I don't know you," he said, "but whoever you are, you're in the wrong place, priest."

"You don't know me, Patrick," Blancanales said, holding his hands still at his sides, "but, I know you and what you're doing isn't right. You can't let the pain you feel bring death to hundreds of innocent people."

"There are no innocent priests." Renfro's eyes went wild, and a Glock appeared in his hand. "All of you bastards are guilty of centuries of crimes. If I could kill each one of you individually I would, but I can clean out this nest of vipers and hope that others will follow my lead and kill the rest of you."

"They won't, you know," Blancanales said calmly, ignoring the pistol. "Doing this won't make you a hero to anyone. Instead, the story of who you are and why you did this will become common knowledge. Everyone will know what happened to you at St. Mary's."

"Everyone knows already," Renfro snapped. "I have AIDS, and I've told everyone how I got it."

"Killing people with nerve gas isn't the way to make anyone pay for what happened to you back then, Patrick," Blancanales said. "And neither is that gun in your hand. If you want, I can get you a personal audience with the Pope, and he will see that the man who hurt you is punished."

"No!" Renfro screamed. "They had a chance to make it right before, and they defended the priest."

He raised the pistol to Blancanales's head as he screamed. "I hate—"

"Duck," Blancanales heard on his earphone.

The single silenced pistol shot took Renfro in the center of the forehead. His head snapped back, and he crumpled to the floor.

Lyons and Schwarz stepped out, their silenced pistols at the ready. "Poor bastard," Blancanales muttered.

"Later," Lyons snapped as he scooped up Renfro's fallen Glock.

Schwarz rushed past him to the door of the second room and kicked it open. "Party's over," he said as he covered the three men inside. "Keep your hands where I can see them."

CHAPTER THIRTY

Jerusalem, Israel

Dave Tolly's hands caressed the Israeli army-issue Uzi submachine gun he'd had no trouble buying on the Arab black market. It was ironic that the Jews had developed such a beautiful weapon in the name of peace and God's love. The Arabs had never built anything that even came close to the deadly Uzi. They all armed themselves in the name of God with weapons they bought either from atheist Russians or Christian Western nations.

His Uzi and the Russian AKs his five men were armed with would insure that they'd be able to work unmolested, but he didn't think they'd be needed. The Israeli cops were guarding the equipment he had left behind at their old site, but the Irish Rangers had set up around the perimeter of their new location. There weren't as many of them as there had been cops at the other site, but he trusted them more anyway.

This new site wasn't the perfect place to set off the bomb, but it had the advantage of being on private property. Because of that, there would be no hordes of tourists clamoring around it tomorrow morning looking for places where Jesus might once have done something or other. The fact that this ground surface hadn't even been in existence two thousand years before wouldn't deter the faithful in their search for the unfindable.

Pious lies were Jerusalem's main stock-in-trade, but it wouldn't be long before all those lies were at last put to rest. Less than twenty-four hours, in fact, before the peace that all these people said they wanted finally came to this ancient, blood-soaked battleground. He could hardly wait.

WITH THE night-vision goggles and the high ground, Katzenelenbogen had a good view of the large lot with the two Geo-Tech trucks parked in front of what looked like the openings to small caves or empty ancient tombs. The rocky ground was spotted with large gnarled olive trees that would give them fairly good cover on the final approach once they got through the Irish Rangers' perimeter.

Gary Manning was watching the unloading of the two trucks through his NVGs and turned to Susan Brown. "What do the canisters look like that you keep your source material in?"

"They're stainless steel, about eighteen inches long, maybe eight or ten inches in diameter. They have radiation hazard markings and a registry number on them, why?"

"Items like that are being off-loaded and carried into

that cave," Manning said as he handed her the night-vision goggles. "Check them out."

She focused and saw one of the canisters. "That looks like them."

"How big are the nuclear slugs inside?" he asked.

"Six inches by two."

"And they weigh about eight pounds, right?"

"About that."

"Four of those," Manning said. "Maybe five and a little deuterium is all they need to create a pretty decent bomb if they rig it right."

"But the nuclear material in the source rods is matrixed," she said. "So that can't happen."

"And the matrix is a hard resin, right?"

She nodded.

"All they have to do is dissolve the matrix in an acid to concentrate the source material, use deuterium to enhance the emissions, and they can create a sub-critical meltdown with a powerful release of hard radiation. It's basically a replay of the Chernobyl incident."

Brown handed back the NVGs. "We have deuterium lenses that we use to focus the neutrino emissions, so we can aim them. But they only have a few ounces in each of them."

"How many of those do you have?"

"Counting the spares, six. Geo-Tech was concerned about working over here, so we brought everything we might possibly need if something broke down here."

"That's it, then," Manning said. "They've got the

makings for a neutron bomb down there. No doubt about it.''

"It looks like I'd better get going then," T. J. Hawkins reached for the shoulder bag full of flash-bang grenades. "I'm going to try to draw them off to the northeast, and that should open a gap for you to get through."

"Just throw a few of those grenades and get out," Katz cautioned. "You don't need to get into a running gun battle with those people."

"Don't worry," Hawkins said. "I'm going to do the best rabbit you ever saw."

IT TOOK almost half an hour for Hawkins to make his way around to his initial position some fifty yards from the outer perimeter of Rangers. "I'm ready to rock and roll," Hawkins sent over the com link.

"We're ready," Katz sent back.

As a kid, Hawkins had been fascinated by the story of the young David killing the giant Goliath with a single sling bullet. He had fashioned a crude sling from clothesline and learned how to use it. He never became very accurate with it, but he soon learned to sling a rock about one hundred yards.

The three-foot sling he had this night wasn't much of an improvement over the one he had used as a kid. But he wasn't a kid anymore and had the muscle power to sling the heavy grenade almost two hundred yards. Loading the grenade into the sling pouch, with the weight holding the spoon down, he carefully pulled the pin to arm it.

Rather than twirl it around his head, he took two quick steps forward and sidearmed it. As the grenade left the sling, the spoon flew off and started the five-second fuse delay. The flash-bang was only a few feet off the ground when it detonated right in front of the Rangers.

As the name implied, the grenade went off with a brilliant flash and a crashing bang that sounded like the explosion of a 105 mm shell. The Irish Rangers had been shot at before, and they instantly took what cover there was.

Loading his sling again and holding it ready, Hawkins drew the Beretta from the back of his belt and fired a couple of rounds over their heads to let them know where he was. For this to work, they had to know where the attack was coming from.

Hawkins's shots drew probing fire, and he launched another flash-bang before pulling back to move to his second position. As the man said right after he jumped off the fifty-story building, so far so good.

His second position was to the northeast in the direction he wanted the Rangers to chase him. He tossed another grenade from there and followed it with a couple more harmless pistol shots into the wall across the street.

TOLLY JUMPED when Hawkins's first flash-bang went off. Sticking his head out the mouth of the cave, he saw the Irish Rangers taking cover and heard their NCOs shouting orders.

"What's going on?" Willard asked, looking up from the explosive block he was wiring into the framework of the device. He was an old blaster, but screwing around with radioactive material made him nervous. As soon as he had this damned thing rigged, he was clearing out of this country for good.

"Keep working," Tolly snapped.

"What if we're being attacked?"

"That's why we have the guns." Tolly swung around his Uzi so the pistol grip was readily at hand.

"Jack," Tolly said to one of his other men, "take a look outside and see what's happening."

Jack picked up his folding stock AK-47 and snapped the stock into place. Checking the magazine, he pulled back on the charging handle to chamber a round before walking outside.

KATZENELENBOGEN and Manning had moved close to the masonry wall that surrounded the lot, with Susan Brown keeping right behind them. When the Irish pulled out to chase Hawkins, they quickly moved to the base of the wall. Kneeling, Manning gave Katz a leg up as he hooked his good arm over the top of the wall, pulled himself up and dropped down on the other side.

"It's clear," he sent over the com link.

Manning motioned for Brown to go next.

After being hoisted up, she lay on top of the wall and offered Manning her hand to pull himself up.

Katz took point, going from the cover of one olive tree to the next. He had reached the first of the Geo-Tech trucks when he went to ground. "Sentry," he whispered over the com link.

Manning tightened the sound suppressor on the muzzle of his Beretta as he went forward. Brown followed him, but held back with Katz when Manning moved into firing position.

When the red dot of the sight was centered on the man's temple, Manning squeezed the trigger. Even though he had a magazine of low-power, subsonic 9 mm rounds in the pistol, they were hollowpoints. The bullet mushroomed in the man's brain, dropping him where he stood.

Katz leapfrogged past him to the entrance of the cave, his silenced mini-Uzi resting across his prosthesis. When Manning joined him, on a count of three, they stormed into the cave side by side.

Of the five men inside, three were wearing assault rifles slung over their backs, and they went down first to the concentrated silenced fire. The man sitting in front of his equipment with the wire pliers in his hand tried to push himself out of his chair and get to his AK, but Manning took him out with a double tap to the chest.

Uttering a cry of rage, Tolly launched himself across the cave, his Uzi forgotten. Katz sent a short burst of silenced 9 mm rounds after him, but he seemed to soak up the low-velocity slugs long enough to reach a computer on a table. His fingers were tapping at the keyboard when Manning put a 9 mm in his temple.

"Wait out there for a minute," Manning called softly to Brown. "We need to clean up in here."

HEARING THE THUMPING of boots coming on strong behind him, Hawkins took a quick look around the cul-de-sac he had mistakenly taken. A fine rabbit he was. At the end of the street was a stone wall a dozen feet tall, and the houses all had adjoining walls so there were no alleys to dodge into. Lights showed in most of the windows of the multistory houses, but the building at the end looked to be deserted. Racing to it, he ducked into the doorway and ran up the stairs.

By the time he got to the top floor, Hawkins was winded, but he had to find a place to hide. It wouldn't be long before the Irish Rangers called in the Israeli cops and started a house-to-house search. He hoped that this place was as deserted at it looked from the outside. If it was occupied, he had a major problem.

"Mister!" Hawkins heard a small voice behind him. Whirling, he saw a kid of ten or twelve beckoning to him from an open door in the back of the corridor.

"Mister, come here."

"What do you want?"

The kid pulled on a rope and a set of wooden stairs came down from the ceiling. "Go on roof. Okay?"

This looked like the best bet he had, so Hawkins dug

into his pocket, pulled out a ten pound note and gave it to the kid. "Thanks," he said.

"Go now, mister. Soldiers come."

Hawkins scrambled up the ladder until he reached a trapdoor over his head. Opening it, he stuck his head through to make sure that the roof was deserted. When he saw that it was, he wriggled through and closed the door after him. The roof was flat with no balustrade, so Hawkins didn't even try to stand.

The trapdoor had a rusty hasp, but no way to lock it. Digging into his pocket, he took out one of the pin rings for the flash-bang grenades. Prying open the ring with his lock blade knife, he slipped it through the hasp. That would secure the door short of it being torn off its hinges.

A few feet away, Hawkins saw a laundry rack set up to dry clothes and a large wicker basket beside it. He was crawling over to it when he heard the characteristic whup-whup sound of a chopper's rotors and saw the probing finger of light from the chopper's searchlight.

Pulling the dry laundry off the line, he sat with his back to the basket and draped it on top of him to break the outline of his body. Hearing the chopper's rotors coming closer, he froze and pretended to be an overly full laundry basket. He could see the glare of the spotlight playing across the roof through the clothes and he didn't move.

After seeing nothing of interest, the searchlight operator moved his beam on, but Hawkins still didn't move. The way this was shaping up, it looked like he'd be stuck on the roof until daybreak.

WHEN MANNING and Katz came out, the Israeli stood guard while Manning took Brown inside. The bodies had all been moved back into the shadow so she didn't have to see them, and she forced herself not to notice the blood on the floor of the cave. She was a big girl, but she was in a bit of shock at how violent this had turned out. She had purposefully not thought about what would happen there tonight. But whatever had taken place, it had been as silent and as swift as the wrath of God.

Walking to the table set up under the portable lights, she saw that one of their laptops was set up. "Oh, God," she said when she saw what was on the screen. Blinking letters read "initiation sequence."

It was a well-known cliché, the clock ticking down to nuclear disaster. This time, though, it wasn't the flashing red numbers on a digital clock favored by most directors. This was simply a time readout like the ones found on almost every computer screen, but instead of displaying the time of day, this one was counting down from fifteen minutes.

"You know this equipment," Manning said, looking over her shoulder. "Can you turn this thing off?"

She reached out and started to type on the keyboard. After a few seconds, she stopped and looked at him. "I don't think so," she said softly. "I've never seen this program before."

The assembly of equipment hooked up to the computer didn't look much like a bomb. There were, however, small blocks of plastic explosive in with the other gear, which kept Manning from diving into it and tearing it all apart.

"Shit," he muttered under his breath. "He's wired it with high explosives."

"Can't you just cut the wires?" Brown asked when he pointed them out.

"No, that's the surest way to set it off. Every good bomb-maker knows that old trick. You're screwed if you do, as well as if you don't."

"If this is supposed to be a nuclear device, why did he put the explosives there?"

"Rather than dissolve the slugs to free the nuclear material like I thought he'd do," Manning said, "he designed this to use the explosives to do that by crushing them. If done right, the effect will be the same."

"How are you coming in there?" Katz asked over the com link.

"I'm not," Manning replied. "This is a lot more sophisticated that I thought it would be. It's an implosion-type device, and it looks like it has antitamper features."

"You'd better hurry," Katz said. "I've got an Irishman coming our way."

"I'll take care of him," Brown said. Reaching into her shirt pocket, she took out her Geo-Tech ID card and clipped it to the flap. Picking up a clipboard, she walked to the mouth of the cave as Katz faded back into the shadows.

"Is everything okay?" she asked when the soldier walked up.

"Yes, ma'am," the Ranger sergeant said. "Whoever it was has gone, but my officer said that he would like your people to evacuate just in case. Just for tonight, mind you. We'll have the rest of the company here in the morning."

"If it's okay," she replied, "we'll be just a few more minutes. We're almost done here anyway."

"Yes, ma'am."

WHEN BROWN GOT BACK inside the cave, she saw that Manning was taking the deuterium lenses out of the bomb and was crushing them on the ground. "You figured it out," she said as relief flooded through her body.

"They did a good job," he said, "but it was all controlled by the laptop and they forgot to provide a backup power source for it. I just pulled the battery pack and that killed everything."

"If you're done here," Katz said, "the truck's ready."

"Give me another minute."

"You're just going to leave the nuclear material here?" She didn't believe what she was hearing.

"And why not?" Katz smiled. "It's perfectly safe right here. Remember, it's guarded by the UN."

"I'll drive," Manning said. "And, Katz, make sure that's a tear-gas grenade in your good hand."

Katz grinned. "That's just insurance if the Irish decide to check the cab too closely."

CHAPTER THIRTY-ONE

Jerusalem, Israel

The sun rose over the living city of Jerusalem as it had
every day for thousands of years. The streets weren't
littered with the dead and dying, and the very stones
weren't poisoned.

For a while longer, at least, the unique life of this
ancient city would go on.

As Yakov Katzenelenbogen had told Barbara Price,
he was a man who had developed a personal philoso-
phy and once more he had lived up to it. He had killed
so that others could live. Now, the irony that some of
those he had saved might this very morning be plotting
to kill others of those he had saved didn't escape him.
That was the nature of the human beast. That religious
differences would most likely be the motive for the
planned killings also did not escape him, but that was
the nature of this city.

At least mass murder hadn't taken place there, this
time. But, since this was Jerusalem, there would un-

fortunately be a next time. There always had been and there always would be. Gary Manning and T. J. Hawkins had already departed on the first available flight out, but he had remained behind to take care of a few loose ends. The last thing he had to do to wrap up the mission was to make a phone call to the member of the Israeli Cabinet who had responsibility for oversight of Israel's nuclear weapon program to insure that nothing like this ever happened again.

He would, though, make the call from a phone booth at the airport as he was leaving. Knowing Israeli security as he did, he didn't want to get caught in a national lockdown.

Vatican City

FROM THE OUTSIDE, things looked completely normal at the Vatican. Black-robed priests and nuns scurried back and forth doing the business of the church while hordes of tourists swarmed the grounds, their cameras clicking like gunfire. A dedicated Vatican watcher might have noticed that the Swiss Guard seemed to be out more in force than usual. Small contingents of Italian police, both Roman municipal and national, were also on the site and had vans parked a short distance away.

Inside the administrative buildings of Vatican City, panic had barely been averted. But when the Pope had said that he wouldn't evacuate his quarters for safety elsewhere, that set the agenda for his staff.

In the basement of the library, the door of the decontamination chamber was being taken off to render it useless for now. It wouldn't be able to treat books, nor produce nerve gas, until the door was remounted.

Of the four chemical storage tanks from the back room, only one of them was attracting any attention. It was the catalyst that would twist the molecules of the other three chemicals into a deadly geometry and bind them forever in that form. Without it, the other three chemicals were dangerous, but not much more dangerous than an agricultural pesticide. Exposure might make someone sick, but wouldn't kill them in seconds.

By itself, the catalyst was also relatively harmless. It was a compound that had been developed by the military to be used in conjunction with binary war agent mixes. And, as part of a binary formula, it had to be harmless until it was mixed with the other chemicals so it could be handled by troops. Once this container had been safely removed, the decontamination of the books and manuscripts could continue.

When the process was started up again, however, the new scientists who would be continuing the work would be personally chosen by the Vatican. Also, a team of chemical warfare experts from the Italian army as well as a strong contingent of the Swiss Guard would be on hand to supervise at all times.

Saudi Arabia

THE SWISSAIR FLIGHT out of Riyadh was scheduled to land in Switzerland in a little over three hours. McCarter and James were flying in first-class comfort as befitted their cover stories as UN functionaries. Rafael Encizo was back in coach, jammed in between two oil-company men, but he didn't mind at all. Right now, being alive felt really good, no matter where he was. All he had to do was to keep breathing until the 747 landed in Geneva, and he'd be home free. The same couldn't be said for the three men of the Gold Star construction crew in Mecca who hadn't been killed in the shoot-out.

Islamic justice was swift, and lawyers didn't have much to do with it. Because of the nature of the outrage, the United States State Department lawyers had wisely kept their mouths shut this time. There had been no outcry in the UN about human-rights abuses, whatever they might be, and no talk in Congress of U.S. constitutional rights not being granted for these particular American terrorists.

Everyone concerned was so relieved that Mecca hadn't been blown off the map that the beheading of three men, even American citizens, was no big thing. Not when compared to what would have happened if they had succeeded in their plot.

Phoenix, Arizona

THE BOULEVARD in front of the Betancourt Industries Inc. headquarters in Phoenix had been blocked off. Dozens and dozens of media vans with satellite dishes on their roofs crowded the parking lot in front of the building. Hundreds of cars that hadn't been able to get into the lot were parked two deep along the street. They were all waiting to catch a glimpse of the man who was believed to be responsible for the greatest criminal plot, so far, of the new millennium.

At the appointed time, the man of the hour walked out of his glass-and-chrome palace. Grant Betancourt wore the proper look of concern mixed with outrage as he faced the battery of microphones and TV cameras on the steps of his corporate headquarters. Rather than hold back in the shade of the entrance facade, in a calculated gesture he walked halfway down the steps into the sun where a simple podium and microphone had been placed.

For the first few minutes, he stood while reporters shouted questions. When it appeared that they weren't going to quiet down to let him speak, he turned as if to go back into his building. That hushed the crowd and he returned to his microphone.

"I am as stunned at this outrage as anyone," he said, his voice tight as if he were keeping a great rage under control. "To even think of attacking religious sites as was apparently intended is unspeakable. I still have trouble believing it, but I know that it was planned and that it was almost executed. It was only through the grace of God that this was prevented not once, but three times.''

He paused to let his eyes sweep the crowd. ''I have seen media reports saying that I was somehow associated with Roy Givens and his heinous crimes, and I am here today to refute those charges. As a man who keeps abreast of the social currents in American society, I was, of course, aware of the organization known to you as Rainbow Dawn. I couldn't have told you, however, what their purpose was beyond what they publicly stated. Nor have I ever met Roy Givens.

''I am willing to accept whatever blame may be found in the fact that I contributed money to the United Nations Commission on Cultural Heritage to fund these projects. As a wealthy man, I am aware of my responsibility to give back to humanity, and I think my record of charitable giving speaks for itself. Nonetheless, I feel that I need to explain how I came to sponsor these three particular projects.

''Some time ago, I was approached by the UN's Commission on Cultural Heritage and was presented with a list of proposed projects they were seeking sponsorship for. After reviewing the list, I chose these three because I thought that they would benefit the three largest religions in the world. The nature of these projects were all quite different, but they were all things that the religious leaders involved felt needed to be done. I proposed to underwrite the costs involved, and the Commission accepted.''

His eyes flashed. "Needless to say, I didn't know what my money was really being used for. Had I known of Givens's plan, or even of his involvement in these projects, I would have moved heaven and earth to stop it.

"So," Betancourt said, his voice rising, "rather than point a finger at me, I suggest that you ladies and gentlemen of the media take a good look at the inner workings of the United Nations and in particular the so-called Committee on Cultural Heritage. How and why that organization could sponsor those projects without knowing exactly who would be doing the work is nothing less than criminal. And let me assure you that it will be a cold day in hell before I ever involve myself in anything that has to do with the United Nations again. Thank you."

"Mr. Betancourt!" a voice rose out of the crowd. "Do you—"

Grant Betancourt turned and climbed the steps back into his headquarters. It wasn't until he was inside his building that he allowed his face to relax, but when he did, it formed a smile.

Stony Man Farm, Virginia

"CAN YOU BELIEVE that crap!" Barbara Price was completely outraged at what she was seeing on the live CNN broadcast from Betancourt's headquarters. "How can that rotten bastard get away with this?"

"He can get away with it, Barbara," Hal Brognola pointed out, "because we still don't have anything to tie him to the activities of Roy Givens and Rainbow Dawn."

"How about that security force he sent to L.A.?"

"They came from one of his subsidiary companies, yes. But we can't prove that he ordered them into action. The records at Security Plus, Inc., show that Givens signed a contract with them because he was concerned about all the negative publicity the Dawners had been getting in the fallout over the Jennifer Wayne incident."

"So Givens hires a private army from one of the world's best security contractors, which just happens to be one of Betancourt's companies?"

"Happenstance," Brognola said. "Any good defense lawyer would tell you that, and Betancourt has his pick of the litter when it comes to lawyers."

"Bullshit."

"You know that and I know that, but we don't have enough to take it to court and this little media circus today will insure that we'll never be able to."

"Then, of course—" Brognola's jaw tightened "—we still have the Oval Office factor to work with."

"Does the Man have any idea yet that we were involved with the takedown?"

"Let's put it this way—he hasn't asked and I haven't told."

"What are you going to do when and if he does?"

"Lie through my teeth." Brognola smiled. "There are some things that the President really doesn't have a need to know.

"And another thing he doesn't need to know is that we're going to keep an eye on Betancourt for the rest of his sorry life. And when we find the slightest excuse, he's going down hard."

"That suits me."

"I rather thought that it might."

* * * * *

*The heart-stopping action
concludes in Doomsday Directing,
Book II of the* Armageddon Project,
available February 2001.

James Axler

OUTLANDERS®

TIGERS OF HEAVEN

In the Outlands, the struggle for control of the baronies continues. Kane, Grant and Brigid seek allies in the Western Islands empire of New Edo, where they try to enlist the aid of the Tigers of Heaven, a group of samurai warriors.

Book #2 of the Imperator Wars saga, a trilogy chronicling the introduction of a new child imperator—launching the baronies into war!